The Clothes of Nakedness

Benjamin Kwakye

Black Star Books and Head of Zeus would like to thank the following organisations: The Miles Morland Foundation, The Ford Foundation, and Africa No Filter. This publication was made possible through their support.

First published in the Heinemann African Writers Series in 1998 by Heinemann Educational Books

This edition published in 2023 by Black Star Books and Head of Zeus, part of Bloomsbury Publishing Plc.

9 7 5 3 1 2 4 6 8

A catalogue record for this book is available from the British Library.

ISBN (PB): 9781035900619
ISBN (E): 9781803288284

Typeset by Siliconchips Services Ltd UK

Printed and bound in Great Britain by
CPI Group (UK) Ltd, Croydon CRO 4YY

Head of Zeus Ltd
First Floor East
5–8 Hardwick Street
London EC1R 4RG

WWW.HEADOFZEUS.COM

About Apollo Africa

The original Heinemann African Writers Series was launched in 1962 with the publication of Chinua Achebe's *Things Fall Apart*, Cyprian Ekwensi's *Burning Grass* and Kenneth Kaunda's *Zambia Shall Be Free*, with Achebe himself acting as an editorial advisor. Over the next 40 years, the series continued to publish the best writing from across the African continent.

One of the founding aims of the Heinemann series was to make books by African writers available to as wide a readership as possible. Apollo Africa – a collaboration between Black Star Books and Head of Zeus – is proud to continue this work, ensuring novels, essays, poetry and plays from the original series are once again made available to readers all over the world.

With eternal love and gratitude
To Father, B. S. K.; and Mother, Abena

Acknowledgments

The writing of a novel is often long and solitary. Even so, a number of people help to make it pleasant so that it is less laborious and more a process of love. In this regard, I must acknowledge a number of people without whose support and encouragement I might not have completed this novel. Foremost, my gratitude goes to my sisters, Mary and Susana, and my brothers, Ebby, Samuel, Benjamin (Snr.) and Moses. I must also express my thanks to my new colleagues at Abbott Laboratories and my former colleagues at Porter, Wright, Morris & Arthur, especially the soccer team. In particular, I am grateful to those who read portions of the manuscript and offered their suggestions even when the possibility of publication seemed dim: Robert Tannous, Mike Underwood, Don Streibig, Pedro Dallarda, Belinda Reynolds and Mollie Grever. I need also to acknowledge the support of Ceda Ogada, Kwadwo Ofosuhene, Dominic Asante, William Anspach, Brian Basil, Sean Alexander, Vincent Aikins, Chip Cooper, Eric Yarboi, Bob and Lorinda Nutor, Patrick Nutor, Kim Shumate, Tom Grever, Craig Fullen, and Kwadjo and Marylin Adusei-Poku. I am thankful to Jean Hay for giving me the opportunity to publish and to the Heinemann group, Ruth Hamilton-Jones and Ayebia Ribeiro-Ayeh, as well as Alison Kelly, for their help and support. Thank you very much.

If Nakedness promises you clothes, hear his name.

Akan Proverb

It is the fool whose own tomatoes are sold to him.

Akan Proverb

Not enjoyment, and not sorrow,
Is our destined end or way;
But to act, that each to-morrow
Find us farther than to-day.

Henry Wadsworth Longfellow (A Psalm of Life)

Chapter One

He moved slowly, like a bored chameleon. It was as though his steps were a chore performed with difficulty but necessary for the accomplishment of compelling objectives. At his sides, his arms swung steadily, unhurried, like noiseless pendulums. The only swiftness in his movements was the sharp motion of his tongue, flickering through his lips and back again. Perhaps his eyes moved quickly too, surveying people and places as he passed by. Or perhaps his gaze was fixed unwaveringly ahead. It was impossible to tell, because his eyes were always hidden behind a pair of dark sunglasses, his barrier against the curiosity of those who were drawn by his unnatural quality of energy and power.

This was the man they called Mystique Mysterious. Male and female, child and adult, all referred to him by that name, in which they combined their respect for him, their fear of him, the fascination they felt for the unreachable person behind the shades.

Mystique Mysterious came to a halt a short distance from a large kiosk standing alone on a compound to his right. The nearest habitation on that side of the road was a little further down. 'What a waste of precious land,' he muttered to himself as he moved on towards the kiosk.

KILL ME QUICK, said the sign above the entrance. Mystique

Mysterious allowed himself a moment to contemplate the asininity of these words. Still, he could not help but appreciate their ability to amuse. He chuckled and stepped into the kiosk. The interior was dominated by a bar, and on the left corner of the bar was emblazoned another sign: FOR CREDIT, COME TOMORROW. Mystique Mysterious chuckled again.

His eyes, still through his dark glasses, studied the room and its occupants. A woman of about forty was engaged in light-hearted conversation with her customers. Mystique Mysterious concluded that she was beautiful and that age had cheated her of beauty only a little; her features, unwrinkled as yet, exuded an affable and easy charm that many of the young women lacked. As for the customers, there were three of them, occupying stools at the bar. They glanced at him, waiting for him to take the initiative. Instead he looked around at the other contents of the room. Near the entrance, he observed two tables, each arranged carefully with a set of five chairs; at the far end of the bar were two large barrels, apparently used as storage for extra supplies of liquor. The sole illumination of the kiosk came from a dim sixty-watt bulb hanging from the ceiling. When Mystique Mysterious was satisfied with his scrutiny, he walked over and sat on an empty stool and stretched his hands over the counter of the bar.

The woman of the bar recognised Mystique Mysterious, smiled in his direction and said with an easily discernible eagerness to please, 'Welcome, sir. What can I get for you tonight?'

As on most nights, Mystique Mysterious did not desire to drink, being wary of what he considered to be the ill effects of alcohol. It dulled the intelligence, and he needed to preserve the keenness of his mind in order to attain his prize. Yet evils such as alcohol had a place in his scheme, so he had to endure and even participate in them. 'Give me quarter,' he said in a voice inflated with authority.

The woman measured the liquor carefully to ensure it was a quarter of a beer bottle. She poured the contents into a glass and placed it on the counter. Mystique Mysterious thanked and paid her. The smell of the liquor hit his nostrils hard and he winced a little. He could handle the more diluted stuff, but not this *akpeteshie*, distilled locally from sugar cane or palm and possessing an incredibly high alcoholic content. The Kill Me Quick kiosk prided itself on the purity of its beverages, hence the strength of the smell from the glass in front of him. He took a sip and almost winced again as the liquor burned his mouth and stomach. But because he could not show such weakness, he maintained his composure, fighting the urge to grimace as most did when they drank the liquor.

The attention of the other customers was still fully focused on Mystique Mysterious. He relished it for a moment longer, while he lit a cigarette. He pulled on the cigarette, blew out the smoke and placed the cigarette to burn out on a tin defly cut to serve as an ashtray. Then he enquired of all three men at once, 'How are you gentlemen today?'

'Fine,' they replied in unison. Closest to him was Gabriel Bukari. Even seen through dark glasses and in the dimness, Bukari's eyes betrayed tension and sadness. He was a gentle man and his friends believed him to be kind-hearted. But the unhappiness born of several months of unemployment had taken effect. Mystique Mysterious smiled, for he was glad that Bukari was jobless. He had plans for him, and the best way to effectuate such plans was to approach him in his hour of utmost need when he was most vulnerable and ready to be influenced.

'Did your day treat you well?' asked Mystique Mysterious, this time of Kojo Ansah, the man seated next to Bukari. At a glance, even to a stranger, Kojo Ansah's nature was clear. He was a man renowned for being deficient in expression and proficient in contemplation. Mystique Mysterious did not approve. He did not like the fact that this silent man held thoughts closed to him, beyond reach. What use is a man's thoughts if he does not express them?

'The day was good,' was Kojo Ansah's terse reply. He spoke with utter indifference, allowing the words to flow slowly from the hollows of his mouth. 'The day was as good as a day must be.' Having expressed this compact thought he relapsed into a deep and cloudy pool of muteness, dense and impenetrable as night. His eyes left Mystique Mysterious and focused on the glass of water sitting on the counter in front of him. He looked intensely into the glass and seemed satisfied with its contents: it was an unmistakable sign that he desired to be left alone.

'That is very good,' Mystique Mysterious said. 'We can only hope that today is no worse than yesterday. We must be content if this simple hope is met by the end of the day when the sun sets and the stars splatter the sky.'

Kojo Ansah did not reply and Mystique Mysterious turned his attention to the third man in the bar. This was Kofi Ntim, also known as Philosopher Nonsense, an unsightly man with a huge forehead and a vast, balding skull. As if to compensate for the want of hair on his head, his eyebrows sprouted in one continuous thick brush of hair. His nose and lips offered nothing that his friends— who were not above jeering at him for his ugliness—could laugh at; but his jaw jutted forward and downward sharply like the tip of a spear. On it, and this was partly what had earned him the nickname Philospher Nonsense, he grew a goatee that accentuated his lengthy chin. And his ears were so disproportionately large they seemed to be attempting to take flight from the rest of his head. In addition, Kofi Ntim was short, standing below five feet.

Yet he was not bitter. It was as if he possessed a raging spirit that would not succumb to self-pity. Ever in high spirits, he was full of jokes and both sensible and senseless quips that he sometimes couched in philosophical terms. Perhaps it was the only escape, the only means of inoculating his sensibilities against an unremitting barrage of taunts intended in jest but still capable of striking painfully at the emotions. Perhaps it was for this reason, too, that he reciprocated, when the opportunity arose, and mocked whomever he could.

Mystique Mysterious wondered why nature had so cruelly moulded Kofi Ntim. Even he, who was supremely in control of his reactions, had to stifle a powerful urge to laugh by speaking instead. 'The drink is strong today, is it not?'

'Ah, the drink is strong. So what? Is that not why you bought it? People are always complaining about one thing or the other. If it were weak you would be jumping up and down complaining how the liquor of nowadays has lost its power, how you used to drink strong drink in your youth and how the young ones of today have lost it,' Kofi Ntim replied with typical irreverence. But his tone lacked bite, despite the irritable choice of words.

'No, I don't complain. I was complimenting Madam here for keeping her liquor clean.'

'You surely were not.'

Mystique Mysterious itched with amusement. His thin smile widened into a grin, exposing his teeth. 'You certainly have a way of expressing your thoughts. I must compliment you on your eloquence, even if I disagree with you.' He had learnt from experience to refuse to be baited into argument, playing instead the part of the diplomat, the detached gentleman. Observers might not notice one instance of his being defeated in intellectual debate, but these things added up: the subconscious fed the active mind its morsels, one by one, until they became fully grown unfavourable opinions.

Kofi Ntim came back. 'I know why you said it in the first place.'

The bait was out again, and Mr Mysterious was curious. 'Why did I say it?'

Kofi Ntim took a long sip of his drink and allowed it to burn his mouth before swallowing. 'You do not have the stomach for strong liquor, you. So you must complain all the time. You are like this weakling here.' The last remark was directed at Kojo Ansah, the quiet one, who drank only water and juice. Kofi Ntim went on. 'A man has to imbibe like a man; drink strong, powerful liquor that burns your insides like fire. I do not like hearing nonsense such as "I do not drink liquor" or "This alcohol is too strong." There's no alcohol so strong that a real man can't drink it.'

The woman of the bar queried: 'How about women? Can a real woman drink liquor like a real man? And watch your mouth. Don't you know this is a big man you are talking to?'

Kofi Ntim ignored the first part of the question. 'As for you, Auntie Esi, sometimes I wonder why you sell this stuff at all. Maybe if you drank some of what you sell, you would have more sense in your head. I can talk to anyone anyway I want.' Then he looked in the direction of Gabriel Bukari and asked, 'Or, Bukari, am I not speaking the truth?'

Out of deference to Esi and Mystique Mysterious, Bukari did not respond. He looked at Kofi Ntim and Mystique Mysterious with an uncertain expression, avoiding eye contact. Finally his eyes came to rest on the counter. 'Or have you also become a weakling like Kojo Ansah, who cannot even talk?' Kofi Ntim pressed.

'Why don't you say something reasonable?' Esi asked.

'I was not talking to you, woman!' retorted Kofi Ntim. 'I was talking to this mute coward called Bukari.'

Finding Kofi Ntim's rumblings annoying, Bukari blurted, 'Why don't you shut up and learn some sense before you open your mouth again?'

'Don't tell me to shut up, you unemployed fool. You are so stupid nobody will employ you.'

'Look who is calling me a fool. You who are so stupid that everyone calls you a philosopher of nonsense.'

'Why are you insulting me, Bukari?'

'Why did *you* insult *me*?'

'I did not insult you, I only called you an unemployed fool, which is true.'

'Neither did I insult you. I only called you a stupid philosopher of nonsense, which is true.'

Anyone would think they were the worst of enemies, ruthlessly tearing at each other's throats. But Esi, who had witnessed such exchanges many times before, knew them better than that: their anger flared up easily and was quickly forgotten.

'Ignore them, sir,' she said to Mystique Mysterious. 'They are only being silly. They do that all the time.'

'I can imagine,' Mystique Mysterious replied.

'Watch your non-alcoholic mouth, woman,' warned Kofi Ntim.

He turned his attention back to Bukari and was about to pursue the quarrel, but Mystique Mysterious intervened. 'Do you come here often?' he asked no one in particular, trying to steer the conversation elsewhere.

'That, sir, is none of your business,' Kofi Ntim responded. 'Why, will you buy me a drink, or what?'

'Maybe,' replied Mystique Mysterious.

'Go ahead, then. What are you waiting for?'

Mystique Mysterious ordered Kofi Ntim a drink. Kofi Ntim was surprised by this show of generosity, though he did not show it. Why would anyone, especially a stranger, buy him a drink *gratis*? He was not used to acts of benevolence, no matter how small. He, the target of mockery, the specimen of human ugliness who others treated as a source of amusement and not much more. Was his luck about to change? Was a propitious god smiling on him today? Was this the beginning of a deviation in the course of his hum-drum life?

Life? He was past the stage when he had contemplat-ed daily the cruelties of his existence. His earlier years had been spent looking in the mirror and grieving over his unattractive physique and near-repulsive countenance. What others told him was confirmed by his own eyes. In his position, many would sink into an abyss of self-loathing that might eventually become twisted into a violent hatred of the rest of the world, so that they were transformed into a walking time-bomb, ready to detonate at the least prov-ocation. Others would choose a less hostile response, yet no less painful: a psychic numbing of sorts, endeavouring to banish any sense of sadness, any feeling of inadequacy, projecting a constant radiance of joy or a cavalier attitude towards life, a facade to conceal the inner pain. Kofi Ntim belonged somewhere in this latter group. In his adult years, although he sometimes lamented his fate, he did not wallow in it. Instead, he concentrated on feeling and spreading hap-piness. He could explode, but his ammunition consisted of jokes and irreverent remarks intended to bounce off his targets.

At the moment, he looked at the drink Mystique Mys-terious had ordered as it was placed in front of him and blinked deliberately, as if he could scarcely believe that it existed. He lifted the glass to his lips and drank with pleas-ure, sinking almost three-quarters of the contents. Then he smiled, but he did not thank his benefactor.

'The evil of alcohol.' It was Kojo Ansah, the quiet one, who spoke.

'How do you know it's evil when you don't drink it?' Kofi Ntim retorted.

Kojo Ansah did not respond: he did not desire to enter into a meaningless argument with Kofi Ntim. He had spoken and warned them. As if to defy Kojo Ansah, Mystique Mysterious ordered a half glass of *akpeteshie* for Bukari. Bukari thanked him and drank greedily. Mystique Mysterious beamed inside. Not only words mattered; actions mattered too. Leadership did not have to have a moral basis. One could gain control of men and women by other means—by enticing them and making them dependent. At the moment, he knew there were four happy people in the kiosk: himself, who had bought the drinks; Esi, the proprietor, who had increased her sales; and Kofi Ntim and Bukari, who had benefited from his acts of apparent generosity. Only Kojo Ansah, the quiet one, remained outside the circle.

So the men who wanted to drink did so. Their tongues loosened and they talked freely and Mystique Mysterious listened carefully, digesting every word and feeding on whatever he heard. Esi, ever the polished hostess, kept them alive with smiles and conversation, but the night was growing old and the traffic of bodies that came and went from the kiosk dwindled and eventually ceased.

Those who remained at the bar were becoming weary, especially as the effects of liquor became manifest in those who had imbibed: Gabriel Bukari's eyes grew bloodshot and Kofi Ntim slumped across the counter like a sagging bag. Esi began to yawn, but she could not dismiss these customers who were the chief patrons of her business. Even the teetotaller, the silent one who had neither strained his body with liquor nor exerted his lungs with speech, showed signs of weariness and, like Esi, yawned repeatedly. Only Mystique Mysterious, sitting upright, did not appear jaded. Since his eyes were hidden, no one could tell how exhausted he was. All they could see was an unfatigued body, which surprised them all.

'Well, nature has its demands. I have to leave now,' said Kojo Ansah. Without further ceremony he walked to the entrance of the kiosk.

'Bye, Kojo, come again,' Esi said.

'Sleep well,' bid Bukari.

'Go with the devil,' said Kofi Ntim.

'As for you, Kofi, you never speak any sense,' Esi remarked.

'Don't bother stating the obvious,' Bukari said.

'I suppose it's time for me to leave too,' Kofi Ntim announced once Kojo Ansah had left.

'I will leave with you,' Bukari informed him.

'No, don't. I have some news for you,' said Mystique Mysterious to Bukari.

Bukari was puzzled. 'What news?'

'I have to tell you alone.'

'What is so important and so secret that you have to tell him alone?' queried Kofi Ntim. 'Let's go, Bukari. This man can have nothing good to tell you. All he can do for you is buy drinks.'

'You will be happy if you listen to me, but you will regret it if you listen to your friend here,' Mystique Mysterious said to Bukari.

'All right,' Bukari replied.

'Oh, you fool, you're going to listen to him?' Kofi Ntim affected indifference and swallowed the dregs of liquor in his glass. He was about to leave when he seemed to recollect something. His face lit up as he asked, 'Esi, will you warm my bed with your body tonight?'

'You shut up! Learn some sense.'

'What is senseless about wanting you tonight?'

'You have lost your head.'

'Why don't you want to come home with me?'

'Because you're ugly,' Bukari intervened on Esi's behalf. 'No woman wants you.'

'Shut up, you urchin,' Kofi Ntim barked at Bukari. Then he addressed Esi again. 'One day you will come to your senses, Esi. One day you will see how sweet it is to have me.' Esi smiled, but did not speak. 'Oh well, if you don't want to come with me, I'll go home alone.' Kofi Ntim leaned over the counter and reached for Esi, but she had already anticipated him and moved quickly aside. Accepting defeat, Kofi Ntim danced his way out.

Mystique Mysterious waited a little, then turned to Bukari and said, 'Gabriel Bukari.' He deliberately pronounced the whole name for effect: it was more commanding of attention. 'I will give you some good news if you walk out with me.' Bukari had already accepted the offer in his mind, and he nodded. The men bade Esi farewell and walked out.

Outside, the moon glowed brilliantly amid glittering stars. Mystique Mysterious remained silent, knowing that this would increase Bukari's anxiety. He would draw this man in slowly. They walked side by side at a pace deliberately kept slow by Mystique Mysterious. After a while

Mystique Mysterious looked up at the sky and whispered, 'Isn't it beautiful, this night of moon and stars?' Before Bukari could reply, he continued, 'But sadly, some people can't even appreciate the night's beauty because they do not have the ease of mind to do so. Many are swallowed by sadness, by concerns that deprive them even of the simple joys of life, the joys that come to us free of charge, for everything else comes at a price. There is a simple truth, Gabriel Bukari, that many people ignore: a man can't enjoy the pleasures that are free unless he has access to those that come at a price. Nature's gifts uplift the mind, but how can a man appreciate this when he has heavy problems on his mind? Problems that threaten his very survival as a human being?'

Mystique Mysterious paused. Bukari's anxiety was turning into anger. Had this man detained him only to propound such meaningless philosophy? He felt a strong urge to express his anger, but he was in formidable company and had to be careful, so he forced a wide grin and his teeth glittered against the darkness of the night.

Mystique Mysterious resumed his speech. 'Contrary to what you are thinking, I am not talking nonsense, Gabriel Bukari. But I can understand why you will not appreciate my words of wisdom at this stage and I will not bore you very much with such talk.'

Bukari was thankful. At last, he was about to learn what business Mystique Mysterious had with him. But not quite yet.

'How is your wife, Fati?'

Bukari gasped, amazed and honoured that Mystique

Mysterious knew his wife's name. But he did not ask any questions: this was Mystique Mysterious, the cryptic man, the enigma you did not try to fathom. 'She is well, sir, and she thanks your mouth for asking about her.'

'And your son, Baba?'

So this detail, too, was known to the great man. 'He too is fine and thanks you.'

Mystique Mysterious said, 'I'm very glad to hear that. I know that you, Bukari, have been deprived of life's enjoyments.' He had taken the lead. Having lured and impressed this man, he could drop the formality and build a safe zone of comfort. Since most of Gabriel Bukari's friends called him Bukari, he did the same. 'Bukari, you don't have the means to enjoy the things that come at a price; you must change that. You must think of your wife and son. They want to live the best of lives and they are looking up to you. You can't fail them and I know that you don't want to fail them.'

Bukari found much truth in these words. 'These things you say, why are you saying them to me?'

Mystique Mysterious smiled and reached into his pocket for his pack of cigarettes. He offered them to Bukari, who took one and put it between his lips. Mystique Mysterious produced a box of matches and lit the cigarette in Bukari's mouth. He was in control: he could afford to appear to be at Bukari's service. As Bukari began to puff on the cigarette, Mystique Mysterious said, 'But today, your luck is about to change for ever, Bukari. I offer you something that will put food on your table, not from your wife's income, but from your own pocket. I offer you the opportunity to walk proud and confident, knowing that you are bringing in a wage. Bukari, my friend, I know you are a driver and I am offering you a job.'

'A job!' Bukari cried, unable to cover his enthusiasm. 'This is incredibly good news! I have been unemployed for—'

'Eight months.' Mystique Mysterious completed the sentence.

This time Bukari was not surprised by the extent of Mystique Mysterious's knowledge; he was only impressed. 'You mean you have a taxi for me?'

'No, I don't have a taxi, but I know someone who does, and he is looking for a driver. It's an old Ford, but it is in very good condition.'

Bukari listened eagerly, pulling hard on the cigarette and blowing out huge puffs of smoke. He did not care how old the car was: a car was a car.

Mystique Mysterious continued, 'I looked around and I said to myself, "Bukari has been without work for a while. He has a wife and a son to feed. He needs this job, so let me give it to him." And here I am offering it to you.'

Bukari was elated. 'So, what should I do now?'

'I will come and get you tomorrow evening, then we will go and see the man who owns the taxi. After that, you will have a job. Trust me.'

'I do!'

'Good, Bukari. Be ready at eight tomorrow evening. Sleep well.' Without waiting for Bukari to say any more, Mystique Mysterious turned and walked away. Bukari watched as darkness descended and swallowed him. The night: immense, vast, powerful, intriguing and mysterious as the man. Then Bukari threw away his cigarette stub and walked on, full of joy, breathing the night's therapeutic air deep into his lungs. His nerves calmed a bit, but his mind buzzed with the new possibilities opened up to him by Mystique Mysterious.

Chapter Two

Fati heard the shrill cry of a cockerel from the distance. She turned sideways on her mattress and felt the body of her husband still wrapped in sleep beside her. Not wishing to wake him, she turned and lay on her back again and, leaving a space between their bodies, tried to spread her limbs, but the mattress was not big enough and her leg made contact with the bare floor. She winced at the cold. If only she could empty her mind—forget the chores awaiting her—she might be able to get a little more sleep. For a moment she seemed to succeed: her body and mind drifted slowly towards unconsciousness. But before she could attain the stage of complete sleep, the cockerel crowed again and again.

Despite the familiarity of this routine, Fati still found it difficult to resist the invitation of morning slumber. She would have liked to go on simply lying there, thinking of nothing, just savouring the uncorrupted smell of the morning. But now the call for Moslems to prayer came soaring over the din of fowls with a power not easily to be ignored. Fati could hear the usual stirring of her neighbour, Issaka, who was not one to miss a call to prayer. Opening and shutting her eyes several times, she began to come alive herself.

She raised her upper body and looked around the room.

There was not much to see. Opposite, a blank wall stared back at her; past the body of her husband on the left was another wall, undecorated except for a few scribblings contributed by Baba in a fit of madness. The young men of today had no sense of responsibility; why he would scribble on the wall was beyond Fati. In the left corner, where the walls met, sat two suitcases and a portmanteau. Clothes were strewn on top of these and on the floor—evidence of her husband's carelessness. There was a rickety table to the left of the mattress, covered with a piece of lace, with a few necessities like soap and toilet paper arranged on top.

Fati rose from the mattress and selected a piece of cloth to wrap around her nakedness. Then she looked back at her husband, still drowned in sleep, and wondered how anyone could sleep so soundly through the mounting din of morning. Drivers were stirring on to the roads now: she could hear the roar and whistle of engines. Through the unshuttered window, rays of sunlight were beginning to reach the room—though the old window screen was so clogged and darkened with dirt that the light struggled to penetrate. A pity that the screen was not equally effective against the entry of mosquitoes. Age had worn holes in it, and sometimes—even in oppressive heat—they were forced to shut the windows to stem the onslaught of the insects.

Fati slipped her feet into a pair of slippers and walked into the second chamber which they used as a living room during the day and as Baba's bedroom at night. Baba, like his father, was still sealed in the envelope of sleep. The living room did not contain much more furniture than the bedroom, but it had two windows opposite one another and was therefore airier. There was an armchair in the corner —old and dilapidated, with one torn cushion for a seat and one for a backrest. Next to it was a cupboard containing four glasses (which were merely decorative and hardly ever used), three tins of sardines and two cans of evaporated milk.

Fati looked at the supine body of her son, his upper torso bare because the cloth he used as a cover had slipped to his waist, and her heart swelled with love. She had every reason to feel disappointed with a son who at sixteen was a high-school truant. She knew what many in her neighbour-hood thought: her son, Baba, the product of her womb, was worthless. Good natured, yes, but still worthless. But she was convinced that he possessed intelligence which had not as yet been revealed; and in spite of the facts she had com-plete confidence in him and loved him dearly. As she looked at his sleeping form, so calm and apparently unperturbed, as though at perfect peace with the world, Fati was thankful that he was there. It was irrelevant what he did, because his presence alone was reason for joy.

With one hand Fati picked up a bucket from the corner of the room. In it was a smaller pail, a tablet of soap and a sponge. With the other hand she took hold of a broom lying nearby. Outside, she placed the bucket down and leant for a while on the broom, spreading out its fronds, musing and looking around her. There were three buildings in the com-pound, enclosing an area for common use which opened on one side on to the gutter and the pot-holed street.

Fati bent forward until her upper body was almost par-allel to the ground and began to sweep the compound.

When she had finished, she laid the broom down close to the entrance to her building, picked up the bucket and hurried through an opening on the left-hand side of the compound. This led to the common lavatory and bathroom. Fati removed the pail, soap and towel and held the bucket under the tap on the outside wall of the bathroom. While the water rose slowly in the bucket, she listened to the stirring of life in the compound. Then she entered the bathroom and closed the door, which squeaked with old age and neglect. She bathed, rinsed and wiped herself dry with her towel.

As Fati re-entered the compound, her neighbour, Issaka, emerged from the building next to hers. 'Eei, Fati, good morning,' Issaka said by way of greeting.

'Morning,' Fati replied. Instinctively, she tightened the piece of cloth shielding her nakedness with her left hand while she held on to the bucket with the right.

'Did you sleep well?'

'Yes, Issaka, I did. How about you? Did you sleep well?'

'Thanks be to Allah, I too slept very well.'

Fati was about to proceed past Issaka after this exchange of pleasantries when Issaka cleared his throat. Fati knew her neighbour and preempted his initiative. 'What is it you want, Issaka?' she enquired.

Issaka affected embarrassment; his eyes narrowed shyly and a coy smile rose from his lips and made dimples in his cheeks. Then he rubbed his fingers together as though he were nervous and said, 'Fati, you know I have a new baby?'

'Is that what you wanted to tell me, Issaka? You've had

the baby for at least seven months and the whole town knows it.'

'I know, Fati, but with our comings and goings we sometimes forget a neighbour has had a baby.'

'Thank you for reminding me, but I have not forgotten.'

'How foolish of me to think that you would forget. Pardon me, Fati. But as a good neighbour I know that you know that new babies mean new mouths to be fed.'

Fati was quite fond of Issaka, but sometimes he got on her nerves. Losing patience, she snapped at him, 'So?' and began to walk on.

Issaka realised that things were turning against him. 'I was wondering if—' He paused, again feigning embarrassment. But Fati's quick dash for the door to her room snapped him out of his reticence. 'I was wondering if you could lend me a tin of sardines,' he said at last.

Fati stopped and asked with incredulity, 'What? Issaka, is the baby going to eat sardines?'

Suddenly Issaka developed a stammer. 'I... we... err... must... muu...'

'When did you forget how to talk, Issaka?'

Instead of speaking, Issaka grinned, exposing teeth so separated from one another that they appeared inadvertently splattered in his mouth like little ivory apostrophes on a large dark page. Fati waited for an answer, but none came. Her patience was completely gone and again she made for the door.

'Oh, Fati, don't go away like that,' Issaka said, following her.

'Are you coming in here with me?'

'The sardines, Fati, the sardines.'

'What sardines?'

'The tin you are going to give me.'

'Who said I was going to give you anything, Issaka?'

'Oh, but Fati, we have already settled that issue. Allah bless you.'

'Issaka, what issue?'

'The issue of the sardines.'

'Issaka, get this into your head. I have no sardines for you.'

'But, Fati, you have some in your room. I saw them there the other day with my own eyes.'

'They are not for you.'

'I know that, this is why I am asking.'

'You will ask for ever.'

Fati stepped into the living room and closed the door, ignoring Issaka's supplications, but she made the mistake of leaving the door unlocked and as soon as she was inside Issaka pushed it open and popped his head round it. Both Bukari and Baba were awake—Bukari reclining in the dilapidated armchair while Baba slouched on the floor against the wall. They were listening to a small radio which Bukari held in his lap. It was tuned to the local service of the Ghana Broadcasting Corporation.

Issaka stepped into the living room and uttered opening pleasantries. 'Allah bless you, Bukari. And you too, Baba. I know he has kept you both very well.'

'We are all well, Issaka,' Bukari answered for both.

'My baby too is doing well, thank Allah,' Issaka said and cleared his throat.

'Good,' Bukari said rather curtly, anticipating a demand. Wearied by Issaka's persistence, Fati simply set the bucket on the floor and disappeared into the bedroom. 'Issaka, what do you want?' Bukari queried.

'Oh, my friend Bukari, you won't even ask me how I am or how my wives and children are. Must you ask me so crudely what I want?'

'Look, Issaka, if you don't have anything better to say, leave us in peace.'

Issaka took a step forward, disregarding Bukari's request. 'My friend, Bukari,' he said. 'I only want one tin of sardines for my baby's sake. Bukari, I do not want three, I do not want two, although if you give me two or three I will take them gladly. But I am not greedy. I only want one.'

Bukari shook his head vigorously in disbelief. 'Issaka! Your head must be absent from your neck. I have been unemployed for how long, Issaka?' Issaka averted his eyes, stared at his feet and said nothing. Bukari supplied the answer himself: 'Eight months, Issaka.' He held out eight fingers to emphasise the extensiveness of the period. 'Eight months I have been unemployed, Issaka, and you won't come and give me food. No, the little that I have, you want to take away from me. The road is your face, Issaka; go and leave me in peace.'

Issaka changed his strategy. 'Hey, Bukari, if you won't give, I will take myself. After all, it is only food. Allah gives food for free!'

'Then why don't you go and ask Allah to feed you? When did you last hear Allah giving free food? He has stopped doing that.'

'Don't blaspheme!'

Issaka hurried to the cupboard, opened it, snatched a tin of sardines, and ran away before Bukari could prevent him. Bukari fumed but resigned himself to the loss and went back to listening to the radio. Soon, however, the door was flung open and Issaka walked into the room again, without the tin of sardines. That he would dare to return surprised both Bukari and Baba and they stared at him, speechless. Tension began to mount in the room as Issaka returned the stare, his eyes sparkling with triumph.

Issaka tried his luck a step further: 'Hey, Bukari, I forgot the key to the sardines. It isn't attached to the tin. Do you have it anywhere?'

Anger began to build into rage.

'Bukari, answer me now! Do you have the key to the sardines?'

The rage was complete. Bukari jumped forward, but tumbled to the floor and fell on his buttocks. Issaka howled with laughter. Hearing this, Fati pushed her head out into the living room in time to see Bukari, still sitting on his buttocks, attempt to reach for Issaka's ankles. Issaka was quicker and moved his feet away so that Bukari caught empty air and nearly fell on his face in the attempt. Fati could not deny the funny side of Bukari's posture, but she did not want to annoy him further so she suppressed her laughter and withdrew into the bedroom. Even Baba smirked, but he erased the smirk from his face before his father noticed. Before Bukari could get to his feet, Issaka made his escape.

Slowly, Bukari rose and walked outside. Issaka was not

in sight, but there was plenty of activity in the compound at the moment. The family in the opposite building was up and about, and Bukari saw Jojo's Father standing in front of his door. Next to him was Jojo's Mother, standing arms akimbo, arguing with her husband. The parents of Jojo went by the names, 'Jojo's Mother' and 'Jojo's Father' because the point of reference in their lives was their five-year-old son. No one remembered their actual names any more. Jojo emerged from indoors and said something to his mother. Jojo's Mother took him by the hand and led him back indoors.

'Good morning, Jojo's Father!' Bukari hollered across the compound.

Jojo's Father noticed Bukari and replied, 'Good morning, Bukari. How are Fati and Baba?'

'They are well. They thank you for asking. And how's the family?'

'By God's grace the family is well.'

The men relapsed into silence. In their silence, sounds around them became more discernible: the murmur of sooty liquid running along the gutter at the roadside, the little chirps of chicks scratching around the compound in search of food. One chick spotted a grain of corn and hurried towards it, but the mother hen pecked the corn itself, depriving the chick of its prize. From the other side of the road the bleating of a goat mingled with the growl of a speeding, dust-raising car.

Presently, the man everybody called Madman appeared, narrowing his eyes at Bukari and Jojo's Father. Bukari said, 'Good morning, my friend. How are you today?' Madman did not reply, but stepped forward to peer at the two men more closely. Bukari repeated the question and was rewarded with a smile.

Jojo's Father tried his luck. 'You are looking sharp today. Have you received some good news that you are not telling us?'

This approach yielded better results. 'Yes,' Madman said.

'Yes? We thank God,' replied Jojo's Father, not bothering to seek clarification.

As though he were hearing the word for the first time, a merry look appeared on Madman's face. 'God,' he said softly. 'God created the hen. And do you know God created the chicks? The hen, the chicks, God.' He pointed to the parade of fowls nearby. 'And speaking of hens do you know that they have a beak, two eyes, nice feathers, and a tail? And do you know that in years past we have killed them and eaten them in our soups? We have! When we go to parties we kill them and fry them and eat them. Do you know that? Do you? Right here in Accra, right here in Nima. That is why I must leave and go to Bombay some day. Maybe I will leave for Bombay tomorrow so you can live in sin killing hens for your soup and stew.' Madman paused a while to catch his breath. Then, as Bukari and Jojo's Father listened, he enlarged upon his plans to get to Bombay, which consisted mainly of swimming across the ocean on the back of a lizard.

'You mean a crocodile?' Bukari asked.

But Madman was adamant. 'No, a lizard! A lizard!' he bellowed. When he was satisfied that they understood him, he looked at them with blazing eyes. To Bukari he then said,

'I am fine today,' apparently in response to the question Bukari had posed several minutes earlier. Madman saluted both men in military fashion and walked away.

Bukari chuckled at Madman's theatrics. He waved goodbye to Jojo's Father and went back indoors. Baba was staring out of the window. 'Father, I am going to walk around a little bit,' he said. Bukari nodded and Baba left. Bukari sat in the dilapidated armchair and thought back to the night before. He remembered Mystique Mysterious's promise and believed what he wanted to believe: that his ill luck was about to be reversed. Eight months of unemployment, the losing battle between hope and despair. Eight months of depression and drunkenness. Eight months of rancour and tension with his wife. While Fati had had to support the family, he had been made to feel inadequate; not by her actions or by anything she had said but by his own sense of failure. He had rebelled by whining and nagging. But now the gloom was about to be dispelled. Mystique Mysterious was the bearer of new light. Tonight would decide it. Beaming, Bukari leapt to his feet and walked into the bedroom to deliver the good news to Fati. She was on her knees, folding and arranging clothes.

'Fati, I have good news!' Bukari's voice rang with hope and confidence. Fati rose and smiled. She had not heard such life in his voice for a long time. As she stood before him, her face lit up with anticipation, her slender neck rising up from the rounded landscape of her body like the delicate stem of a flower rising up from fertile soil, Bukari experienced a rush of affection and desire. He reached out, gathered her into his arms and carried her to the mattress.

After their love-making, he told her the news. Buoyed up by the pleasures they had just experienced and their shared hopes of impending improvements in their lives, they lay side by side, oblivious to the passage of time and to the sounds of fowls and humans from the compound and the street. It was *their* world now, filled with endless potential. But gradually the sun rose in the sky and the heat of the day intensified. Fati, already behind with the day's work, hurried outside to prepare for her afternoon sale.

Alone, Bukari, head resting on open palms, eyes shut, allowed his mind to roam into the depths of time before. The memories were clear. Eight years old in the north of Ghana, the town of Wa. His father came: a lean figure who wore his soul, his feelings both positive and negative, all his innermost thoughts, in his eyes. Anger, joy, approval and disapproval—all of these his twelve children and two wives understood perfectly from the expression in his eyes. They knew from the look in his eyes when he wanted to be left alone and when he desired company. And whatever his wishes were, they must be complied with, for it was not wise to provoke his ire. When he raised his fists, the effects could be catastrophic. Bukari remembered once when he beat his mother. She nearly died from the bruises and swellings and had to be nursed for weeks by her co-wife. Bukari hated him for that and had sworn never to beat his own wife.

He had only fond memories of his two mothers. He was the offspring of the elder wife, but both were mothers to him and he treated them both as such. There never seemed to be any jealousy between the two women, and if the man of the household showed little affection, they compensated with an abundance of it. Bukari's natural mother was a seemingly inexhaustible well of strength and vigour, running tirelessly around the house from morning to evening. Her energy was so powerful that she had plenty to spare for her family: she was the source which, when their own reserves were low, they tapped for replenishment. Even when she left for the market, her presence lingered on at home. And she always returned with a gift for her children, all seven of her own and all five begotten by her junior in marriage.

When she died from a snake bite, the radiance was gone from the house. There was no joy, no vibrancy, no promise. Bukari's father aged instantly, as though all the years in his life had waited for that event to become manifest. So Bukari, who was fifteen by that time, decided to leave Wa and try his fortunes in Accra, the capital. He had heard how the streets of that city glittered with lights at night as if the sun had never retired; how sophisticated the women were, possessed of grace and panache; how opportunities were arrayed like ripe fruits, within reach, ready to be plucked by the industrious; how men and women chased after their dreams and realised them, drove fast cars, drank expensive drinks and lived in gorgeous mansions. This was the time to move on. He had dropped out of school. His senior mother was dead, his father was dying, his junior mother was struggling to support the family. If he did not leave he would only be a burden on her. So despite his father's protests, he borrowed money from his junior mother and left for Accra. He was lucky, for his junior mother had a cousin there who agreed to take care of him.

Only a month later, his father died and he had to return

to Wa for the funeral. Perhaps the father had been unable to bear it when his favourite son left home, contrary to his wishes. Or perhaps the cause of death lay elsewhere. They never found out. Bukari, returning for the funeral after a month in the city, commanded a new level of respect, benefiting from the human tendency to revere travellers, those who have visited distant places, walked exotic streets, seen new or different things, survived in a strange environment. His family felt the void created by his father's death and pleaded with him to stay home. But the allure of the city, with its freedoms and promises, outweighed the wish to be among loved ones. Besides, this town had the unpleasant memory of death. He returned to Accra where his junior mother's cousin, himself a driver, taught him the art. After his brief apprenticeship, the young man from Wa was ready. He found employment as a driver for one of the wealthy men of the city. He had come a long way since. Now there was Fati and Baba.

Chapter Three

When evening came, the temperature dipped as the heat of the afternoon yielded slowly, like a stubborn adversary, to the gentle breeze of sunset and then to the chilly wind of dusk. Mothers and fathers, their day's work done, turned to recreational activity, while the youngest children gathered round their grandparents for company. Other areas, however, continued to bristle with life. In the suburb of Accra called Nima, within an area known simply as 441, young men lounged on street corners. They sat on whatever they could find: broken stools, bricks, even stones—anything large enough to accommodate their narrow buttocks. Many held in their hands fresh plantain leaves containing rice and beans, or *kenkey* and fish, bought from nearby vendors who set up shop at that time of the evening to capture the patronage of those who had spent a long day toiling at work, had been paid little, and now craved food to fill their stomachs and conversation to soothe their minds.

The conversation shifted from topic to topic, from the hustles of the day and the problems of ordinary men like them, to the selfishness of rich folk, who used their labour, smiled disdainfully into their faces, flashed money in front of them and then paid them little. They spoke with eloquence but without passion; as though they were, if not content with their lot, at least resigned to it, and their complaints were mechanical: things to be said and forgotten and then repeated and forgotten, day in and day out. This was their ineffectual way of vengeance: to join one another in maligning their bosses, the big men whom they simultaneously envied and despised, to whom they were indebted for being there to hand out a little money at the end of the month. In this world of theirs, they could criticise these people, heap them with insults, cover them with scorn. Together, and with words, they could savour a triumph over their bosses which they could not achieve with their actions.

This done, they turned their attention to their families. Since most of the street-corner men were unmarried, their families consisted of parents, siblings, aunts, uncles, and the like—the full array of the extended family system comprising all blood relations. They bemoaned the stresses of being members of an extended family in which everyone had a say in everyone else's affairs. This was Accra, modern and sophisticated, where traditional systems and practices were under siege. Yet the power of the extended family was still felt by all of them: no man or woman was beyond its reach. But even as they complained about their lack of freedom, they were partly grateful for what they had. An uncle could interfere in their lives and they resented that, yet they knew that if they got into trouble that same uncle would help them out. The family might sometimes seem to imprison them, but without it many of them would probably be homeless.

Finally, they discussed their love lives, picking on one

another and making jokes to lighten their hearts and put smiles on their faces.

Then from somewhere—no one was quite certain where—Mystique Mysterious entered the private world of the gathering. A deferential stillness fell on the group as they watched his approach. For a period, he did not speak, studying their faces under cover of his dark glasses and relishing in his heart the respect he commanded among these men. His unspoken feelings were partly exposed by the curious smirk on his face; it seemed as if he was mocking them, flaunting his power in silent challenge.

Mystique Mysterious found an unoccupied stool and sat on it. The conversation that had died completely was revived, but only in the form of whispers. Faces turned furtively, and here and there agitated voices murmured into ears as the crowd struggled to remain calm. Finally, Mystique Mysterious said, 'It's a good day, no?' The question was directed at no one in particular, and there was no oral response—only, instead, a collective nodding of heads. Mystique Mysterious reached into his pocket and produced four packets of cigarettes. 'I have something for you all,' he remarked, and the men stretched their necks to see what he had. He tortured them a little before beginning to pass the packets around. The men grabbed the cigarettes hungrily, and when enough had gone around he produced lighters and passed them around as well. The crowd was impressed: for many of them lighters were luxury items. Some fumbled in excited attempts to get the devices to spark, so that they had to be aided by their more sophisticated friends. Mystique Mysterious lighted a cigarette himself, but he merely held on to it and occasionally put it to his lips and pulled without inhaling. The crowd puffed greedily until the air was dense with smoke.

Mystique Mysterious eyed the man sitting closest to him until the young man—looking away in a vain attempt to ignore the scrutiny—burned with discomfort, praying silently that Mystique Mysterious would spare him the intense, disquieting gaze. At last, Mystique Mysterious said to him, 'This cigarette is not strong enough, is it?'

The young man hesitated. If he disagreed he would be contradicting Mystique Mysterious; if he did not, he would probably sound ungrateful. 'It is strong, but maybe not,' he said. Let Mystique Mysterious read what he wanted from the ambiguity.

'You could try something stronger.'

'Like what, sir?'

Mystique Mysterious did not answer. Instead, he reached into his pocket again and produced a roll of marijuana. He sniffed it and offered it to the young man, who took it without hesitation or question. But when the young man looked at it more closely, he realised what it was. 'But sir, I don't smoke marijuana,' said he.

'Why?'

'I don't think it's good for me, sir.'

'Nonsense! It is the source of knowledge, the beginning of all wisdom. Don't let anyone to tell you it isn't good.'

'But it is also illegal to smoke, sir.'

'Nothing I give you is illegal! I am what is legal and what is not. Don't you know that?' The young man stared. 'Light it and smoke,' ordered Mystique Mysterious, with such authority that the young man felt afraid to disobey. He found a lighter, lighted the roll of marijuana and pulled heavily on it. He waited, contemplating the effect, and then he pulled on it again, and again. Soon, a sedate look settled on his face and he smiled contentedly.

'Pass it around,' Mystique Mysterious requested. The young man took another puff and passed the diminishing roll to the next person, who smoked and passed it on. Mystique Mysterious observed happily as the roll went from hand to hand, from mouth to mouth. He produced more rolls. Even if they did not become addicts, so that he could make some money out of them, this act of free giving would endear him to them, or make them feel indebted to him, so that they would not easily rebel against him. The conversation livened as the marijuana eased the discomfort his arrival had first caused. As the smoke grew more dense, Mystique Mysterious got up and left, as quietly as he had come. Nobody noticed him leave.

Dusk was gradually giving way to the thickness of night as Mystique Mysterious made a detour into the back alleys of Nima. There he found Bukari's son, Baba, and his friends, idling, seated in a dim corner of a ruined structure that might once have been a stall. Mystique Mysterious observed them for a moment before approaching them. When the boys noticed him, like the 441 crowd before, silence fell on them, and they too looked at Mystique Mysterious in awkward admiration.

'Baba,' said Mystique Mysterious. 'How are you, my son?' To be addressed directly by Mystique Mysterious was to achieve instant stardom: Baba gained immediate respect from his friends. Baba himself was speechless. That this important man would single him out was too much for him; he merely stared, open-mouthed. Mystique Mysterious came closer, until he stood next to the younger man. He slipped his arm paternally round Baba's shoulders. 'Come with me, Baba,' he said. Baba followed him away from the rest. Mystique Mysterious delved into his pocket and produced a bundle of money. He held it out so that Baba could see its thickness before handing it over. 'This is for you, Baba.'

Baba was shocked. He stood motionless, staring at the money as though it were a treacherous viper to be feared.

'Take it, my son, and enjoy youself a little bit. Go and watch films with your friends, your girlfriend. Buy yourself some good food. Do whatever you want with it.' Still Baba hesitated. Mystique Mysterious helped him by taking his limp hand and slipping the money into it.

Slowly, Baba brought the money closer to his body— cautiously, like a hunter who is fearful that the prey may disappear at any time into the thicket. Then he squeezed it, as if to ensure that it was really there. He struggled to speak and managed to say a weak 'Thank you very much.' What he was unable to put into words was clearly expressed, however, by the glitter of gratitude and admiration showing in his face.

'Do not behave as if you had seen a ghost, my son, Baba.' Mystique Mysterious said. He hoped to gain Baba's trust by addressing him as a father would. 'I know you need the money since your father has been unemployed for so long and you don't do any work. I am a good friend of yours, although you don't know it yet.' Then he disappeared, leaving Baba dazed.

When Mystique Mysterious knocked, Bukari jumped anxiously from his seat and hurried to open the door. The two men shook hands. Then Mystique Mysterious's eyes travelled to where Fati sat mending clothes. She got to her feet and approached him. He felt his body tremble with desire when he shook her hands, and was surprised that this poor, ordinary woman could so effortlessly stir his loins. So nervous and uncomfortable was he that he immediately reminded Bukari of the need to take care of business.

Even in darkness, the transition from Nima, beaten down by poverty and squalor, to the adjoining luxurious estates of Kanda, was so stark that the opulence of Kanda was exaggerated in the mind. Most of the dwellings were built during the colonial period or soon afterwards, and although they had aged, care and refurbishment had kept the structures and surroundings impressive and charming. Their elegance was more powerful than the forced and cultivated ostentation of the more modern suburbs of the city.

Mystique Mysterious and Bukari entered the grounds of a bungalow. On their far right sat a rectangular structure that served as the guest house, a little isolated from the main quarters and unlit. Close to the guest house was a garden bench, while nearer to the street stood two swings and a see-saw. A large, well-manicured lawn, outlined with sparkling lights, was bisected by a bitumen and gravel drive, one arm of which curved away to a garage beside the guest house, while the other—culminating in a circle in the middle of which rose a palm tree—led up to the main house.

Bukari and Mystique Mysterious walked up to the veranda and knocked on the door. A girl of about fifteen opened it and peered curiously at the visitors. Mystique Mysterious asked, 'Is Mr Denyi in?' The girl nodded and beckoned the visitors inside.

'Please have a seat,' she said.

Mystique Mysterious sat immediately, but it took Bukari a while to do so. He appeared extremely flustered by the plush surroundings: the wall-to-wall carpet, the softness of which he could feel even with his sandals on; the television; the stereo; the artwork on the walls; the deep-cushioned sofas and armchairs. All this, contrasting so greatly with his own drab living room, aroused awe and desire in his mind. His thoughts burrowed off into the labyrinth of possibilities that would be open to him if he were rich and presented him with images of the happiness he would have if he were fortunate enough to possess wealth.

'Have a seat.' Mystique Mysterious echoed the words of the girl, jolting Bukari back to reality. Bukari walked with caution, almost on tip-toe, over to the sofa, and perched reverently on the edge.

Henry Denyi soon appeared. He was a man with congenial disposition and a pleasant face that would not be noticed amid a throng of men. In Bukari's eyes, however, his appearance seemed dignified by wealth. Even his enlarged belly seemed not the careless type, but regal and cultivated. Henry came up to the two men and shook hands first with Mystique Mysterious and then with Bukari, who stood up to receive the handshake as a sign of respect. Henry sat down adjacent to the visitors and said, 'How are you, my brothers?' His voice was low but strong.

Mystique Mysterious did the talking for both visitors. 'We are both very well. And how are you?'

'By God's grace I am well.'

Without flirting with time Mystique Mysterious said, 'We have come about the taxi.' Henry nodded and Mystique Mysterious continued, 'Remember I told you this morning I had found you a gentleman to drive it?'

'Oh yes,' replied Henry. 'Oh yes.'

Gesturing in Bukari's direction, Mystique Mysterious said, 'This is the gentleman I mentioned.'

Again Henry nodded as he studied Bukari. 'Well, I am glad you were able to come today,' he remarked. 'My friend, what is your name?'

'Gabriel Bukari, massah.'

'Well, Gabriel, I believe you are a good driver?'

'Yes, massah, I am.'

'I vouch for him,' Mystique Mysterious said, to prevent any further interrogation. Bukari was exceedingly grateful for the help.

'Very well, I have no reason to doubt you,' Henry said. He went on, 'There are certain basic rules I have, Gabriel. They are simple and so long as you follow them we will have no problems. You understand?'

'Yes sir, massah.'

'No matter what happens, no matter what you do, you must have the car back here by eight every evening. If you intend to work overtime, you must obtain my prior permission. Is that clear?'

'Yes sir, massah.'

'I have no set amount you need to make a day. Bring me whatever you make, but I expect it to be reasonable.'

Bukari was surprised at this last remark. Wherever he had worked previously, he had always been required to reach a set target. Once he reached the target everything else was his to keep, in addition to his monthly salary. On good days, he made a lot of money; on bad days, he had to supplement the takings with money of his own in order to reach the target. It was as simple as that. This new arrangement would give him some discretion and he was not sure if that was good or bad.

The men proceeded to discuss salary. Then Henry Denyi handed Bukari the keys to the taxi. It was agreed that Bukari would start the next day. The taxi would be waiting for him: all he had to do was start the car and go to work. Bukari was near frantic with joy and expressed his gratitude profusely, first to Henry Denyi and then to Mystique Mysterious when they left the bungalow.

Mystique Mysterious bided his time, accepting Bukari's gratitude with equanimity. Bukari fell into a trap he did not know existed when he said, 'I do not know how to thank you.'

'Bukari, my friend, there is a simple way to thank me.'

'There is? Tell me and I will do it, for what you have done for me is a very nice thing indeed.'

Mystique Mysterious smiled. This one had been easy, too easy. He capitalised further on Bukari's gratitude. 'Bukari, you know there are a lot of people who want jobs. It is extremely difficult to find work these days. You know the pain and emasculation you feel when you can't provide for your family. You know I could have picked anybody, but I chose you because I like you, Gabriel Bukari. I could have named any price, and you know that I too must eat. So I ask for only one little thing. All I ask is that you give me fifteen per cent of your monthly earnings.'

Bukari was astonished. He had never heard such a preposterous proposition, and he wanted to reject it outright, but his sense of gratitude precluded that course. He tried to think of words in which to frame a polite rejection, but the pressure was on and he had read the veiled threat in Mystique Mysterious's words. Before Bukari could compose himself, Mystique Mysterious pressed. 'Will you deny me this simple request, Bukari? You know I did not have to pick you, but I did. Will you deny me a small accommodation so that I too can eat?'

Bukari did not understand what Mystique Mysterious meant by accommodation. The urge to yowl in anger was strong, but it was quelled by the other man's threatening gaze. Reluctantly, Bukari agreed to Mystique Mysterious's terms. The two men shook hands and parted company.

Alone, Bukari stood and weighed the significance of the agreement. Perhaps, after all, Mystique Mysterious was right: there were so many people looking for work and so many of them would gladly make the same bargain if they had the chance. Having settled it in his mind that he had made the right deal, Bukari felt his pockets and found enough money for a drink—thanks to Fati's beneficience, the woman who had stomached without complaint his unending whining and unpredictable explosiveness in the past few months, who had sensed that pride made him refuse her outright offers of money and had fallen into the way of leaving a few bank notes on the suitcase in their bedroom, where he could see them and take them when she was out. This was the face-saving compromise her kind and tactful nature had devised. It was more bearable to take his wife's money if he did not have to look into her eyes. Even so it had been a painful period for him, but his fortunes were about to change and Bukari promised himself that from now on he would ensure that all Fati's needs were abundantly met. He whistled his way to Kill Me Quick.

When he arrived, the moon had eaten deeper into the night. The earlier crowd had dispersed: there only remained a couple perched on two chairs in the corner of the kiosk. But the usual friends were at the bar: Kojo Ansah, the quiet one; Kofi Ntim, also known as Philosopher Nonsense, and Esi, the proprietor. Bukari beamed into the room, his elation obvious.

'Have you won the lottery, or what?' Kofi Ntim enquired. 'If you have, you must give me my share before I curse you.'

'As for you, Kofi, not only do you have the face of a clown, but you also have the mind of a turkey,' joked Bukari.

'Shut up! Foolish man like that!' Kofi Ntim countered.

Esi said, 'May I get you something to drink, Bukari?'

'What can an unemployed idiot afford? He doesn't have the money to pay for drinks,' said Kofi Ntim.

'That situation has changed as of tonight,' Bukari announced. 'I have a job. Starting tomorrow, I begin driving a taxi.'

'That is great news. I am happy for you, Bukari,' Esi said

as she prepared to take Bukari's order. 'I think this calls for a celebration.'

'Ah! As for you, Esi, if Bukari has a job, should you not give him some liquor for free? How wicked and money hungry can you be? Give the man a free drink for once,' Kofi Ntim chided, and Esi knew she could not argue with him.

'I will give you a free drink, Bukari. I think for once Kofi has spoken sense.'

Then Kojo Ansah, the quiet one, spoke. 'Congratulations, Bukari. This is very good news and I am very happy for you.'

Esi said, 'You must thank God that you have finally found this job.'

Kofi Ntim said, 'Why must he thank God now that he has a job? Did he blame God when he was unemployed? Why must God take all the credit and never the blame?'

'Eei, Kofi Ntim, watch your mouth. Don't you know that bad things come from the devil and good things come from God?'

'Says who?'

'Says the Lord.'

'Why should I listen to what he says?'

'I will not argue with you, Kofi Ntim, and for your soul's sake, I hope you are not serious. But be careful, there are certain things not to be said in jest.'

'Let me speak my mind, woman! Is God not a friend? Why can I not say whatever I like of him as I do of my friends?'

'Kofi Ntim, do not speak with such foolishness.'

'Give Bukari the drink and stop arguing with me.'

Esi shook her head and poured Bukari a half glass of *akpeteshie*. Bukari thanked her and took a considerable gulp.

'How about me?' queried Kofi Ntim.

Esi replied, 'How about you? Did you get a job today?'

'I already have one.'

'I know. That is why you are not getting anything for free.'

'You are a very wicked woman, Esi. I have a job already so I do not get a free drink? Is Bukari not our friend? Should we all not have a big celebration when he receives such good news?'

'Good idea, Kofi. You should buy your friend a lot of drinks.'

'It is not for me to buy friends drinks, it is for you to give me and my friends drinks for free.'

'Kofi, there is a lot of common sense in the world. Why don't you learn some?'

'Oh, Esi, at your age you should know that common sense is not something you learn. You are born with it. I wasn't born with it and there's nothing I can do.'

'I'm glad you realise that you do not have any sense.'

'Oh no, I didn't say that.'

Esi turned to the others for support. 'Did you not hear him say that he does not have any sense?'

Bukari nodded and said. 'Yes, he said that.' But Kojo Ansah maintained his neutrality by remaining silent.

'Why don't you listen before you speak? I said I was not born with *common* sense. I did not say I have no sense,' Kofi Ntim explained.

'I don't see the sense in what you are saying.'

'I have no common sense; I have superior sense.' Kojo Ntim said, and Esi chuckled and busied herself with wiping the counter.

'So who are you working for?' queried Kojo Ansah, the quiet one.

'I don't think you know him, Kojo.' Bukari replied. 'He is a big man who goes by the name of Henry Denyi. He lives in Kanda.'

'As for some of you people, don't you have any sense of pride at all taking foreign names like Gabriel and Henry? You had to sit down for Europeans to come and give you names.' Kofi Ntim quipped.

Bukari ignored Kofi Ntim, and Kojo Ansah said, 'How did you meet him?'

'Mystique Mysterious got me the job. He is the one who introduced us.'

'That's very interesting.' Kojo Ansah remarked. 'Why would Mystique Mysterious get you a job?'

Bukari squirmed a bit. Kojo Ansah's line of questioning was making him uncomfortable. Bukari was tempted to relate the exact happenings of the evening, but he was shamed by them, so he said instead, 'He is a very nice man, Mystique Mysterious.'

Kofi Ntim retorted. 'No man is that nice. Someone you really don't know and are not related to?'

'Why not? Anyway, you are talking too much. This is a night for drinking and celebration, not for useless talk.'

'I don't like this.' Kojo Ansah murmured, and went back to the solace of silence.

But he had opened the door for Kofi Ntim, who said, 'Yes, why would Mystique Mysterious get you a job?'

'He is a good man, I told you.'

'There is no such thing as a good man. All men are evil, but some have some good in them.'

'All men are good, but some have some evil in them,' replied Bukari.

'I don't believe this, you must have paid him a bribe,' insisted Kofi Ntim.

'I paid no bribe,' retorted Bukari.

'What are you trying to hide?'

'I am not trying to hide anything.' Bukari turned to Esi for help. 'Esi, am I trying to hide anything?'

'As for this one, Bukari, I can't say.'

'Don't I have any friends here?' Bukari complained. 'I thought I would come over here and celebrate with my friends, but what do I get? Nothing but questions and accusations.'

'I believe you, Bukari,' Esi said.

With burning eyes, Kofi Ntim looked into his empty glass and thundered, 'My glass is empty and you will not fill it up, Esi! What is this world coming to when the seller of the good stuff fails to fill the glass when it is empty?'

Esi filled the glass halfway and said, 'Kofi Ntim, don't yell in my kiosk like that. Do you think you are the only one here?'

'I can yell as loud as I want. Who am I afraid of?'

'Your mouth will lead you to trouble one of these days,' Esi warned.

'His mouth is bigger that his face,' Bukari noted. 'It's a miracle it fits on his face.'

'Shut up! Foolish man like that! Bukari, one of these days, I will slap that face of yours till you cry for mercy,' warned Kofi Ntim in jest.

Bukari laughed. He drank a bit and beat his chest as the liquor burned it. Then he relaxed and smiled. The friends talked a little while and then parted company. Night had fallen, plunging the town of Nima into deep darkness, unrelieved by either the twinkle of stars or the glimmer of the moon.

When Bukari arrived home, Baba was still out, so the living room was empty. Bukari entered the bedroom. Even in the darkness he could tell that Fati, lying on the mattress, was awake. Bukari undressed and joined her.

Fati waited until Bukari was comfortable, then asked, 'What happened today?'

'Things went well. I have the job.'

'I am so happy.'

'I am too.'

'When do you start?'

'I start tomorrow.'

'So soon?'

'Yes, and I can't wait. It's been too long.'

'Then you had better get some sleep. We will talk some more tomorrow. I know you will have a busy day and you need all the sleep you can get.'

'I know, but my body aches with such anxiety I don't know if I can fall asleep.'

'I know, but you must try.'

'I will try. Good-night.'

'Good-night, my dear.'

Fati turned on her side. Bukari contemplated her and said, 'Fati, I thank you for all your understanding and patience and support throughout the past eight months. I don't tell you often, but you are a wonderful woman and I am blessed to have a wife such as you.'

Her heart was full of affection and hope and she said with false nonchalance, 'That is nothing. Now you really must get some sleep.'

'Good-night, my dear,' he said.

'Good-night again,' she replied.

In a minute Fati was asleep, Bukari could hear her snoring softly. He looked at her for a long time. From outside came the intermittent whirr of passing cars and the persistent chirr of insects. A little later, as Bukari still lay awake, Baba opened the door to the living room. This was unusual, for Baba stayed out late and by the time he came home Fati and Bukari would normally be asleep. Bukari felt an urge to walk into the living room and hug his son and tell him the good news, but something restrained him. Soon, he could tell that Baba was asleep, for Baba began to snore loudly. It was a while later before sleep erased Bukari's mind of its anxieties and hopes. As he fell asleep, he smiled with a sense of victory—of having triumphed over an unkind destiny. Whether the bargain with Mystique Mysterious would render the victory Pyrrhic remained to be seen, but for the moment he was content as sleep weighed down his eyelids and eventually closed them.

Chapter Four

'Collect your piss, you fool!'

A brutish voice exploded near Baba's ears.

'I said, collect your piss, you fool!' the voice came again.

Baba turned around quickly from the spot on the wall he had just made wet with his urine. When he saw the source of the voice, he shivered a little and suppressed the insult he had been preparing, for the man he saw was a towering giant of a human being: a tall, muscular, lean body with a huge head and terrifying face.

'Did you hear me?' the menacing one asked.

Trembling with fear, Baba said, 'But what have I done? I did nothing but piss on the wall.'

'Foolish boy! Why did you piss on it?'

'My body felt like pissing.'

'Your body felt like pissing? Why did you do it on the wall? Is it your mother's wall?'

'No, but it is not your mother's wall either.'

'How do you know I don't live here, fool?'

'This is the wall of a public school. Nobody lives here.'

'Shut up and collect the piss.'

Baba wanted desperately to hurl insults at this idiot who was insisting that he perform an impossible task. He measured the distance between himself and the menacing stranger and concluded that he did not have enough space to bolt, so he settled for a more conciliatory strategy. 'Chief,' he began to plead, as the stranger took a step, closer, 'I won't do it again. I beg you with God.'

Still the man came closer. It was too late to do anything now but kneel and plead. This seemed to touch the threatening man. He halted and looked down at Baba with contempt. 'Never do that again, fool! You hear me?'

Baba nodded vigorously. 'I hear you, chief.'

'Say I will never urinate on walls again.'

'I will never urinate on walls again.'

'Good. I will leave you this time, but if you ever do it again I will break your head until it splits like a broken stick.' Satisfied, the man turned his back on Baba and started walking away.

Baba waited until the man had widened the distance between them. Then he got to his feet and began to follow at a safe distance. When he felt the time was ripe, he began to unleash insults. 'Big fool like you, why don't you pick on someone your size?' The man walked on, apparently unaware that the insult was meant for him. Baba repeated himself and this time the man stopped briefly, but did not turn around. 'Ah, God has cursed some people,' crowed Baba, as the man walked on again. 'Look at your head, ugly as a frog's. Your legs are like a crooked bamboo and your face is so ugly even monkeys run away when they see you.'

The man stopped again and turned around to face Baba, who squeezed his features into a contortion, pulled out his tongue and began to dance, jerking his hips from side to side. This seemed to provoke the man and he began advancing towards Baba, but Baba went further in the opposite direction so that the distance between them remained safe. Suddenly the man started to run, hoping to cancel Baba's advantage with surprise. But Baba had maintained enough distance between them; he began to run away. For about a minute, the man pursued Baba, who darted to one side of the street and then the other. The man began to pant heavily and, realising that he probably could not catch up with Baba, stopped and walked away again.

Baba was thoroughly enjoying himself. He went back to his game of insults and taunts. 'Hey, what a wonder I see. This man has no arse behind him to support the waist. I wonder how he shits, for where will the shit come from? Ah, I see—it comes from his mouth.' Baba pointed at the man and began to laugh. His face twitching with rage, the man turned again and stood staring. By this time, Baba's theatrics had begun to draw a crowd, mostly teenagers sympathetic to him. A spaniel walked by and Baba picked up a stone and hurled it in the dog's direction, saying, 'You foolish dog, go and wear underwear. ' Then he looked at the man, pointed a finger at him and said, 'Foolish man, you see this dog? You are like him. You are both stupid and you both wear no underwear.' Baba danced again, pushing his hips to the left as far as they would go, to the right in similar fashion, then forward and backward. 'Bad dancing does not kill the earth,' he said. The man started to advance towards Baba again, and Baba began to retreat.

He was not so lucky this time. He inadvertently bumped into an older man, who reached out, grabbed his arm and said, 'You young men of today have no respect for your elders. In my days you would not dare talk to an older person like that.' Baba looked into the older man's face, bespectacled and as stern as pain. He was bald and wore a small beard.

'Let me go!' Baba yowled, and tried without success to wrestle his arm free. Meantime, the menacing man was approaching fast. The agitated crowd of teenagers realised Baba was in trouble and began to berate the bespectacled man.

'Let him go, old man.'

'You two old fools just like to cheat small boys and girls.'

'Hey, bald man, leave him alone.'

'Jesus is my barber! Why not go and bother your own children?'

At this last expression, the crowd erupted into thundering laughter. Baba continued in vain to try to free himself, while the belligerent stranger drew closer, impervious to the hostile calls from the crowd. Then an agile young girl in the crowd picked up a stone and hurled it at the bespectacled man. The bespectacled man had two choices: he either had to let Baba go or be struck by the stone. He chose the former, jumping to the side to avoid the missile. Baba made immediate use of his freedom to run away. Both his adversaries pursued him for a while; but they soon grew tired and gave up. The crowd dispersed in all directions, but Baba was sure to run in the same direction as the girl who had thrown the stone. Eventually, as she reduced her sprint to a trot, he caught up with her. She turned around, and when she saw Baba her face lit up with a smile. Baba slowed his run into a casual walk. 'Thank you for saving me,' he said.

'Oh, that was nothing. I didn't do anything.'

'It was not nothing. Do you know what they would have done to me? I know their type. They would have whipped me until I begged for mercy.'

'I know. I am glad they did not have the opportunity.'

'Why did you help me, anyway?'

'I don't know. It just felt like the right thing to do.'

Baba seemed disappointed. 'Is that the only reason?'

The girl sensed flirtation brewing and looked away with a shyness that was at odds with her earlier show of defiance. Baba studied her. Her face was beautiful, and it was unblemished by the acne which afflicted most of the girls her age. Her charcoal-black hair graced her head like a calabash or a crown. Her eyes glittered under a thick brush of brows. Her face was narrow, but her nose and lips were full. Her ears coiled neatly on the side of her head and were adorned with multicoloured earrings.

Baba liked her. 'They call me Baba,' he said.

'They call me Adukwei.'

Baba felt a tightening in his belly and chest. It was strange feeling, which he had never experienced before—at once unpleasant and pleasant. Embarrassed, he turned his gaze away from Adukwei, towards the sky, but the sun cut into his eyes and made him squint. He placed his palm on his forehead as shield and said, 'It is a hot sun today, you see?'

'Indeed it is,' Adukwei replied, still smiling.

'Do you want to sit a little bit under that tree?' Baba pointed to a neem tree nearby.

'Yes.'

They strolled towards the tree. As Adukwei walked

beside him Baba stole glances at her; she noticed this and smiled wider. She did not know why she had thrown the stone—defiance, perhaps—but she was happy she had done it. Baba had such a simple, innocent face. His features were sharp, but his eyes were subdued. Adukwei looked at him openly, watching tiny beads of sweat forming on his face and dampness spreading under his arms. She could almost feel the heat and energy of his young body.

They reached the neem tree and sat underneath it, in its dark, comforting shade. 'Thank you again for helping me.' Baba repeated.

'Like I said, it was nothing. Why were those two bothering you anyway?'

Baba said, slightly abashed, 'I urinated on the walls of the school.'

'So? Why is that a problem?'

'Ask again. The man—not the one with spectacles, but the other one—he told me to collect my urine.'

Adukwei giggled. 'He actually said that to you? So you collected it all back, I suppose?'

'He is such a big fool.'

'It's funny, isn't it? I did not really care who was right or wrong, I just knew I was on your side. It's often like that with grown-ups—I get so angry with them. I fight with my mother all the time.'

'How about your father?'

A sudden shadow fell on Adukwei's face. She looked down at the ground and started playing with the sand, cupping handfuls in her palm and letting them slip through her opened fingers. 'My father is dead,' she said sorrowfully.

'I'm sorry.'

'That's all right. He died eight years ago. I was about seven then. I still think about him a lot, though. I can't forget him. My mother has pictures of him everywhere at home.'

'I don't talk to my father much, but I can't imagine life without him. My father will not die.'

'You are funny. Everybody dies eventually.'

'Not my father.'

'You must like him very much.'

'I don't know. Sometimes I think I do, sometimes I think I don't.'

Baba leaned his head against the tree and closed his eyes. The strange feeling Adukwei had induced was still there, but it was not as overpowering. He felt more at ease with her already. He pondered his next move. Should he hold her hand? Slip his hand over her shoulders? Or simply grab her and hug her and hold on? But what if she recoiled in terror or exploded in anger? Adukwei sensed Baba's problem and wished that she could help him: reach for his hands, hold them in hers and reassure him that everything was all right. But she believed she was not supposed to take the initiative. Patiently, she waited. Meanwhile, Baba had remembered the money Mystique Mysterious had given him. He turned to Adukwei and said, 'I have some money with me. Why don't we go and watch a film?' Adukwei's heart burned with joy, but she said nothing, feigning indifference to the idea. Baba pushed: 'What do you say?'

'I don't know,' said Adukwei.

Baba could not afford to lose now. He heard Mystique

Mysterious's voice suggesting that he should spend the money on his girlfriend. 'Listen, Adukwei, do come with me. I will buy you something to eat—ice-cream, whatever you want.'

'I am not hungry.'

'All right, I won't buy you ice-cream, we will just see the film.'

Adukwei hesitated a bit longer, and then agreed.

Baba grinned triumphantly. 'We can catch the twelve o'clock film at the Opera if we hurry.' He got up and helped Adukwei to do the same. As they walked back to the street, he debated reaching for Adukwei's hand, but decided against it. He did not want to frighten her off by moving too fast. They boarded a *tro-tro* mammy truck and passed through the Kanda Estates and then the Ringway Estates. When the driver's mate began to collect the fares from the passengers, Baba promptly paid for Adukwei and himself and hoped that she admired him for it. Then the truck went through Ridgeway Estates, past the Parks and Gardens and the American Center.

Downtown, Baba and Adukwei got off and walked towards the Opera. Posters, some tattered with age, were arrayed on the walls of the cinema hall announcing what times the various Chinese, American, British and Indian films were playing. A throng sprawled outside the hall, talking and arguing. As Baba and Adukwei joined the others they saw a teenager spraying fresh urine on the wall. They remembered the events of before and laughed.

The crowd snaked into a long, slow-moving queue heading

for the box office. The next film was playing at 12.15. It was already twelve o'clock and all were anxious to purchase tickets. Baba and Adukwei joined the queue, wondering whether they would get tickets before the movie started. Then Baba noticed his friend Otto standing towards the front of the queue. Without hesitation he prodded Adukwei and they both hurried forward. Otto grinned enviously when he saw Adukwei beside Baba.

'Let me get in front of you, Otto,' Baba entreated. 'Otherwise we won't be able to get in before the film starts.'

'No problem,' replied Otto confidently.

Baba introduced Otto and Adukwei, but before either could speak the three of them were bombarded by angry insults from the crowd behind. Baba ignored them. The best way to deal with them was to pretend he could not hear. Then a husky voice yelled, 'Your mother!' with such force that Baba turned. The man who had shouted approached, and Baba recognised him immediately as Opera-Champion-Atta—tough, menacing, and skilled in the martial arts. Behind Opera-Champion-Atta came fawning subordinates, always striving to please their unpredictable leader. A quick debate raged in Baba's mind. Under different circumstances, he would bolt at once. But because he had Adukwei beside him, he did not want to show such weakness. Yet if he did not, he could suffer the ignominy of a thrashing.

Before Baba could decide what to do, Opera-Champion-Atta was staring down his face. Baba was reminded of the menacing man. Had he escaped one only to be thrown into confrontation with another? Opera-Champion-Atta growled, 'My friend, get out before I smash you to pieces!' Baba's heart contracted and his knees felt weak, but he did not budge. Otto looked from Baba to Opera-Champion-Atta and back again, debating whether he could diffuse the rising tension. He feared for his friend—and even more for himself. If he were to become involved in the simmering squabble, he would be asking for trouble. Meanwhile, Adukwei stood by calmly and observed. Baba's silence and inaction infuriated Opera-Champion-Atta. 'I said get out of the line before I spank your buttocks like a little baby.'

A chorus of 'Get out!' emanated from his disciples.

Still, Baba stood mulishly, unstirring. Opera-Champion-Atta's infuriation was building into rage: he took a step closer to Baba and readied himself to strike. But Baba was doubly blessed that day, and help came from an unexpected source as Adukwei moved quickly and interposed herself between Baba and Opera-Champion-Atta. She placed her hands on her hips, stood akimbo, pushed out her chest and with a calm voice said to Opera-Champion-Atta, 'You leave him alone or I am going to have to fight you myself.'

The crowd stared excitedly at the unfolding contest. Opera-Champion-Atta's face stiffened at the surprising challenge, but soon eased to an amused smirk. 'And who are you? His saviour?' Adukwei did not respond. From the big man's followers came calls for him to wipe her out with his fist; some of them even volunteered to do it on his behalf. But Opera-Champion-Atta only looked over Adukwei's head at Baba, frowned at him as if in warning that their fight would resume some other time, then, smiling, walked away.

Otto stared at Adukwei in admiration and disbelief. 'You are something. Nobody would dare do what you just did.'

'You have to show these people that you don't fear them,' she advised. 'Otherwise, they will walk over you like dirt.'

Baba was relieved, but a little embarrassed. Twice that day she had done what he could not do for himself. She was clearly of leonine courage. His feelings towards her began to develop from admiration to adoration. Thanks to her, they had won the respect of the crowd: there were no further protests about their staying at the front of the queue. When Otto and Baba had bought tickets, they all entered the cinema and occupied three of the few remaining seats. The hall was filling up rapidly and a clamour of voices echoed around its four walls. Vendors walked back and forth, peddling an assortment of chewing gums, chocolates and toffees; Baba bought some chocolate for all three. The film had not yet started, though it had been due to start ten minutes before. Meanwhile, still more people were coming in. There were no empty seats left, so latecomers had to stand. Baba tried to relax, but suddenly he felt a jolt as his chair was pulled from underneath him. For a moment it seemed as if his bent body remained suspended in the air; then he tumbled to the floor on his buttocks. He cursed and stood up, ready to do battle. It was too late, however, for Opera-Champion-Atta—was walking away, with one sneering backward glance—chair in hand. Baba stared at him with rage, but there was nothing he could do. Revenge had been exacted.

'Don't worry.' Adukwei said. 'You can share my chair with me.'

'Is there enough room?'

'I will sit on your lap.'

Baba could have leaped up into the air. To have Aduk-wei on his lap was a dream. Before he could speak again. Adukwei was up, yielding her seat. He took it and Adukwei sat on his lap. His arms hung awkwardly beside him until Adukwei took them and wrapped them around her. She cupped his hands in hers—Baba's nirvana.

The lights went out and the room exploded into a thunder of catcalls and whistles, the audience's own prelude to the film. Then the reel began to roll and the first images filled the screen. But suddenly, almost at once, some technical problem caused the screen to go blank. It was the projectionist's turn to swallow abuse:

'Ei, operator—your mother's!'

'Operator, foolish man! Open the lights!'

'Operator-imp, did you not drink porridge today?'

Finally the mechanical failure was resolved and the film was shown. Throughout, Baba's mind rested on the girl sitting on his lap: a beautiful girl who was not afraid of anything, a girl quite unlike most girls. She would be his if he played his cards right. If he did not? He would... he did not know what he would do.

When the three left the cinema, a solemn calmness appeared to have fallen on Baba. Was this love? He would find out. Otto excused himself, realising that he was becoming an impediment. Baba and Adukwei walked through the streets of downtown Accra and Baba spent his money freely, buying Adukwei a snack here and a treat there. Then, as their talk grew still easier, Baba was emboldened and reached for her hand. They walked, they giggled, and time, unnoticed, crept on until evening fell and they returned to Nima.

'I have to go home now,' Adukwei said.

'Why not come with me?' Baba implored. 'We will go somewhere quiet and sit, just you and I.'

'I'd be glad to, but I have to go,' she replied. 'My mother will begin to worry if I don't return soon.'

Baba was disappointed, but he did not make a fuss. He said earnestly, 'Today was a great day for me.'

'It was for me too,' Adukwei replied. 'Thank you for all the things you gave me.'

'I enjoyed doing it.'

'But you should not spend so much money, Baba.'

'It's nothing.' Baba's heart pounded as he searched for words to arrange a date with her. 'We should see each other again,' he said.

'I think so too.'

'Tomorrow.'

'Oh, no. I can't. My mother will need me at the market tomorrow and at home in the evening.'

'The day after tomorrow.'

'That will be fine.'

'Good. Shall we meet under the tree near the school at noon?'

'Yes,' she said. 'Bye now.'

'Bye, and thank you for saving my life twice today.'

Adukwei chuckled as she walked away. Baba suppressed a longing to race after her and grasp her, to prolong her presence beside him just a little. He felt he was losing something precious, as if a part of him were being slowly severed while he observed, passively and in pain. He stood motionless and saw the distance embrace her. But as he remained there, reliving the day, a smile formed on his lips and grew into a grin; and when he finally turned and walked away, he felt an invulnerable satisfaction novel to his young heart.

Chapter Five

It was interesting the way they interacted. Love was expressed in shells of taunts. When one called the other a simpleton, or otherwise mocked him, it was merely a manner of expressing empathy, for if they failed to resort to such mockery theirs would be a world of bare frustrations. There were very few options. An insult was the opportunity to be aroused and to respond in kind, spicing up the conversation. No ill will, no grudges. It was a game open to all, and those who participated enjoyed it, on the whole. Even Kojo Ansah, who did not join in by choice, was made a reluctant participant.

Presently, Kofi Ntim asked, 'Did you get your injection today?'

'What injection?' Esi queried.

'Ah, you people don't know anything. Must I be the only knowledgeable person?'

'Tell us, Kofi,' Esi entreated.

'I was in town today and was going past the Trade Fair Site when I saw all these people there. I wondered what was happening, so I went in and I saw some government officials injecting people for free, so I went and got myself injected too.'

Esi asked, 'What was the injection for?'

Kofi Ntim sounded irritated. 'I don't know. Why should I care? I got the injection because they were giving it for free. Me, when I see something for free, I don't let it pass by me—I take my share.'

The room shuddered with laughter, even from Kojo Ansah.

'Kofi Ntim,' said Bukari. 'You really must learn some of the sense floating around in the world. That is also free and will do you more good than going for an injection when you don't know what it's for.'

'Shut up!' Kofi Ntim retorted. 'You are all jealous because you were not there.'

It was then that Mystique Mysterious stepped into the room. As if he carried a magnetic charge, all heads turned in his direction.

'What can I get you to drink?' Esi enquired, after a pause.

Mystique Mysterious seated himself at the bar next to Kofi Ntim. He pointed to the bottle in front of Kofi Ntim and said, 'I will have what he is having.'

Esi fetched him the drink. 'Here you are. Enjoy.'

'Thank you,' Mystique Mysterious said. 'Let us drink to Gabriel Bukari, a man who has found the joy of work again.'

They all drank, including Kojo Ansah, who drank a little water. Kofi Ntim opined. 'As for me, I drink not to the joy of work, but against its slavery.'

'Shut up, Philosopher Nonsense!' Bukari thundered.

Mystique Mysterious said, 'Bukari is happy again, thanks to good friends.' He had to make sure they all remembered the benefactor.

'Bukari thanks you and we all join him in thanking you,' Esi said.

They knew. They had been reminded and Mystique Mysterious was satisfied. 'It is nothing, nothing at all,' he remarked.

'It *is* something. You are taking a large bite out of my earnings,' Bukari thought to himself, but dared not say aloud.

'Listen,' Esi said to Mystique Mysterious. 'You are always welcome here in my kiosk. In fact you don't have to pay for that drink. It is free—to thank you on Bukari's behalf.'

'Thank you.'

'Don't be silly, Esi. How can you be grateful to someone who has led another to the slaughterhouse of labour?' Kofi Ntim questioned. 'You should be whipping and chasing him away from here.'

Bukari found Kofi Ntim's irreverence for Mystique Mysterious confounding: he would never dare to speak like that. But Mystique Mysterious studied the faces in the room and concluded that the others did not take this philosopher of nonsense seriously. There was no need to engage in an argument with Kofi Ntim. Instead, he replied simply, 'You must work to eat, my dear friend.'

As if on cue, the others lifted their bottles and glasses to their lips and drank. Presently, Mystique Mysterious asked, 'What do you think, Bukari?'

Bukari replied, 'I agree that a man has to work to eat, and that work brings pleasure. Kofi Ntim always talks nonsense and I will not sit here and argue with him since there is nothing in his head. I must be going back home now.'

Without realising it, Bukari had helped Mystique Mysterious accomplish his objective. As a reward, Mystique Mysterious patted Bukari on the shoulders and said, 'Sleep well, my friend.'

'Why must you go so soon?' queried Kofi Ntim.

'I have to wake up early tomorrow. Some of us have real work to do.'

'Some of us have only been on the job a day and we are already showing off.'

'I have a wife and a son at home.'

'You sleep well,' said Esi.

Kofi Ntim said, 'Oh, Esi, your attitude will cost you your business. Don't you know that the longer he stays the more drinks he buys and the more drinks he buys the more money you make? Where is your common sense, woman?'

'Leave me alone,' Esi requested.

Bukari ignored their little exchange and walked out. He was followed shortly by Kojo Ansah, the quiet one, whose eyes had begun to weigh heavily with slumber. Left alone with Kofi Ntim, Mystique Mysterious ordered a beer for him.

'To what do I owe such generosity?' Kofi Ntim enquired.

'It is a lucky day for you,' Mystique Mysterious replied.

'It is indeed. If you buy, I will drink.'

Soon, however, Kofi Ntim began to yawn. 'I must leave now. Even the strongest must yield to nature's call.' He looked at Esi and there was mischief in his eyes. He said to her, 'Esi, when are you going to bless my bed with your beautiful presence?'

'Leave me alone, Kofi.'

'As for you, Esi, you don't know what's good for you. One of these days you will realise I am the one for you.'

'Yes, when I am dead.'

Kofi Ntim pulled on his goatee, shrugged and walked to the door.

'Wait. I am coming with you,' Mystique Mysterious told him.

'Bye, you two, and sleep well,' Esi said.

The men walked out. Both were silent for a while, pondering what was on the other's mind. Mystique Mysterious tried to wear Kofi Ntim down with silence, until curiosity should overcome him. But Kofi Ntim was clearly outside those claws. He had an air about him that suggested indifference, and in the end Mystique Mysterious was the one who felt compelled to speak. 'Kofi Ntim, how would you like to make some money?'

'What kind of question is that? Everybody could use a little more money these days.'

'I thought you would say that. Well, I can guarantee you more money. I know you are not making much as a labourer for the City Council. Cleaning the city is good, but it does not make you rich.'

'It feeds me.'

'Barely.'

'How do you know where I work anyway? I didn't tell you. Was it Bukari?'

'I know everything. Remember that.'

'What is it you want from me?'

'It is not what I want from you, but what you want for yourself.'

'What do I want for myself?'

'I am offering you a job.'

'Tell me more.'

'How would you like to start driving a taxi?'

'Like Bukari?'

'Yes, like Bukari. It will pay better than you are paid as a labourer, you know that.'

Kofi Ntim came to a halt, pulled on his goatee for a while, and then commenced to walk again. 'I must admit that the idea is tempting.'

'It is, is it not? You can't say no to it.'

'But why are you offering it to me?'

'What do you mean, why?'

'Do you own the taxi?'

'No.'

'What is in it for you?'

'A friend owns the taxi.'

'Do not tell me you are doing this just to help your friend, without any benefit to you.'

It was Mystique Mysterious's turn to halt. This was not the way he had planned it. 'I can see you are a very cynical person, Kofi. You don't believe I may be offering you this job because I want to do my friend or you a favour?'

'No! Nobody does good for nothing, especially not you.'

'That is not true.'

'Yes, it is. Nobody does good just for the sake of doing good. We always do good as a means to an end, never as an end in itself.'

'That is an interesting view, but it is seriously flawed.

What do you say to all the philanthropists who give out money to the poor without asking for anything in return?'

'Look, some of them are disguised misanthropists who conceal their true natures under the cloak of good works. I agree that not all are like that. Some do it because they have what you could call good hearts, but even they are doing it so that their hearts will remain good. They do it because it gives them a sense of happiness, or perhaps it assuages a sense of guilt. "Why is it that I have so much, while others have so little? Let me give some away so that I may convince myself that I have not done my fellow humans ill." Whatever it is, the end is something other than just helping people. So when you tell me you are offering me this job because you want to help a friend or help me, I cannot believe you.'

Mystique Mysterious found Kofi Ntim's unexpected eloquence daunting and his reasoning sharper than he had anticipated. For a moment he was befuddled into silence. He had never expected that out of the rubble of Kofi Ntim's apparently skewed thoughts and expressions could emerge such coherent observations. Never mind whether the philosophy was true or not in general terms. What mattered to Mystique Mysterious was that it was true regarding his own intentions.

'Well,' he said. 'I disagree, but I will not argue with you. You are entitled to your view. And perhaps in this particular case you are right. I will tell you what I want.'

Never before had he disclosed his interest before the deal was done; but now, he had no choice. 'You will be making much more money than you are making now. The increase will be significant, but I don't ask for much, Kofi. Since I am the one who found you the opportunity, I too must be compensated. I ask that you give me fifteen per cent of your monthly salary.'

Kofi Ntim grinned. 'I knew something like this was coming.'

'Certainly, it is a fair deal,' Mystique Mysterious said.

'It may be, depending on how long you expect the fifteen per cent.'

'I am a fair man. I ask for fifteen per cent the first year and then ten per cent the following two years. After that, you are free to keep everything you make.'

'That is too long! Three years?'

'Think about it, Kofi. It is only three years of your life. Imagine all the money you will earn even with my cut compared to what they pay you now.'

'Money is not everything. At least now I have my peace of mind.'

Mystique Mysterious made no rejoinder to this, but decided to press Kofi Ntim for a decision.

'Well, is it going to be yes or no?'

Kofi Ntim pulled on his goatee. 'I will do it if you will come down to five per cent the first year and two per cent the second year.'

'Now, do not insult me, Kofi Ntim.'

'I think I have offered a fair counter-proposal.'

'I can't accept it.'

'Then I am sorry, we can't work together. Thank you for thinking about me—and good-night.'

Mystique Mysterious rubbed his chin. 'Wait!' he called,

as Kofi Ntim began resolutely making tracks. 'You should not walk away from such a good deal. How about twelve per cent the first year and nine per cent the remaining two years?'

Kofi Ntim walked on. 'Six per cent the first year, four the second. After that, I pay you nothing.'

Mystique Mysterious was almost desperate. 'Seven per cent year one, five per cent year two.'

Kofi Ntim, the man they called Philosopher Nonsense, stopped and turned back. When he was close enough, he extended his hand and the two men shook. Mystique Mysterious had been forced to accept a lower rate than he had intended, but he had still made the deal—it was better than nothing. His time was precious and he did not want to start afresh looking for new prey for this particular job. Certainly he could find another man, but that would take time. Before he made such offers, he had to satisfy himself that the recipient was one who would not default on the deal. If they defaulted, he had his own way of dealing with them; but that too was time-consuming. He had studied Kofi Ntim. The man was full of sarcasm and nonsense, but he was sincere in many ways and that sufficed. Many of his friends could not be trusted, and lack of trust made for bad business. So Mystique Mysterious congratulated himself on having closed with Kofi Ntim, even on reduced terms. For his part, Kofi Ntim too was pleased. He could look forward to increased earnings, and even if he retained less than he earned, this was a beginning. It was an opportunity to escape the downward spiral of material privation. If he set his marbles straight, they might fall in the right places and raise him outward and onward to brighter things. Had he not demonstrated his acumen by negotiating Mystique Mysterious's cut downward? If he had done that, he could do better in the coming days.

'I like your ways, my friend,' Mystique Mysterious told him after they had shaken hands. 'We are cut from one cloth. I think we can do business together.'

'I hope so.'

'We will. You have a week to prepare yourself. I trust that will be sufficient time to quit your job.'

'Yes, but there is one problem. How do I know that you will stick to your side of the bargain? What if I quit and there is no taxi waiting for me?'

Mystique Mysterious's face hardened. 'I have done business with many people, my friend. No one has dared question my integrity. I always live up to my promises.'

Kofi Ntim said, 'You can't blame a man for seeking assurances.'

'You have to take the risk. You have my word. There is nothing else I can do if you don't trust me. The choice is yours.'

Kofi Ntim captitulated. 'That is good enough. I will be ready in a week.'

'Good.' Mystique Mysterious's face softened again and he became jovial. 'That is very good, my friend. I will come and get you tomorrow so that you can meet your new boss. Wait for me around six in the evening. I will come to your home.'

'Do you know where I live?'

'I know everything.'

Mystique Mysterious turned his steps in one direction and Kofi Ntim in another. Many of his friends would be delighted to have this opportunity, Kofi Ntim reminded himself. Even so, he felt uneasy, though he could not put a finger on the source of his discomfort. Instinctively, he lifted his eyes to the sky as though to thank the stars for his good fortune and in the hope that their brilliance might dispel his doubts. But the answer was not there in the sky, he knew. It lay somewhere in the mind and in the heart. He was ill at ease because he had made a deal with a man he neither knew nor trusted. He tried to convince himself that providing he was careful, all would work out for the best. But he walked home in a deeply contemplative mood.

Chapter Six

The neem tree cast a shadow on the bare brown earth and over Adukwei and Baba. It was a few minutes after noon and Nima was slumbering, for the sun has a way of bringing sleep. While a soft breeze rustled the leaves of the neem tree, Baba and Adukwei sat with their backs against the trunk, their legs pulled up to the chest.

'I am glad you came today,' said Baba.

'I am glad too,' replied Adukwei.

Out of insecurity, Baba said, 'You know, I was thinking that perhaps you would not come.'

'I told you I would and I don't break promises.'

Baba was like one who has chanced upon a treasure he cannot reconcile to the drab reality of his life. 'Well, you did, but I thought you were just playing with me.'

With a serious expression Adukwei looked into Baba's eyes and said, 'Baba, I want you to know that I don't play games.'

Baba felt a deep yearning to express the desire in his heart for her, but his sense of machismo and male pride warned him that such fondness for a female was a sign of frail masculinity. Yet resistance was like a punishment to his heart. He had to say something. Against his instincts, he told her, 'I missed you so much, Adukwei.' Instantly, however, he regretted the admission and tried to distance himself from it. 'I can't believe I just said that.'

'What do you mean?'

'Don't worry.'

Adukwei tried to look into Baba's eyes once more, but he averted his gaze. She said, 'Baba, you should not keep things from me. We should be honest with each other if we are going to remain friends. Baba, what is it that makes you regret having said that you missed me?'

Baba hesitated. Then, as if spurred on by a new impulse, he raised his head high and said, 'Adukwei, you have done things to my heart that no one has ever done before. I find it hard to believe that after meeting you only once this has happened to me. I've been thinking about you all the time. When I go to sleep, you are the last thought on my mind. You are my first thought when I wake in the morning. And even in my sleep it as if you are with me. I dreamt about you last night and the night before.'

Having confessed all this, he simultaneously felt relief and fear. He was relieved that he had summoned the courage to express his feelings, but he was afraid that despite her apparent fondness for him she would reject his advances, especially when so frankly and forwardly expressed.

Adukwei paused and collected her thoughts. 'I was hoping you would say something like that,' she confided in return. 'I have been thinking about you too, a lot. Yesterday, without realising it, I mentioned your name in the kitchen and my mother heard me and asked about you, so I told her and she seemed very interested. Would you like to meet her?

You know I'm her only child, so she takes special interest in my affairs.'

Baba was free from his cage of fear, and freedom led him to say the words he had thought he would never utter. 'I believe I love you, Adukwei.'

'I believe I love you too,' Adukwei said.

'This is the happiest day of my life. I think it calls for a celebration. Maybe we should watch another film?'

'I would like to, but I can't because I have to go to the market to help my mother. Don't worry, there will be plenty of time for celebration.'

'Oh.'

'But you can come with me to the market. I am sure mother will be glad to meet you.'

'I do not know if—'

'She said herself that she would like to.'

'But—'

'You should come with me, Baba.'

Baba did not want to disappoint her and threaten the fragile structure he was building. 'All right, I'll come with you. Maybe we can visit my mother too.'

'That suits me well.'

'They got up and walked on. It took a while to reach the Mallatta Market. Although the casual observer might not notice, the Mallatta Market is an institution, an instance, a spectacle, a mosaic and a soul all rolled up into one. It is an institution of buying and selling, an instance of human endeavour, a spectacle of bustling bodies and a mosaic of food, and it is a place with a soul of its own. It has a character, and it has a set of customs and unspoken laws. There is the law of haggling over prices, for example. If a seller were to tell you, 'These three tomatoes are worth this much,' you could agree and take the tomatoes at that price. But you could say instead, 'No, I will give you a little less for them.' Then the seller might say, 'Why don't you buy six and I will reduce the price for you,' and you could either agree or bargain further until you reached a mutually acceptable price for a certain quantity of tomatoes. Without this system, there would be no trade.

The air and the ground still seethed with the day's heat. The bitumen surface of the street was hot enough to penetrate footwear and warm the soles of the feet. Adukwei and Baba stood for a while and observed the kaleidoscope of market activity: bare upper torsos, some muscular, some flabby, bathed in sweat; bodies in motion packed so close together that it took concentration to avoid collisions; feet clad in assortments of footwear milling on pavements scattered with debris; a scavenging vulture on top of a decrepit stall, biding its time; an ice-cream vendor yelling for business; a man dressed in a suit, sweat meandering down his face, negotiating some sort of deal with a vendor of stationery. Then the two young people crossed the street and entered the market proper, where a colourful array of food—cassava, yams, cocoyams, rice, beans, meats and fish, oranges, guavas, mangoes, bananas—was arranged on stalls to attract a trade. Those sellers whose stalls lacked canopies protected themselves from the sun with large sombrero-style hats. Baba said something to Adukwei, but she did not hear him: his voice drowned as traders haggled noisily over prices and the market women cried forth to attract business. He repeated himself in a louder voice. 'Are we close to your mother's stall?'

Adukwei halted at that very moment. 'Here we are,' she said. Baba looked to his left, following the movement of Adukwei's head, and his eyes came to rest on her mother. No one needed to tell him; she was an older and slightly fatter replica of Adukwei: the soft features, the thick eyebrows, the full nose and lips, all blended into another Adukwei. 'Mother,' said Adukwei. 'Here's my friend Baba.'

Adukwei's mother extended her hand genially and said, 'How are you, Baba?'

Baba took her hand. There are two types of handshakes. One is limp and casual, the other is strong and full of heart. Theirs was the second type. 'I am fine,' he said.

'My daughter mentioned you yesterday. I am glad to see you.' Noticing the sweat on Baba's face, she said, 'You must be thirsty. Let me get you some water to drink.'

She reached behind her for two plastic cups and filled one with cool water from an earthenware pot. She gave Baba this cup and he gulped down the water as she filled the second cup for Adukwei. By the time she was ready to give Adukwei hers, Baba had already emptied his. Adukwei noticed and said, 'Baba must be thirstier than me. Why not give him this cup as well.' Adukwei's mother obliged and gave Baba the second cup. He quickly drained half of its contents and was about to pour the rest away when Adukwei reached for the cup and drank what remained.

'You two come inside the stall,' Adukwei's mother said. 'You must be hungry. Let me get you something to eat.'

'I would very much like to,' replied Baba. 'But I have to

go. I need to meet someone soon.' This was untrue; he lied without knowing why.

'Very well, but do come and visit soon.'

'I will.' Baba said his farewell and left with Adukwei. 'Now let's go to see my mother.'

Fati's stall was not far away. As Adukwei and Baba approached, she noticed them and called, 'Hello Baba!' and then, with considerable surprise, 'Hello Adukwei. How are you, my dear child?'

Adukwei replied, 'I am well. And how are you, Auntie Fati?'

'Thank God, I am well too.'

Baba was bewildered. 'Don't tell me you two know each other,' he said.

'Don't act as though you've seen a ghost, Baba,' Adukwei said. 'I didn't realise your mother was Auntie Fati. I know her quite well.'

'Indeed,' Fati corroborated. 'I didn't know you knew Baba,' she added to Adukwei.

'We met yesterday,' Adukwei said.

'The day before yesterday,' corrected Baba.

'Well, that's good,' Fati opined. 'Let me get you something to eat or drink.'

'Thank you, Auntie Fati, but my mother gave us some water,' replied Adukwei. 'I must leave before she begins to get angry that I am not helping her.'

'I understand, my child. Give your mother my regards.'

'I will. Bye, Auntie Fati. Bye, Baba.'

'Bye, Adukwei, and take good care,' Fati said.

Adukwei started to leave. Baba realised he had not

arranged their next rendezvous, so he hurried and caught up with her. Fati looked on as her son whispered into Adukwei's ear. Adukwei nodded and then walked away while Baba stood motionless and watched her. Fati observed an intensity in Baba's gaze she had not seen before. She waited patiently until he unbound himself from the trance.

'My son,' Fati said. 'I see you have been up to certain things. You have met Adukwei and her mother.'

'Yes, I have.'

'What is going on? You have not told me anything.'

Baba hesitated. He knew his mother was the only person he could talk to without fear of being mocked, but he was not sure it was appropriate to discuss his emotions with her. The relationship between mother and son may be a loving and trusting one, but there are certain things often left unspoken, for some of them might disturb the delicate balance of interaction between parent and child. But if he could not confide in the woman who bore and raised him, then in whom could he confide? Friends? They would listen, but they would also tease him. They could advise, but with what knowledge, what experience? They might like him, but sometimes their liking was tainted by jealousy.

'Mother, what do you think of Adukwei?'

'I don't know her very well, but I think she is a good girl. And I like her.'

Baba scratched his chin in thought.

'Baba, do you have something you want to say to me?' Fati asked with a mother's intuition and understanding.

'Mother, I want to tell you something, but you can't tell anyone, not even Father.'

Fati did not like keeping things from her husband, but when it came to her son, compromises were sometimes necessary. 'You tell me, Baba. It will be our secret.'

Baba found assurance in her words. 'Mother, I have been having certain feelings lately that I don't understand.'

'And do these feelings have anything to do with Adukwei?'

'They do, Mother. I don't understand why, but when I see her I feel blissful and joyous and the feeling builds until it is as if I am going to choke on it.'

'Son, it could be that you are in love with Adukwei.'

'No!' Baba exclaimed, so vehemently that his own reaction surprised him. Though he yearned to accept his emotions and swim in them without worry, he was afraid of what they could do or where they could lead. Even at his age, he understood the loss of independence that love for another could entail, the sacrifices, the compromises. He was fighting love by denying it, struggling with the immemorial conflict between heart and mind.

After a few seconds he recovered a little. 'Mother, do you believe in such a thing as love?'

Fati was unprepared for the question, for she had not expected her son to doubt love. When she was his age, she lived and breathed love. Nor was it a mere romantic desire to feel: it was a deep, emotion, common to her mind, her heart and her soul. And time had proved her right. At fifteen, she was in love with the only man she had ever loved: Baba's father, Gabriel Bukari.

Fati smiled and, as she remembered, a tranquil air seemed to encircle her. Her body appeared swallowed in a deep calm and her face shone with a peaceful look. The memory was so visible to her it was as if a reel of film were projecting images in her mind's eye. When she spoke again, her voice was steady and reassuring. 'I am going to tell you something, my son. I have never told you this before, partly because it never came up and partly because I thought you were not old enough to hear it. Forgive me if you think I have wronged you, but I hope you understand that I kept this a secret because I believed it was for your own good. My son, listen to the story of how you came to be. And son, there are things I am going to say that will surprise you or perhaps even shock you. Come in here away from the sun and sit next to me.' Baba complied, his curiosity aroused, his ears attentive.

Fati continued, 'You know how we have been telling you that my father is an old farmer in the North of the country, living with the rest of my family?' Baba nodded. 'And you know how we keep promising that we will take you there on a visit one day, but we never do?' Again, Baba nodded. 'Well, the truth, son, is that my father is not in the North. He is right here in Accra and he lives in the Airport Residential Area.'

'Airport?' asked Baba in surprise. 'Only rich people live there. How can your father live there when we are so poor?' The revelation that he had a relative who was possibly wealthy was more significant to him than the fact that his parents had deceived him. 'Mother, how rich is he? How come he lives in Airport and we live in Nima?'

'Be patient, Baba. Be patient and I will explain everything to you. My father, your grandfather, is a very rich man as you rightly think.'

'How rich? He must be very rich to live in Airport.'

'I will not be able to explain anything to you if you keep interrupting me. You must be patient and quiet and listen. Like I was saying, your grandfather is a very rich man. His name is Ahmed Yussef and he is a very devout person, a principled Moslem, staunch and disciplined in his aim of living a pious life, a life above reproach. And he is also a very astute businessman. You see, he imports all kinds of goods from abroad: clothing, cars and what have you. He also exports things like artwork and rice. And he owns a large herd of cattle and runs a transportation business. As you can see, he is a man of wealth. But he never allows business to interfere with his quest for spiritual purity. In that regard, he is held in very high esteem by his peers.

'He married more than once. He married three women. My mother was the second wife and she had five children. My other mothers had eleven children altogether, so there were sixteen of us: five girls and eleven boys. My father belonged to the old school that believes that sending women to school is a waste of time, for he used to say that a woman's place was in the house, keeping home and raising children. So he sent my brothers to school, but he never sent any of the girls. While our brothers went to school, we helped to keep the house and improve our cooking skills so that we might be good wives and mothers in the future. We were a little resentful that we had to stay at home while our brothers went to school and came back to boast of the knowledge they acquired in the classroom. They used big English words in the house and we did not understand. But we admired them so much, our brothers who were educated and spoke English. It was a happy homestead, I think. Not because of wealth alone, but because there were good hearts. You see, Baba, my father was a generous man and had a big heart, as did my mothers. Even if they did not tell you how much they loved you, you knew it was there, you knew you could count on them.

'You may be wondering what happened to end this for me. I will tell you: it was the result of my love for your father. I was a mere fifteen-year-old girl when I met him. He is a handsome man even now, but he was even more handsome in those days, just like you, my son. You see, my father hired your father as a driver and the first time I saw him I thought he was an angel. I thought I was going to die of love. Your father was on my mind all the time and I could not sleep or eat properly.'

Baba grinned, rejoicing as every child rejoices at the thought of love between their mother and father. Fati went on, 'My secret love for him was eating into me and I had to bare my soul to somebody. But who? I was ashamed to tell my brothers and I was afraid to tell any of my mothers, nor could I tell my father. So I went to the object of my love, the cause of my confusion. I went to your father and told him how I felt. That, for a girl, especially a girl from a family as religious as mine, was a very bold thing to do. But sometimes your emotions can lead you to things you never would have thought possible. Anyway, I told your father I was in love with him. And his response shocked me. I had expected him to laugh in my face. But no. He told me he had been experiencing similar emotions, but he was afraid of expressing them. How could he, a mere commoner, dare to express his love for a wealthy man's daughter, his master's jewel?

'So that started it all. We had to be extremely discreet. Your father feared the consequences if we were found out and so did I. So our relationship was limited to hugging and kissing when we got the chance. This went on for a long time, until one day our emotions rebelled and we went all the way. You understand what I mean by that, I am sure.' Baba understood. 'Only once, and I became pregnant. I was only sixteen then. I tried to keep it a secret, but you know how a woman's body and her moods change when she is pregnant. My mother suspected it and she questioned me until I admitted the truth. But I only told her I was pregnant: I refused to tell her who was responsible. She told my father out of loyalty to him and he was furious. I had never seen him so angry before. He threatened to do all sorts of things to me if I did not tell him who was responsible, but still I refused. I don't know why your father did it, but he volunteered the information to my father. Perhaps it was out of love or perhaps it was his conscience—he and I never discussed it—but he came forward.

'As you can imagine, your father was immediately sacked. My father could not forgive me for the disgrace I had brought on him and the family. I, his daughter, who should have showed piety and dignity, had allowed myself to be taken by a commoner, a Christian, outside wedlock. He threw me out of the home and disowned me. Your father and I got married. So, my son, that is what happened. And you were born and I have never regretted my actions.'

'So you have never seen your father since?' Baba queried.

'No, I have not. And it hurts that I can't see him. I don't understand why he was so harsh with me, but not everything that happens to us can be understood.'

'How about your mother?'

'I see my mother from time to time. She stops here at the market when she gets the chance and we talk a little. But she has to be very careful. Who knows what will happen if my father finds out?'

'How about your other mothers and your brothers and sisters?'

'They too try to stop by when they get the chance. Sometimes they bring me money to help me a little. They tell me my father is ailing now and I wish I could see him. It will be terrible if he dies before I get the opportunity to do so. My mother says she will try to reconcile us, but so far she hasn't been able to. I suspect my father will not hear her.'

'Does she know me?'

'She knows who you are. She has seen and observed you, but I could not let you meet her because I was afraid.'

'I would like to meet her, Mother.'

'Now that you know the story, you shall. I will arrange it. But your father does not know I am telling you this. You are a grown up now and I trust that you will keep this to yourself. When the time is right, I will tell him.'

'I will not tell, Mother. You can trust me.'

Baba was fascinated by the story. That they had lied to him all this time was insignificant to him. What mattered was their courage and the sacrifices they had made in order to be together. He understood why his mother had chosen that moment to reveal the secret she had kept from him for so long. The message was clear: Fati believed in love and her story was an illustration. But still he was not completely satisfied. 'Do you ever have doubts?'

'Doubts?'

'Yes, doubts about your decision. Do you not wonder how life would have turned out if you had chosen to do things differently?'

Fati was surprised that her son could already fathom that life offered such choices. 'Son, nobody goes through life without some doubts. When you make a choice, you wonder what might have been if you had chosen otherwise. Yes, I have wondered how life might have turned out if I had not met your father, if I had not become pregnant, if my father had not disowned me, if I could still see my family. There have been days when I have wept and my heart has been heavy. But what keeps me going is that I have you and your father. I have never doubted that the decision I made was the right one, that being with you two is the key to happiness for me.'

'So, Mother, you love without question?'

'It is not possible to love without question. But it is possible to experience love that is so deep it can never be exhausted and so strong it cannot be broken. My love for your father, and for you, is of that kind.'

Baba took a moment to absorb this wisdom before posing his next question. 'Why is it so difficult to tell another person that you love her. I mean, I find it difficult. I—'

'I know what you mean, Baba. It is hard for us to express love because that means stepping into a new and awesome pair of shoes. Shoes that carry with them a great responsibility, close to a divine responsibility. But you will find the courage to step into those shoes if you remember that they can also bring great joy.'

'Thank you, Mother,' Baba said.

Fati looked upon her son with empathy and replied, 'I hope I have not confused you, Baba.'

'Not at all, Mother. You have clarified a lot for me.' He clasped his hands together as though they held a precious gem that might escape. 'I have to go now, Mother,' he said.

'Okay. Be careful, Baba.'

When he was gone, Fati said to herself, 'My son the truant has found love.' But even then, she could not be sure he really had found love. There were other emotions which could masquerade as love. Could it be the stirring of lust, for example? A passing infatuation? She could not tell. She could only hope that his young heart was leading him in the right direction.

Alone, she again revisited her past. This time the images were more vivid and detailed. Her father, towering over her with a stern face, yelling until his voice hurt her ears; picking up a cane and threatening to lash her until she divulged the secrets of her shameful love; her mothers, tears running down their faces, pleading with her father to exercise patience, pleading with her to tell the whole truth; her sisters, cowering in corners and whispering among themselves, afraid to come to her aid for fear of bringing their father's fury on themselves; her brothers, silent but with sympathetic eyes. Then her mind's eye sharpened its focus and her father's face was magnified, displacing everything else. The expression of combined rage and disgust was so powerful even in memory that it still aroused her fear and remorse.

Her mind's camera quickly refocused and showed her an image to soften the pain: Bukari, his affections, his geniality, his bravery. When many would have fled from the wrath of a wealthy man and the responsibility of caring for a pregnant woman, he had come forward of his own volition, looked her father in the face and claimed responsibility for her pregnancy, risking everything. When she heard what he had done, she was angry that he would be so foolish, but proud that he would be so brave.

Bukari! Gabriel Bukari! Their love had held them steady all these years. It was an anchor that refused to break, a warmth that devoured all fears, a lullaby that drowned all sorrow.

There had been strains on it, of course. Especially recently, when he became unemployed and was for the first time unable to provide for the family. But the anchor had held fast even through that, and now they were in calmer waters. If Baba had found a love like theirs, then he too would know happiness as far as was humanly possible.

Chapter Seven

The twilight crowd of 441 gathered under a subdued silvery moon. Earlier, the thunder had guffawed so loudly and the rain had fallen so heavily that the men and women of Nima had withdrawn fearfully into their homes to watch as the torrent splattered the earth and a fierce wind rattled rooftops, shook eaves and trees and sent litter in the streets swirling out of sight. With every ear-splitting clap of thunder the people held their breaths and prayed, as cataclysmic visions filled their heads. When the apocalypse did not occur—when the storm had passed—they emerged thankfully from their shelter to enjoy the sight of gutters running with fresh water, the feel of cool damp earth beneath their feet and the sweet smell of rain in the air.

The 441 crowd ate: fried plaintains, fried fish and boiled rice, beans and *kenkey*—the usual rich combination to accompany their usual mixed diet of talk. While they were alternately chewing, laughing and lamenting, Mystique Mysterious drew up nearby in a bright red Mercedes Benz. He stepped out of the car and approached them, dressed as always in an expensive dark suit, flashy shirt and shades. This evidence of his wealth aroused the admiration of the other men, but also their resentment. None of them could afford smart clothing, and few of them had money enough to afford a bicycle, let alone a fast car. But their resentment remained unspoken because poverty, unaware of its collective power, fears wealth.

Mystique Mysterious came to a halt and surveyed the gathering. Then he produced a cigar from his pocket and put it between his lips. The men eyed the cigar and smiled. Presently he produced more cigars and passed them round. Soon the crowd was enveloped in clouds of smoke. Mystique Mysterious continued to puff, knowing that in his little act of cigar smoking, the crowd found an affinity with him. He was not the wealthy man walking in clouds of luxury, untouchable and beyond reach. He was a mortal, just like them, sitting among them, sharing a pastime with them and conversing with them. They could claim him as one of their own and he had a place with them. So they smiled and told him stories and Mystique Mysterious pretended interest and laughed with them. For a while Mystique Mysterious and the 441 crowd were the same.

Sensing his advantage, Mystique Mysterious put his hand into his jacket and brought out a stack of cash. This he began to distribute, while the bewildered but money-hungry men blessed him and his progeny. Then he produced a quantity of cocaine, and this too he passed around. The crowd sniffed on it and again thanked him for his beneficence.

While the men were busy with the drugs, a little boy no more than seven wandered out into the street and stood there absent-mindedly. He did not notice the oncoming car and would have been hit had not Mystique Mysterious intervened by running out, grabbing him and carrying him to safety. The car missed them by a split second, and but for Mystique Mysterious's intervention, the boy would have died. The crowd witnessed it all and they praised Mystique Mysterious for his kindness and bravery. Mystique Mysterious himself did not know why he had done it. He had acted more from instinct than anything else and he thought himself undeserving of the praise, but he was glad that it came, because it added to his power. Once the excitement caused by the incident died down, he quietly left. Long after the growling of his car had died away, the 441 crowd continued to bless him and to reiterate among themselves what a great man he was.

At about this time, Bukari arrived at Kill Me Quick. He noticed the Mercedes parked in front and—wondering which wealthy person was calling on the lowly kiosk—stopped for a moment to appreciate the glamour of the car, his heart beating faster with the desire to drive one like it. Wrenching himself back to reality, he put the thought out of his mind and entered the kiosk. Present as usual were Kojo Ansah, the quiet one, and Kofi Ntim, alias Philosopher Nonsense. Mystique Mysterious was also there; and, surprisingly Madman.

Mystique Mysterious welcomed Bukari with exaggerated glee. 'There you are,' he said. 'Come and join us for a drink. We are celebrating Kofi Ntim's first day on the job and I have invited our friend here to join us for the celebration.'

The last reference was to Madman, who nodded his head vigorously and launched into a lecture. 'Drink and happiness,' he began. 'Happiness and drink. They are one and the same thing. Because drink is what we take into our system and when we do that we say, "We are having a drink, let us drink till we drink all drinks." So we drink a bit and then a bit more and happiness comes to us. As for being drunk, it is nothing but happiness. When I was in Tokyo, I...'

'You have never been in Tokyo,' interjected Kofi Ntim.

At this remark, Madman seemed to take offence, he frowned at Kofi Ntim. 'I have been in Tokyo. I will go to Tokyo. Drinking is like going to heaven where all the trees are nice. At this juncture, you may ask, what is a tree? A tree is...'

Kojo Ansah broke his silence and intervened with unusual anger. 'Now, you wait a minute. Are you trying to suggest to us that drinking brings happiness?'

'Drinking is happiness,' replied Madman. 'Drinking is happiness.'

'That is a foolish thought,' said Kojo Ansah.

The response from Madman was swift, churlish and unexpected: he stood up and swung his arm awkwardly and caught Kojo Ansah in the mouth and again in the chin, forcing Kojo Ansah to hold on to the bar-counter to keep from falling off his stool. By now, Kojo Ansah was agitated too. He jumped off the stool, erect and prepared.

'Nobody calls me foolish and gets away with it!' Madman bellowed.

The two men might have exchanged further blows, but Bukari moved promptly between them. They glowered at one another for a while longer, but then their anger died away, leaving Kojo Ansah feeling ashamed and foolish. Kofi Ntim chuckled and Esi hit him on the shoulder to warn him against inflaming the situation. Kofi Ntim grinned at her humorously. 'Esi, you see, at long last you are showing affection for me. No woman hits a man on the shoulder unless she loves him.'

Esi laughed. 'Kofi Ntim, when will you get it into your head that I am not interested in you? Not yesterday, not today, not tomorrow.'

'That's what you think, but I know you love me.'

Madman said absent-mindedly. 'Love is the liquor in the glass and it is all like water. Water is the place for the fish, and at this juncture, one may wonder, what is a fish?'

They all knew Madman would begin a lecture on fish and none of them was interested in hearing it, so they were thankful when Kofi Ntim interrupted. 'Hey, why are you drinking so slowly? Or don't you know how to drink like Kojo Ansah here?'

Madman laughed mirthlessly. 'You think you can drink? You don't know what you are saying. I can take more drinks than anyone in this town.'

'Maybe with little boys,' Kofi Ntim replied. 'You are among big men now, my friend, and you can't last in such company.'

'What? Don't insult me. I challenge you to a contest right here, right now.'

'No problem. I accept your challenge, but you must pay.'

Mystique Mysterious, enjoying himself, said, 'I will pay for as much as you both can take.'

Esi rolled her eyes disapprovingly, but she had too much respect for Mystique Mysterious to express her thoughts openly. Mystique Mysterious ordered *akpeteshie* for Kofi Ntim and Madman and they drowned it as soon as it was placed before them. It was not just the quantity they consumed, but the art and speed with which they drank that demonstrated their prowess. Mystique Mysterious ordered another round, and another, and another. After four more rounds, Madman was visibly affected. His eyes were heavy and he mumbled incomprehensibly.

Mystique Mysterious ordered yet another round. This time Esi lodged her protest. 'I think they have had enough,' she said softly, hoping to make her point without riling him.

'Do not be foolish, woman!' Kofi Ntim yelled. 'It is none of your concern how much we've had. You must be happy we are giving you business.'

Esi looked to Bukari for support. Afraid of opposing Mystique Mysterious directly, Bukari suggested a compromise: 'Why not have just one more round?'

'Fair enough,' agreed Mystique Mysterious.

Madman mumbled meaninglessly again.

Esi got the drinks and Kofi Ntim swallowed his immediately, but Madman's attempt was a complete failure: as he lifted the glass to his quivering lips his hands shook so violently he spilled half of the contents on his shirt. Bukari tried to assist him by removing the glass from his hands, but was brushed away. Then Madman tried again. He managed to pour the liquor into his mouth and even swallowed a little bit, but most of it was regurgitated in a stream of liquor and saliva that splashed all over the bar. The others recoiled. Esi fetched a cloth and began to wipe up the mess. Madman was slobbering now. Saliva collected at the corners of his mouth and dripped down on to his chin. At this point he lay deep in the pit of inebriation, past any semblance of sobriety.

Esi was concerned. 'You have to get him out of here before he passes out or vomits all over the place,' she said.

'As for you, Esi, all you care about is yourself and how he is going to vomit in your bar,' Kofi Ntim shot back. 'See how selfish you are?'

'I think Auntie Esi is right. We better get him out of here and into some fresh air,' suggested Bukari.

The others agreed, but when it came to doing the task, Kofi Ntim slid away and Kojo Ansah showed no interest in helping. 'Kojo,' Mystique Mysterious said. 'We need to get him out of here. We need help.' It was clear that 'we' referred to everybody but Mystique Mysterious himself.

Kojo Ansah replied with vehemence, 'You help him. It was you who encouraged the drinking and bought the drinks.'

That Kojo Ansah would so boldly defy him surprised Mystique Mysterious and for a moment he could not find any words. But he acted swiftly to reestablish his authority by saying to Bukari. 'You will take him out?' Though framed in the form of a question, it was an order. Bukari understood and nodded; he had no inclination to disobey and he wanted to help Madman anyway.

Esi tried to persuade Kojo Ansah, 'Kojo,' she said, 'Will you please lend Bukari a hand? I am begging you.'

Again, Kojo Ansah's response was angry and quick. 'Why can't you ask him to do it?' he replied, referring to Mystique Mysterious.

Esi ignored the question. 'I am begging you, Kojo.'

'No!' Kojo Ansah said with finality, and there was a flame of anger in his eyes that Esi had not seen before.

In a way, Mystique Mysterious was glad that Esi had also failed. It would have been a major defeat for him if she had succeeded while he had not. He crossed to the doorway, looked outside and motioned to Bukari. 'Bring him over here.' Bukari slid Madman's arms over his shoulders and helped him to his feet. Madman was so unsteady that Bukari had to support his full weight and slowly guide him out of the kiosk.

'Look at him,' jeered Kofi Ntim. 'And he calls himself a man. A few drinks and he is walking like a rabbit. Next time when men are drinking he will not come close. Foolish man like that.'

'Shut up!' Esi told him.

Kofi Ntim ignored Esi and followed Bukari outside. Mystique Mysterious asked Bukari to place Madman's sagging body on the ground. 'He needs fresh air, you see. Why not unbutton his shirt?' Bukari did so. Then Mystique Mysterious said, 'Ah, I know what we have not done. He still has his shoes on. Bukari, remove his shoes. It is all in the shoes, gentlemen.'

Bukari began removing Madman's shoes, but without warning Madman came back to life and weakly kicked his legs, catching Bukari on the chin. Bukari paused, then tried again. Again Madman kicked out, but Bukari was expecting the kick this time and dodged it.

Kofi Ntim said, 'Bukari, you are learning, huh? You don't step on a fool's balls twice.'

Bukari then grabbed Madman's feet and pinned them to the ground. Madman began to struggle, and made his first comprehensible speech in a long time. 'Not my shoes. Please, not my shoes.'

'He doesn't want his shoes removed,' Bukari noted superfluously.

'Don't be stupid,' said Kofi Ntim. 'Are you going to listen to a drunkard or are you going to take his shoes off? Take them off.'

Bukari looked at Mystique Mysterious for guidance. Mystique Mysterious advised him to remove the shoes and he did so quickly, before Madman could put up another fight. At once he was assaulted by a putrid stench that came from Madman's socks. It smelled like rotten eggs and meat and Bukari jumped up in disgust.

Kofi Ntim said, 'No wonder he didn't want his shoes removed. But one would think a man like that wouldn't care about such things.'

The three men stood looking at Madman, who now seemed perfectly calm, eyes shut, features relaxed. 'I think he will be fine here,' Mystique Mysterious said. 'He will recover and find his way back home.'

'I think you should put him in your car and drive him home,' Kofi Ntim suggested.

'No, not a good idea,' replied Mystique Mysterious. 'He needs fresh air.' With that he went back into the kiosk. Bukari rolled Madman on to his side so that he would not choke if he vomited later. Then Kofi Ntim and Bukari went back inside.

Mystique Mysterious smiled at Kojo Ansah, the quiet

one. 'My friend, you don't look very happy tonight. I think you should come with me. I have something to tell you and things to show you to make you happy.'

'Thanks for your concern,' Kojo Ansah replied. 'But I am not interested.'

The response surprised everyone in the kiosk. Kojo Ansah had spoken in a tone which conveyed disrespect. Mystique Mysterious too was taken aback and wondered for a moment what tactics to employ. Should he pressure Kojo Ansah, or persuade? In the circumstances, he decided, the use of force was impractical. For the time being he would take a conciliatory approach. 'Come on, you don't know what it is I have to tell you or show you. I promise it will be worth your while.'

'I don't care. I'm not interested.'

The atmosphere grew tense, but Mystique Mysterious responded quickly; he could not let his failure linger in the minds of the others for long. 'Well, suit yourself.' He turned to Bukari and asked, 'Would you like to go for a ride, my friend?' Bukari accepted and the two of them left.

A mischievous grin spread across Kofi Ntim's face. 'Let us talk about you, Esi.'

'What do you mean?'

'You know exactly what I mean.'

'No, I don't.' Esi said. But she did. Esi had no sexual interest in Kofi Ntim, but she tolerated and sometimes encouraged his flirtations.

Kofi Ntim continued. 'Oh, my dear angel, need I say anything? Is your beauty not beauty that makes every man shudder? Are you not fit only for gods like myself?'

Esi smiled. 'When the rain falls, I am the fish swimming in the puddles towards your door. When the sun shines I am the bird bearing the leaf of love in my beak only for you.'

Kojo Ansah said, 'With a sweet tongue like yours, Kofi, you could win the heart of any woman.'

'But you don't understand, Kojo,' replied Kofi Ntim. 'I could win any woman I want, but Esi is the only woman I want.'

Esi suppressed a chuckle and said, 'I am really blessed and honoured to have the attention of a man who can win any woman he wants.'

'You surely are, and although you think you don't love me, you will realise soon that I am the one for you.'

Esi smiled and said nothing. She allowed Kofi Ntim the comfort of his thoughts; he deserved, like everybody else, to be kept hopeful by fantasies. Kojo Ansah drained the water in his glass and said he was leaving. Kofi Ntim decided to leave with him, and both of them said good-night.

Outside, they saw Madman, still asleep on the ground. 'Do you think he will be all right?' Kojo Ansah asked.

'I am sure he will be fine. Nobody will bother a man like him.'

They walked on in the night. A composed quiet had settled on the town: the calm after the storm. Kojo Ansah turned to Kofi Ntim and said, 'In all seriousness, Kofi, watch how you go with Mystique Mysterious.'

'I know how to deal with his type.'

'I don't know what to say to Bukari. I wish I could talk to him, but somehow he seems distant these days.'

Kofi Ntim said, 'I am sure Bukari knows how to look after himself.'

'I hope so. For his sake, I hope so.'

They walked in silence until they reached the junction where they had to part company. Kofi Ntim asked, 'Kojo, do you think Esi likes me?'

Kojo Ansah reflected and replied diplomatically, 'She is a nice woman and well disposed towards you.'

'I make lots of jokes about it, but I really like her. Do you think she could like me also?'

'The joking may be your mistake. Why not be serious with her? Let her know how you feel, instead of joking around. Maybe she will take you seriously.'

'Even one like me?'

'Do not put yourself down, my friend.'

'I am being realistic. I know what people think of me.'

'Kofi, you don't understand the wonders of the heart.'

'I wish it had wonders to perform for me.'

'Believe, my friend.'

Kofi Ntim stood for a little while, thinking. Then he smiled and said good-night to Kojo Ansah and the two men walked their separate ways.

Chapter Eight

By now, the night sky, swept free of clouds, was strewn with bright stars. Mystique Mysterious drove Bukari from Nima through Kanda and down Ringway to the Kwame Nkrumah Circle. He brought the car to a stop near the Orion Cinema, where a dwindling crowd was pushing its way into the hall for a late film.

'How are you enjoying the night, my friend?'

'It is a nice night: I am enjoying it perfectly well.'

'How would you like to enjoy it to the fullest? You, Gabriel Bukari, have not learned how much life has to offer.'

'I don't think I understand what you mean.'

A smile was on Mystique Mysterious's face and it carried mischief. 'I will show you, my friend, I will show you.' He looked out of the car and then pointed to a cluster of young women gathered by the side of the street. 'See these women, Bukari?' They are among the ingredients in the pot of life. You, my friend, have decided to live your life with only one woman. Now, don't get me wrong: you have made your choice, and I can't quarrel with it. But that should not stop you from reaching out and feeding on life's delicacies now and then.'

Bukari was still confused. 'I'm not sure I understand what you are getting at.'

'Look at the women and understand.'

Bukari looked. 'Are you saying that marriage should not bar promiscuity?'

'Ah! You are beginning to see the light.'

'But if that is what you mean then I don't agree. If you are happy and satisfied with your wife, why should you reach outside of the marriage?' He only dared to contradict Mystique Mysterious because Fati was involved.

'But are you satisfied?'

'Of course I am. I am perfectly happy with Fati.'

Mystique Mysterious's loins twitched with desire at the mention of Fati. 'I don't doubt you, but you must still desire other women every now and then. Look, you don't go to the river and then wash your face with spittle, do you?'

'Maybe not, but you do not have to go to the river at all.'

'Ah, but that is where you are mistaken, my friend.' Mystique Mysterious's voice assumed a more serious tone. 'You live in the middle of the river. Look around you.' He pointed to the young women again. 'Look at them, Bukari. Look at their young faces, fresher than morning dew, their skins smoother than the grass the dew falls on. Ah, look at their behinds, their breasts. My friend, even you must want a taste of that nectar.'

'Wanting and doing are different things.'

'Ah, so you do want?'

'I did not say that.'

Mystique Mysterious grinned and without another word stepped out of the car and walked towards the young women. Bukari could see the admiration on their faces as he approached, their eyes following him coyly. When he began to speak to them their faces relaxed and grew seductive. Bukari could not hear what he said, but the young women were smiling winningly, determined to hold his interest. Soon, Mystique Mysterious and four young women walked to the car. Mystique Mysterious opened the rear door and all four women slipped into the back. He got into the driver's seat and introduced the women to Bukari: Ama, Jane, Akua and Grace. Bukari nodded in their direction and they giggled. In the little time before the car started to move, he studied their faces and concluded that they were not past their early twenties. Their mannerisms reinforced this conclusion: they giggled childishly and acted as if they had no cares in the world.

Mystique Mysterious drove them to the Cantonments area, to a large three-storey building. All six entered, Bukari reluctantly. Mystique Mysterious gestured for them to sit and turned on a little red lamp which suffused the room with sleazy light. He went into the kitchen and returned with a bottle of schnapps. 'Let us have a little celebration,' he said, reaching into a cabinet for six glasses. Bukari flinched at the speed with which the young women quaffed down their liquor. Mystique Mysterious turned on the stereo and a reggae tune filled the air. 'Reggae is too heavy for the occasion,' he said. He chose a cassette and inserted it into the tape deck. 'Jazz is the voice of the soul, the spirit of the heart. The young women giggled. 'To health and happiness,' he toasted. 'Drink up, Bukari. What are you afraid of?'

Bukari rose and walked to Mystique Mysterious and whispered, 'I want to talk to you, please.' The smile on

Mystique Mysterious's face vanished and he placed his arm round Bukari's shoulder and guided him to the kitchen.

'What is it now, my friend?'

Bukari asked, 'What is going on, sir? I don't think it's a good idea to be here at this time with these women, drinking, sir.'

Mystique Mysterious, his hand still resting on Bukari's shoulder, replied, 'I am showing you that there is more to life than you know. These women here want fun and you and I are going to give it to them.'

'I am married. You know that, sir.'

'Surely, but that should not stop you. I thought we had agreed on that already.' Bukari looked troubled and Mystique Mysterious continued, 'Look, I know you are thinking about Fati, but you shouldn't. We will have some fun, you will feel refreshed, you will go back home and nobody will know what happened. Trust me, you can do whatever you want when you are with me and not get caught. You can get away with murder.'

Bukari replied weakly, 'I don't know—'

Then they heard the voices of the young women from the living room. 'Just listen to them. Are you not aroused? You've seen their bodies, Bukari. Are you going to turn your back? They want you, Bukari. Don't be foolish. Be a man, Bukari. Don't disappoint me. We will go back, we will have some fun. I will drive you home, and everybody will be happy.'

After a brief moment of indecision, Bukari nodded his agreement and they returned to the living room. The bottle of schnapps was half empty and the women were tapping their feet and snapping their fingers to the music.

'Are you having fun?' asked Mystique Mysterious.

Ama nodded, Jane smiled and Akua grinned. Grace said, 'Oh yes, we are.'

'The music is very good,' Jane said. 'I like mellow music.'

'I like mellow music with red lights,' Akua opined, and giggled.

'It doesn't matter what lights you have, give me slow music, and I am happy,' intoned Jane.

Grace said, 'It's not the music or the lights, it is the booze that matters.'

Ama said, 'I'll tell you what is best: you need red lights, alcohol, good music and dancing. It is all useless without the dancing.'

Mystique Mysterious said, 'What a wonderful idea. But since there's only one man for every two women, we are going to have to improvise.' He helped Ama and Grace to their feet and took their glasses from them. He opened his arms and gathered them both to him, and began to sway slowly. Bukari did likewise with Akua and Jane. For almost ten minutes they danced. Passion was in the air, inhibitions were falling away.

'I'm getting tired of dancing,' Mystique Mysterious said. 'I would like to continue this upstairs.' He led the way to the second floor and guided Ama and Grace into one bedroom and showed Bukari, Akua and Jane another.

Hours later, spent and fulfilled, they drove back to the Kwame Nkrumah Circle. Mystique Mysterious bought some fried pork and they all ate. Then he took the women aside and said something to them; they seemed satisfied and left.

Mystique Mysterious returned to Bukari and said, 'You see, my friend, everything has gone as I told you. I will now take you back home and all will be well.'

Bukara felt both guilt and fear. He felt guilty not only because he had cheated on Fati but also because he had not thought about her during the act itself: she had been forgotten while he lay in the arms of other women. He felt fear because he dreaded being caught. Life without Fati was unimaginable. Yet he had to admit that he was beginning to feel a return of the sexual power he had experienced when he first slept with Fati. That she, a rich man's daughter, would sleep with him had given him a sense of power to begin with. Gradually that feeling had diminished and only affection remained. Now his consciousness of his own virility was coming back. He had been with two women much younger than he was and they had swooned.

It was close to midnight: Fati would be wondering where he had been all this time. 'I wonder what to tell Fati,' he said.

'What do you mean? Just tell her we went out for a few drinks.'

'She may not believe me. I have never been out this late.'

'You worry too much, my friend. Just leave it to me.'

They returned to an anxious and angry Fati who was pacing the compound while the breeze whispered among dancing shadows and nocturnal insects crooned a night-time chant.

Mystique Mysterious got out of the car and hurried

towards Fati. Before she could speak, he launched into a preemptive apology. 'As for this, madam, I beg you to forgive me for keeping your husband so late.' Bukari stepped out of the car and stood behind Mystique Mysterious. Mystique Mysterious continued, 'I should have brought him home earlier. He insisted it was getting late, that he had to come home to you, but I thought I would show him around a little, you know, take him around the town and enjoy the pleasure of his company. So I ignored his request and next thing I know it is already midnight. I am very sorry, madam, and I hope you understand.'

The depth and length of the apology left Fati speechless. She simply nodded and looked past Mystique Mysterious at her husband, whose face was riddled with guilt. Fati's anger vanished. Why had she allowed herself to get so worked up, when she should have known that her husband was among friends? She smiled sweetly and said, 'That is all right. I am glad you decided to take him around town.'

'I knew you would understand,' Mystique Mysterious said. 'Well, I have to get going. Have a good night, madam.' He took Fati's right hand and placed a kiss on it. As he did so a pleasant weakness ran through him. He hurried to the car and drove off.

When Mystique Mysterious was gone, Fati looked at Bukari in silence. Bukari was compelled to say, 'I am sorry, Fati.'

Fati understood. She was lucky: many of Bukari's peers would not bother to apologise. 'It's time for bed, my dear,' she said. 'I was worried because I had no idea what had happened to you.'

'I know, but this man Mystique Mysterious never gives up. I was at Auntie Esi's when he insisted that I come with him for a ride.'

'Did he invite anybody else?'

'No, it was just me.'

'Where did you go?'

Why was she prodding so? Bukari's mind went on the alert. Had he betrayed himself somehow? He had to tread carefully. 'Oh, a lot of places. We drove through Kanda, Ringway, Circle, downtown Accra, Cantonments…'

Fati soon grew tired of this narration. 'I see. Do you like Mystique Mysterious?'

'Yes. Why do you ask?'

'I don't know. I suppose it's because I don't really know him. I know all your close friends.' Her thoughts travelled to Kofi Ntim, whose head might seem full of balderdash, but who was genuine. She liked him. Kojo Ansah too, though he hardly spoke, seemed full of goodness. She said, 'Kofi Ntim and Kojo Ansah are good people, but this Mystique Mysterious…'

'He is a good man too.'

'If you say so.'

They went to the bedroom.

Fati said, 'I told Baba about us and father yesterday.'

Bukari was surprised, but not displeased.

'How did he take it?'

'Very well. I think our son has found a new love.'

'What? Nobody tells me anything around here.'

'Maybe if you spent more time with him he would tell you these things.'

Bukari knew Fati was right. He asked, 'So who is this person Baba has found?'

'Her name is Adukwei. Her mother works at the market close to me. I think she is a good girl.'

'But is Baba not too young for such things?'

'Huh? How old was I when we met?'

'Those were different times.'

Fati said nothing. Both began to undress. Fati thought back to the day before, when Baba had questioned her about love. She wished she could have been more helpful. He was still a boy who needed guidance. She sighed. Perhaps if she had given Baba a sibling, he would stay home more and not play truant all the time. That was the one thing she regretted in her marriage—her inability to have more children. After Baba it was as if Bukari could no longer fructify her womb: try as they might the second child would not come. Neither prayers nor potions had worked. She had even been told she was under her father's curse for her misdeeds.

They were fully undressed. Bukari went and lay on the bed and Fati looked at him. Where earlier that night there had been disappointment, now there was longing.

'Dear,' she whispered softly, lowering herself on to the mattress beside him.

The response was mumbled.

She moved closer and looked into her husband's eyes. They were heavy with fatigue. She placed one hand on his chest and weakly he put his hand over hers. She watched his eyes close as sleep enveloped him.

Fati lay back in resignation and disappointment. She heard the outer door slam and she knew that Baba was back home. Where could he have been, so long? She could only hope that his prodigality would not stretch beyond redemption. Maybe Adukwei would help him. Presently Baba's snores joined forces with Bukari's. Fati lay awake, alone with her unfulfilled desire. She did not blame her husband.

He had had a long day, driving the taxi back and forth on the street under the hot sun, taking a few drinks afterwards to ease the tension, then being called on to tour the town with Mystique Mysterious. She understood. But understanding did not stop her yearning for the act of love.

Chapter Nine

B ukari met Adukwei and was charmed by her. He took her and Baba to watch a soccer game at the Accra Sports Stadium. 'I hope you enjoyed yourself,' he said to Adukwei when they returned to Nima.

'Very much, sir,' Adukwei said. 'Thank you for everything.'

Then Baba said they had to leave. 'Come and visit us again,' Bukari told Adukwei.

'I will, sir.'

Baba and Adukwei walked slowly to the road and picked up their pace when they were out of Bukari's sight. Baba slipped his arm around Adukwei's waist and she put hers around his neck. They attracted a few stares for displaying affection in public, but they did not care.

'I am glad you came with me today,' Baba said.

'I am glad I came. It was good to meet your father. I think he is a very nice man.'

Baba said, 'Let's get something to eat.'

'That is a good idea. Why don't you come home with me? I will make you something to eat and you and my mother can chat a little.'

Baba remained silent for a moment to give the false impression that he was contemplating the offer. Then he replied, 'It would be nice, but I am famished and I can't wait. Let us get something to eat on the street. It will be much easier.'

'Very well, if you so wish.'

They turned the corner and came to a small stall where a woman stood selling *kenkey*. Baba said, 'Auntie, we will have four balls of *kenkey* and six fish to go with it. Please give us some black pepper as well.'

The woman dug into a large pan and brought out four balls of *kenkey*. Baba gasped at their size. 'Eei, Auntie, these balls are tiny indeed. I can eat all four by myself.'

'Ah, don't blame me,' the woman said. 'The price of maize has gone up.'

'All right, make it six balls.'

Adukwei protested. 'That's too much. Who is going to eat all that?'

'You will. You must eat and grow nicely fat.'

Baba took the food from the woman and paid her. Then he grabbed Adukwei by the hand and led her to a stool behind the stall. The woman brought them a bowl of water and they washed their hands and dipped the balls of *kenkey* into the pepper, breaking pieces of fish to go with them. Adukwei prepared a morsel and fed it to Baba. He gulped on it and licked her fingers. Then she prepared another one and this time teased him a little: as he stretched out his neck to receive it, she pulled her hand back a little and he bit into thin air. This happened a couple more times, until something distracted Adukwei's attention and Baba succeeded in snapping up the mouthful of food.

'You cheated,' she complained.

'No, I am just faster than you.'

Adukwei grinned. Then they changed roles, with Baba feeding Adukwei and occasionally teasing her too. After a while, Adukwei said she had had enough to eat. Then she asked, 'Where do you get the money for all these expenses?'

Baba played for time. 'What expenses?'

'You haven't stopped spending money ever since we met.'

Baba said, 'My parents give me money from time to time.' He did not know why he felt uncomfortable with the idea of telling Adukwei that the money came from Mystique Mysterious.

'I think you should keep your money. Save it for something you really want for yourself. You should not spend so much on me, Baba.'

Baba was bewildered. In his opinion, the way to impress a girl was by spending lavishly on her. 'But, Adukwei, don't you like me showing how much I appreciate you?'

'Baba, you are not rich. You must promise to stop it. You can spend as much as you wish when you start working. For now, it is enough for me to know that you care.'

'But it will be all right if I find a job?'

'Yes.'

They washed their hands and walked to the Kanda Estates. The air seemed to hold the subtle smell of the city: the marketplace with its aroma of fresh food, the breath of the trees, the flagrance of flowers in sleep, and the urban smells of kebab and petrol. At the Parks and Gardens, they sat on a bench .and Adukwei rested her head on Baba's shoulder. Baba looked at the sky and said, 'Adukwei, you are as brilliant as that bright star.'

Adukwei smiled, but said nothing. Her heart churned

with emotion. She longed for Baba both physically and in the spirit. This feeling had started slowly and burrowed deep into her, until now it had reached the point where she wished she and Baba were one, forever inseparable. This, she knew, was the stage of dependency: when she thought of herself, she thought of Baba and when she thought of Baba, she thought of herself. Baba had to be in the picture for Adukwei to be Adukwei. Yet she could envision Baba without her and that frightened her. She sought reassurance. 'Baba.'

'Yes, my sweetie.'

'Do you love me?'

'Yes, I love you. You know that. I love you to infinity.'

'Are you serious or are you just saying that to please me?'

Baba seemed a little peeved. 'Adukwei, why don't you trust me?'

'I'm sorry.' There was a brief silence; then she spoke again. 'Baba.'

'Yes, my sweet one.'

'We will stay together for ever, will we not?'

'How many times do I have to say it? You and I were made for each other. We will be together for ever.'

'Some boys say that without meaning it.'

'I'm not like them. Can you eat without food?'

'No.'

'Can you drink without liquid?'

'No.'

'Can you live without life?'

'No, Baba.'

'Then you cannot have Adukwei without Baba.'

That pleased Adukwei, although she would have preferred

him to say the reverse, for not having Adukwei without Baba was not the same as not having Baba without Adukwei. But perhaps she was reading too much into words.

'We are the luckiest people in the world,' Baba said.

Adukwei guessed why, but still she asked, 'Why do you say that?'

'Must you ask? Do we not have each other?' Baba became thoughtful. 'One day, we will be rich and we will have many mansions and many cars and many children and we will be happy. You like children, don't you?'

'Oh, yes, I like children. How many will we have?'

'I think twelve.'

'What? You are mad.'

'Why? What is wrong with twelve children? I see, you don't think twelve is enough. How about fourteen?'

'Nobody has that many children any more.'

Baba laughed. 'I was only joking, my sweet one.'

Adukwei pretended to be angry and hit him on the shoulder.

But Baba's dreams were serious. Spurred on by his love for Adukwei, his imagination was reaching beyond the boundaries of what many would believe to be realistically possible in his confined and impoverished life. He dreamt of more now than ever before, because he was dreaming for both of them.

'We must be getting back, Baba.' Adukwei said. 'It is quite late.'

And Baba suddenly became aware that darkness had stolen in around them. The rumble of cars had faded and the breath of the city had grown chillier. Holding hands, their fingers interlaced, Baba and Adukwei walked home to Nima.

Chapter Ten

1 July is Republic Day in Ghana, a holiday gladly seized on by the people. At the Labadi Pleasure Beach, the skies were marbled in sapphire and white, the sun hung burning in the heavens, a ball of fire that was reflected in the boiling surface of the sea. Kofi Ntim and Auntie Esi splashed across the wet sand where the waves lapped the shore. Unexpectedly, a bigger wave surged forward and broke around them; Kofi Ntim cursed at the drenching while Auntie Esi laughed. The beach was alive with people, some dancing to music played by a band.

Kofi Ntim thought back to the day before, when he had asked Auntie Esi to accompany him to the beach. It had been a usual night of drinking at Kill Me Quick. When the darkness outside had grown deep, Bukari and Kojo Ansah retired and went home while Kofi Ntim remained with Esi. Kofi Ntim had begun: 'So, Esi, why do you insist on ignoring me so?'

'I don't ignore you, Kofi Ntim.'

'But you do all the time.'

'Don't bother my ears.'

Kofi Ntim changed his strategy. 'You are a religious woman, Esi, are you not?'

'Yes, you know I am.'

From his pocket, Kofi Ntim fished out a small-sized Bible. 'You have heard of the Song of Solomon, have you not?'

'I have not really read it.'

'Well, if you will give me a minute, I will tell you the vital parts.'

'It is late, Kofi. I need to get some rest.'

'You see what I mean? You always want to ignore me.'

Slightly shamed, Esi said, 'All right. What is it?'

'Esi, don't treat me like a hoodlum off the street. Or am I not your friend?'

'Kofi Ntim, why are you babbling like that?'

'Esi, be patient so you can listen and listen so you can hear.'

Esi nodded in resignation and said, 'I am listening.'

Slowly, Kofi Ntim leafed through the Bible until he found the Song of Solomon and began, '"Let him kiss me with the kisses of his mouth: for thy love is better than wine."' He paused and looked into Esi's eyes for her reaction, but he could not find any. 'You see, Esi, my love is better than wine. Will you not taste its sweetness and allow it to intoxicate you?'

Esi was amused and a furtive smile formed on her lips.

Kofi Ntim continued, 'If I haven't moved your heart yet, be patient and hear some more. Are you listening?'

'I am listening.'

'Good. This is the heart of it all, so listen carefully: "O my dove, thou art in the clefts of the rock, in the secret places of the stars. Let me see thy countenance, let me hear thy voice; for sweet is thy voice, and thy countenance is comely."'

'I am flattered.'

'Let me analyse this verse for you, Esi my love. You are in my eyes, like the dove that graces the skies and the fields, innocent and sublime. I desire to see your countenance every minute, every second and every passing moment. Why? Your face is beauty personified. Men and women may travel to the corners of the earth, they may go to outer space and back, yet nowhere can they find beauty to equal your beauty.' Esi prepared to speak, but Kofi Ntim held up his hand and she remained silent. He went on, 'As for your voice, Esi, what can I say about it? When you speak, it is as if the doves have come from heaven to sing in your vocal cords. The soothing harmony, the melody your voice carries sweeps like the evening breeze over my face and caresses my ears with bliss. Bliss, perfect bliss. That is your voice.'

'Kofi, you—'

Again the hand: again the silence. 'So, Esi, when you put voice and face together, what you have is perfect beauty.' This time, Esi did not attempt to disturb the silence created by his pause. Kofi Ntim leafed further through the pages until he found a passage that lit his face. 'Esi, listen to this one,' he said. '"Thy teeth are like a flock of sheep that are even shorn, which came up from the washing; whereof every one bear twins and none is barren among them... Thou hast ravished my heart, my sister, my spouse; thou hast ravished my heart with one of thine eyes, with one chain of thy neck."'

Emotion etched deep lines into Kofi Ntim's face. He held the Bible a little further from his body and began to declaim more energetically. There was an earnestness in his voice which rose powerfully to fill the air. "'Thy lips, O my spouse, drop as the honeycomb: honey and milk are under thy tongue; and the smell of thy garments is like the smell of Lebanon. I sleep, but my heart waketh: it is the voice of my beloved that knocketh, saying, Open to me, my sister, my love, my dove, my undefiled: for my head is filled with dew, and my locks with the drops of the night.'"

He stopped and placed the Bible on the bar counter, breathing heavily. Esi was surprised at his zeal and ardour. She had known three husbands in her lifetime and none had so earnestly and vigorously addressed himself to her. Kofi Ntim's performance had pierced the shell of indifference with which she had viewed him until that moment. While he recovered, she managed to say, 'I am impressed.' Then she added gently, 'But Kofi, I am not your spouse.'

'In my mind you are.'

'Your mind is out of touch with reality.'

'At some point they will intersect.'

Esi smiled. 'You have spoken many words tonight, Kofi. But most were not your own.'

'I acknowledge that others can express certain things more eloquently than I can, but I meant everything I read, believe me.'

'I believe you.'

'Well, is that all you can say?'

'What do you want me to say?'

'Anything on your mind, my dear.'

'Thank you.'

'Is that all?'

'What more do you want?'

It was Kofi Ntim's turn to smile. He was gaining ground, but he needed time. 'Esi, I have a simple request.'

'What is it, Kofi?'

'Tomorrow is 1 July.'

'I know that. Everybody knows that.'

'Well, they are having a party at the Labadi Beach, Esi.' She waited. He said nothing more, so she asked, 'So?'

'You should come with me.'

'To do what?'

'So we can be together.'

'How can we be together when there will be so many people there?'

'Esi, do not play games. You know what I mean.'

'But, Kofi, we are not—'

'I know we are not lovers.'

'That's not what I was going to say.'

'Whatever you were going to say, you agree we are friends?'

'Yes, I agree.'

'So we will go as friends.'

She hesitated before saying, 'All right, I will come with you, but we are going as friends and nothing more.'

A rapture of delight seared through Kofi Ntim. Here he was in the presence of the woman he desired and he was moving closer and closer. Like the tortoise, he would not hurry, certain in the knowledge that eventually he would reach his destination. 'I am glad you have made that decision, Esi. You have made me a happy man. I could climb the tallest mountain.'

'Kofi, you better shut up before I change my mind.'

'Ah, Esi, you will not grant me a moment to relish in my exultation?'

'There is nothing to get excited about.'

'Whatever you say,' Kofi Ntim put the Bible back into his pocket. 'Give me another drink for the road, Esi.'

'Don't tell me you want another drink at this time of the night. It is too late.'

'Only one more, Esi. Don't make me beg for it.'

Esi poured a quarter glass of *akpeteshie* and placed it in front of Kofi Ntim. 'You drink too much, Kofi,' she said in a concerned tone.

'I follow the Bible.'

'Where does the Bible tell you to drink?'

'Did Jesus not turn water into wine? Look, One Timothy, chapter five, verse twenty-three says, "No longer drink only water, but use a little wine for your stomach's sake and for your frequent infirmities."'

'You have a way of using the Bible to serve your mischievous ends. Anyway, my point is not that you should not drink at all. I serve the stuff. My point is only that you should not drink so much.'

'You think I drink too much, but I don't. My body can take it. I am not like Madman who drinks and then starts behaving like a fool. I drink, Esi, but I am not a drunkard.'

'I wonder what it must take to make a drunkard, then.'

'Don't worry about my drinking, Esi. So long as it does not affect my judgement, it is no problem.'

'But that is where we must disagree. I think your drinking does affect your judgement, Kofi.'

'How so?'

'Look at you. You are not a young man. You have worked for a long time now. What do you have to show for it?'

Kofi Ntim laughed without mirth. 'Esi, do you not know I have been making a pittance all my life? What I have earned until now maybe, is hardly enough to make ends meet.'

'Maybe if you cut down on your drinking.'

'Must you always mention my drinking?' Kofi Ntim gulped down a little liquor as though to defy Esi's concern. 'It is only now that I can talk about doing something with my life, now that I am driving a taxi.'

'Well, what are you going to do with your life?'

Kofi Ntim grinned with pride. 'I have been thinking very hard. You know my uncle, the one in Apam?'

'I have heard you mention him.'

'Well, I have decided to ask him for a piece of land. He owns a large parcel of land at Awutu and he does not use all of it. I will go and ask him to lease me a portion that I can use for farming.'

Esi's interest mounted. 'That sounds like a good idea. But what are you going to grow?'

'Maize, Esi. I am going to farm maize, and I should have enough money saved up by the next season to start.'

'Next year? That's a long time away.'

'Yes, I know,' replied Kofi Ntim. 'But little steps are better than no steps. I will move forward even if I don't reach my goal.'

Esi liked this man. Until now, her affection for him had been the same as for the others: Bukari, Kojo Ansah. Now he was beginning to kindle sparks in her of a different kind.

Whereas in the past she had thought Kofi Ntim was only joking when he said he loved her, now she knew he was not. She had travelled this path before and her previous failed marriages had taught her many lessons. The men she had shared her bed with before, and whose children she had borne, were all alike in certain ways. Their love was like the embers of the fire, soon to fade and die. Then the painful part would begin: living in a loveless marriage. When love and desire die, tolerance is the new target to aim for, and tolerance by itself stands on uncertain ground. Three times Esi had tried to hold a marriage together by means of give and take, and three times she had failed. In each case her parents, aunts and uncles had intervened in the final stages to try to salvage the remnants of affection, but in each case she had gone ahead with the divorce, knowing that nothing worth saving was left. The third time her relatives threw their hands into the air in frustration and cried, 'Why can't Esi keep a man?' No one asked why the men couldn't keep Esi. They wondered, 'With three husbands behind her, will our Esi find another man?' They worried, but Esi did not. It had been three years since the last divorce and she did not care.

But now Kofi Ntim had come knocking on her door, cautiously and brazenly both at once. Kofi Ntim, the man they called Philosopher Nonsense. But was he really a philosopher of nonsense? True, he often spoke as though he were incapable of intelligent thought. But was that the real Kofi Ntim? And was he really so ugly? Esi reviewed the details of his appearance in her mind. The sparsely haired head: baldness was not such a bad thing; it added dignity.

The broad expanse of forehead: a pane of skin enclosing weighty faculties of thought. The thick brush of eyebrows: they added character to his face. His jutting jaw: a mark of strength. The goatee: the final proof of personality. Even the large ears could be seen as erotic symbols, the short limbs and torso as expressions of virility. Taken individually, then, Kofi Ntim's physical attributes were acceptable, but when she put them together, the result was not pleasant to the eye. Yet her growing affection was beginning to make this less important. Perhaps in the end Kofi Ntim's ugliness would not matter at all. Time would tell.

Kofi Ntim took another gulp of his drink and winked at Esi in a manner at once innocent and lewd. It was a quality he possessed: the power of paradox. He was ugly, and yet he was beautiful, a unique amalgam of powerful features, a man with a wholesome physique. He was profane and vulgar in speech, yet he was refined, decent, honourable. His thoughts were unfiltered, raw; at the same time, they were sharp, shrewd, witty. At any point he could ascend from the basest of actions to the noblest. And these paradoxes haunted Esi. She could not grasp the essence of Kofi Ntim. The human desire to comprehend others in order to know how to respond made her wonder and worry. If your neighbour is a thief, you guard your possessions; to the foul-mouthed, you deafen your ears and sharpen your tongue; the bellicose you avoid, or else you carry your own weapon. But how to react to one who could not be understood?

It took Esi a while to respond to Kofi Ntim's wink, while her mind worked to put her concerns in perspective. Finally she smiled at him and winked in return. A huge grin spread over Kofi Ntim's face and his eyes held much joy.

Esi's body was weary and her eyes scratchy with the need for sleep. 'I am a little tired, Kofi, and I think you are too. I think we should bid the night farewell.'

'I know, I am tired too.' He finished his drink and took some money from his pocket to pay, but Esi pushed his hand away. 'Tonight, I give you the drink for free, Kofi Ntim.'

Surprised, Kofi Ntim said, 'The gods must be smiling on me tonight.' He prepared to leave. 'I will pick you up tomorrow afternoon.'

'Very well.'

'Good-night and sleep well.'

'Good-night and sleep well,' she echoed.

Kofi Ntim left the kiosk and the night took him into its vast openness. He walked home as though he were floating on air, gliding above the mundane surface of the earth. He was the weightless feather borne along by a soothing wind. He gave himself up to delicious recollection for what had passed in the bar: Esi's words, her smiles, her wink.

The next day, Kofi Ntim waited impatiently for the afternoon, then drove the taxi he had borrowed for the occasion to Esi's home, picked her up and made for the beach. He beamed with pride to have Esi sitting beside him.

Newly curious, Esi asked, 'Kofi, how come you have never told me about yourself, your family?'

Kofi Ntim made no response, but Esi glanced sideways and saw that he was blinking his eyes as if to hold back tears. Scolding herself for having intruded on some private sorrow, she changed the subject. 'This is a beautiful day to go to the beach.'

Kofi Ntim only nodded, still not able to trust his voice. A little later, when he was convinced he had regained control over himself, he said, 'Esi, my life has not been a pleasant one. I don't talk about my childhood because it brings unwanted pain.' His voice quavered.

Esi said, 'You don't have to tell me, Kofi. Sorry I mentioned it.'

'I will tell you,' Kofi Ntim replied. 'I was born so feeble my parents thought I would die in no time. But after about seven months of frail health, I got sturdier and stronger. But they tell me as I gained in health, my mother got weaker and weaker, and a year after I was born, she died. Three months later, the first of my three brothers died. Exactly three months afterwards, the second brother died, and the third, three months later.

'My father was sad, I hear, and he used to tell his friends that he held me responsible for the deaths of his wife and sons; that I was an evil influence. In a way, I think he needed an excuse for his own guilt, for I later learned that the night my mother died, he was in the bed of another woman. He married that woman when I was about five and that worsened my plight. I knew before then that my father didn't like me, but my stepmother was worse: every ounce of flesh in my stepmother bore hatred for me. And she vented her hatred by beating me all the time.'

Tears rolled down Kofi Ntim's cheeks and he let them flow. 'Some days, I actually thought of killing her. I might have tried if she had not stopped. You see, when I was about eight, she had her first child, my sister, Ama. Now she had a new life in hers and she had less time to dwell on her hatred for me. And she had five more children afterwards over a period of about thirteen years, one after the other. By the time she was through, I was too old to be beaten. But the hatred lived on. I was still treated like an outcast.'

Esi asked, 'You never complained to your father?'

'It would not have made a difference. Remember, my father did not like me much anyway. And he began to drink very hard until he seemed to be in a stupor almost all the time. He didn't care what went on in the home. You know, I could have gone to secondary school because I did very well in primary school, but my stepmother bullied me into giving up the idea. I tried to get a scholarship and failed and my parents would not support me in any way. So I had to settle for odd jobs. When I was twenty-three, I got the job at the City Council and left home soon afterwards.'

That is probably why he drinks so hard, Esi reflected. To numb the pain of the memories of such a life of misery. Aloud, she asked, 'Do you see your parents these days?'

'Hardly. My father is senile and frail. I go to see him sometimes. Sometimes he recognises me, sometimes he doesn't. My stepmother is frail too but she still hates me with the same passion as before. When I go to see my father, she still looks at me like I am a monster to be despised. But I go to see my father, not her, and so I bear her contempt silently.'

'You still visit the father who treated you so badly?'

'Yes, and do not ask me why because I am not sure why I do it.'

'You are very honourable,' Esi said.

'Thank you.'

The tears had dried on Kofi Ntim's face; he rubbed at the thin streaks with his palms. They drove in silence the rest of the way, each contemplating the beauty and calm of the skies.

When they got to the beach, it was already packed. 'I can't believe this,' Kofi Ntim said. 'Look at the crowd. Is the whole of Accra here today?'

'People must have their fun. Are you here to complain or to enjoy yourself?'

Kofi Ntim led Esi to the coconut trees and they lay on their backs for a long period of time in silence, against the background of music and voices on the beach. After a while, Kofi Ntim asked, 'Do you want something to drink?'

'I wouldn't mind something soft.'

Kofi Ntim walked to a stall where the logo of a foreign soft drinks company was displayed boldly and a teenager served him his order. He was about to return to Esi when he saw Mystique Mysterious through a thicket of bodies with his arm around a young woman's neck. He looked a little harder and there was no mistaking it: Bukari also was there, and he too had his arm around a woman's waist, and the woman was not Fati. Kofi Ntim watched as the young woman reached up and kissed Bukari on the lips. Bukari smiled and reciprocated.

'My God!' Kofi Ntim exclaimed in surprise. How many times had Bukari not professed his unending love for Fati and Fati alone? Was he now walking the path he had so often condemned?

Kofi Ntim turned and walked to a stall near by and bought four beef kebabs. Sternly telling himself not to allow his day to be spoilt by brooding over something that was none of his business anyway, he returned to Esi. They had their meal, rested a little and then walked down to the open shore. As they strolled along the beach, Kofi Ntim reached out his hand and took Esi's. She did not resist or complain. So they walked hand-in-hand on the shores of the Atlantic Ocean until the sun began to set and the sky became dimmer. They laughed with one another and talked about many things they had never talked about before. Then when the hour grew late Kofi Ntim drove Esi back home.

Chapter Eleven

Bukari was thoughtful as he drove home from Labadi Beach. His life was moving at a faster pace than ever and he was exploring new zones of pleasure, exciting and stimulating but dangerous and uncertain. His nocturnal life was now crammed with drinking and women. The drinking had been routine with him as far back as he could remember, but it had never been this intense. Not only had his consumption now increased vastly, but he was also drinking different things. There was no more local gin and beer: in the company of Mystique Mysterious, he drank only foreign gin, vodka, and beer. Whereas initially he got them free, nowadays Mystique Mysterious insisted that Bukari contribute to the coffers, as he liked to put it. So Bukari paid for expensive foreign drinks, and that put a strain on his pocket. The women too were abundant: Mystique Mysterious procured new ones for every escapade. And Bukari had to pay for them also—indirectly, to Mystique Mysterious, who said they ought to be bought off so that they would not stir trouble. What had begun as an experiment was developing into an addiction, an obsession. Whenever Mystique Mysterious went womanising without him, Bukari's desire grew unbearable. But he could not seduce women on his own; he was dependent upon Mystique Mysterious, who knew exactly which women to pick, what to say, what to buy. He, Bukari, only walked in Mystique Mysterious's shadow and ate the crumbs, but even the crumbs were tasty.

Bukari knew that he was walking dangerous paths. Not only was he draining his finances, but also his physical energies. He could tell that Fati was missing him, that she craved him in a physical sense, but he simply did not have the energy for her. He told himself that in time he would make it up to her: when this phase in his life was over, he would be a good husband once again. In the meantime, he told her that Mystique Mysterious demanded his company, and hoped that she did not suspect the truth.

When he arrived home, worn out with dancing and sex, he tumbled into bed and slept until evening. Then he ate the meal prepared by Fati, sat outside for a while and prepared to leave for Kill Me Quick. But to his surprise, Mystique Mysterious appeared, carrying a bottle of schnapps.

'I think today we should just have a quiet night here. No bars. Just the three of us, right here.'

'I don't know if Fati will approve,' Bukari said.

'She will. Where is she?'

'She is inside mending clothes.'

'Well, then, let's join her.'

Bukari hesitated a moment, but Mystique Mysterious motioned with his head and he obliged and opened the door leading to his living room. Fati was seated in the only armchair in the room with a pair of trousers in her lap and a needle in her hand. She appeared a little flustered by the unexpected appearance of Mystique Mysterious.

'Madam,' Mystique Mysterious said before Fati could

speak. 'Today, I bring you and your husband a bottle of schnapps to share and celebrate the night.'

Fat smiled and replied, 'I am glad you are so thoughtful, but I don't drink.' Then she realised the men were both standing so she stood up and offered her seat to Mystique Mysterious.

'Oh, no. You sit down, madam,' said Mystique Mysterious. Fati complied.

Bukari dragged an upright chair from the corner of the room and offered it to Mystique Mysterious. The only seat left was a stool and this Bukari took for himself. Mystique Mysterious pulled up one of the two decrepit coffee tables in the room and placed on it the opened bottle of schnapps. Bukari provided three cups and Mystique Mysterious half filled one of them and offered it to Fati. 'I'm sorry, but I told you I don't drink.'

Mystique Mysterious passed the cup on to Bukari and filled one for himself. The men commenced to drink while Fati sewed. Then Mystique Mysterious removed a tin of evaporated milk from his pocket, asked for a tin opener, made holes in the tin and poured a drop of milk into each of the cups of schnapps. 'This is delicious, don't you think, Bukari?'

'It's very nice,' replied Bukari.

Mystique Mysterious said, 'I think you ought to try it, madam. With the milk, you can't even taste the liquor. Or what do you think, Bukari?'

'I agree. It tastes mild, almost sweet. You should try it, Fati.'

Fati looked up at her husband with surprise. He had never advised that she drink liquor. Never. What was coming over him? She started to decline the suggestion when Mystique Mysterious poured a little schnapps into the empty cup and added some milk. He shook the cup a bit to mix the contents and said, 'Madam, you will not deny a visitor's request, especially after I have prepared the drink myself. I have taken the pains to buy this drink and bring it all over here, madam. Will you not just take a sip?'

Fati waited for Bukari to come to her aid, looking at him for a signal. But her husband's eyes spoke clearly: do not turn this man down. Fati forced a smile and said, 'Well, if you insist, I will just take a sip. I suppose that won't hurt.' She took the cup in her hands and for a long time stared into it as though it were lethal. Then she looked again at her husband, appealing to him to save her from actually putting the cup to her lips, but he returned the same silent signal as before. She raised the cup to her lips and took a little sip. She found that she could swallow without effort. 'I guess it's not that bad after all,' she opined.

'I told you, didn't I?' said Mystique Mysterious. He looked at Fati's face as she took another sip. The salacious desire began in his groins again and grew stronger and stronger until he felt weak in the belly. He looked away, embarrassed and afraid that he might reveal his weakness. How could he have such feelings for a woman of such common rank? Presently, he buried his embarrassment in the drink and began taking more frequent gulps. Fati too was imbibing more freely now. After a while, the liquor evidently had its effect on her and she became very talkative. The men sat in silence and listened. Bukari with amusement at the transformation in her, Mystique Mysterious increasingly tormented by his susceptibility to her allure. In the end, the feeling was so powerful that he had to excuse himself before he lost all control.

Once outside, Mystique Mysterious stood still a long time in order to clear his body of the desire for Fati. When he was sure of himself, he left the compound and went on to 441.

The usual crowd was assembled. Mystique Mysterious did not waste time. He produced rolls of marijuana and passed them around. The crowd sat and smoked them hungrily.

Mystique Mysterious nudged a man whose eyes were blank, as if his mind were elsewhere. 'Young man, what is your name?'

'Yaw Cake,' the man said.

'Yaw Cake?' Mystique Mysterious asked, to assure himself he had heard correctly.

'Yes sir, Yaw Cake.'

'Well, Yaw Cake, I have a few questions to ask you. Do you think you can answer them?'

'I will do my best, sir. My very best.'

'Good. Do you know the man Kojo Ansah?'

'Yes sir, I do. He is a very quiet man who keeps to himself and doesn't say much to anyone. I know he works as an electrician with the Public Works Department.'

'Well, tell me what you know about him. For example, is he married?'

'Not now, sir. He used to be married a long time ago, but they say his wife died and he has refused to marry again.'

'Did they have any children?'

'No sir, none.'

'I see. And what does Kojo Ansah like doing? What pleases him?'

Yaw Cake did not know the answer to that question, but he was afraid to say so for fear of losing favour. He said, 'Sir, you know he is a quiet man? He likes to go to the Kill Me Quick and listen to his friends talk. They say he does not drink though. He just drinks water and listens to his friends.'

Then Mystique Mysterious asked the question he had been building up to. 'Do you like Kojo Ansah?'

Yaw Cake pondered before answering. If he answered in the negative and that displeased Mystique Mysterious, he could be in trouble. Yet the same might be true if he answered positively. He gambled and answered with the truth. 'I don't know him very well, sir, and I don't like or dislike him.'

Mystique Mysterious nodded. 'I can understand that. How about the others here? Do you think they like Kojo Ansah?'

Yaw Cake reflected a little and said, 'I think they are just as indifferent as I am. They don't like or dislike him.'

'So if he were to take a long vacation nobody would miss him?'

'Oh no, nobody would miss him.'

Mystique Mysterious nodded again. Yaw Cake wondered why such a man took an interest in a nonentity like Kojo Ansah. Without saying anything more, Mystique Mysterious walked away into the back alleys of Nima in search of Baba.

He found Baba and his friends in an unlit alley. There were four of them and all eyed him with awe. Mystique

Mysterious stood a moment to relish the reverence in their faces, then motioned to Baba who leaped to his feet and allowed himself to be drawn away from the rest. When they were out of earshot, Mystique Mysterious said, 'So, Baba, how is Adukwei?'

Baba was stunned into silence. How did he know Adukwei? Who had told him? Mystique Mysterious said, 'I am sure she is well?'

'She is very fine, sir,' Baba said weakly.

'I am glad she is well. You like her very much, don't you?'

Baba looked away bashfully.

'I will tell you what the secret is, Baba,' said Mystique Mysterious. 'You want to keep her, don't you?'

Baba said, 'Yes sir, I do.'

'A young woman as beautiful as Adukwei should not be taken for granted. You can never know what the other men are planning for her. You see, at my age, I know the ways of men. Adukwei is growing and men are beginning to be attracted to her. Some men are older than you are and have ways with words. They know exactly what to say to woo her. Others will use money. I can assure you that if they have not already started pursuing her, they soon will.'

Baba was suddenly filled with fear. Was it possible that another man would seize Adukwei's heart from him? No, not his Adukwei! Yet Mystique Mysterious had opened up the possibility and Mystique Mysterious was an experienced, sophisticated man who knew many things about how women and men interact. So if Mystique Mysterious said it could happen, it could. Baba sought help. 'What can I do, sir?'

'I am glad you asked, Baba, my son. I will be glad to tell

you,' Mystique Mysterious said with confidence. 'You see, the best way to keep Adukwei is to make her believe that you care, that she is not just in your heart, but in your mind also. How? You must buy her things, you must make her feel appreciated.'

'But sir, she does not like me buying her things. She says I don't work so she doesn't like it when I spend money on her.'

'But that is precisely why you must spend on her. By defying her request you will prove to her that you really like and think of her. Let me explain, my son. When she says she doesn't like it when you buy her things, she is just testing how much you like her. If you take her word for it, she will say, "This Baba doesn't like me very much. I show a little disapproval and he doesn't even persist." Do you want her to say that? Certainly not. But if you continue to spend on her, you will be telling her, "Adukwei, I know your concerns and I am willing to prove to you that even if it hurts my pocket, you are the one I enjoy spending my money on because I like you so much." She will like you for that.'

Somewhere, Baba had lost the thread of Mystique Mysterious's logic, but he understood that he was being urged to continue to spend on Adukwei. He would follow his mentor's advice. The problem of money remained, however. How could he put his hands on more cash? He did not have to wonder for long. Mystique Mysterious brought out a bundle of notes from his pocket, counted a bunch and handed them to Baba. The young man was lavish in his gratitude. Mystique Mysterious thought to himself, 'This is a fraction of what your father gives me.' Aloud he said, 'You see, my son Baba, everything can be taken care of, but I tell you there is nothing better than being able to make your own money, being your own man. I can help you do that, my son. Do you want to be able to do that? To have your own money? To work for it?'

'Yes sir!'

'Good, I knew you would. I have a friend who is looking for somebody to help sell newspapers. You see, Baba, it's not a hard job at all. All you do is wake up in the morning, get the newspapers and try to sell as many as you can.'

Baba accepted Mystique Mysterious's proposal without hesitation. Then Mystique Mysterious persuaded him to agree to pay a small commission to his friend, the kind provider of the job opportunity. Mystique Mysterious impressed on Baba that he was only linking employer to employee. Baba readily agreed. Mystique Mysterious slapped him mildly on the back and walked away.

Left alone, Baba wondered why his own father could not be like Mystique Mysterious. It was not that he did not love his father. Although he was past the period of unconditional adulation for parents and had reached the stage where his admiration could be swayed in any direction, his love stayed on course: not adulatory, but affectionate. Even so, he wished he could talk to Bukari and seek guidance on certain matters, but Bukari seemed preoccupied with other things. His mother was empathetic, but she could not teach him the things that a man could teach.

Baba stood long after Mystique Mysterious was gone, lost in thought, oblivious to the yelling of his friends. It was not till Otto picked up a small stone and threw it at him that Baba became conscious of his surroundings again and returned to the group of boys.

'How do you know Mystique Mysterious?' asked Otto.

'What was he talking about?' Ntiamoah queried.

Ofori said, 'Tell us how you know him.'

But Baba's mind was elsewhere. He thought of Adukwei and of the possibility of losing her. Was it really true that she did not mean it when she said he ought not spend so much on her? Even if she meant it, had she not also said that he could spend money on her if he found work? Mystique Mysterious had solved all Baba's problems in one night. With the money from the newspaper job, he would keep her for ever.

Otto asked again, 'How do you know Mystique Mysterious?'

Baba smiled and waited a while in order to cultivate an air of importance. His eager friends pushed closer. 'I can't tell you that,' Baba said. He did not know the answer himself. 'He knows me because I am so important. How can he not know me?'

'You, Baba, ever since you met that girl Adukwei, you have been acting as if you have no head,' Ntiamoah said.

Baba glared at Ntiamoah. 'Why are you picking on Adukwei? She is the sweetest thing the world has ever seen.'

'We are not picking on Adukwei,' said Ofori. 'We are picking on you for having allowed your heart to swallow your head.'

'You are jealous. It is nothing but jealousy.'

Otto came to Baba's assistance. 'There is nothing wrong with Baba. If I had a girl like Adukwei I too would be in love and nothing but love.'

Chapter Twelve

A year passed. It brought many tidings. Some were of great joy and some were not.

In September, Kofi Ntim went to see his maternal uncle with a bottle of schnapps and asked for land. The uncle had deep affection for this one, perhaps because his mother had died in his infancy. 'You city boys never come to visit us,' he complained. 'But it is a great pleasure to see you, my son.' Kofi Ntim did not waste any time in explaining his purpose. His uncle, having heard his request, insisted that he spend the night. The next day they went to Awutu and the uncle made over a large portion of land to the nephew. Kofi Ntim returned to Accra and forgot about the land for a while. Then in December the *harmattan* came and the wind got chillier and he prayed for the season to move on. At Christmas, he bought Esi a bottle of perfume. She was very grateful and her gratitude made him happy. He dreamt every day of his future and continued to save as much money as he could. He also continued to pay Mystique Mysterious a percentage of his salary.

He started to work his land in March, before the rainy season. The process was slow and painful, especially clearing the ground and preparing it for sowing. Every weekend he travelled to Awutu and worked feverishly on the land.

He also hired two hands to help him. After sowing the seeds, he waited and prayed for the rains to fall. In April, the rains were miserly, but in May, they fell heavily. The earth drank deeply and the seeds did likewise. In June, the rains subsided, but they still fell. Kofi Ntim's first harvest was bountiful. He bought sacks, hired a truck, loaded the maize into the sacks and the sacks on to the trucks, and hauled the crops from Awutu to Accra. He found a good market and made a sizeable profit.

When he harvested the second batch, Kofi Ntim was luckier still, for the roads in the northern regions of the country had become so bad that it was difficult to transport food to the South. So in Accra, the supply of food was low and prices rose. Kofi Ntim made more money than he had anticipated. He invested in clothing, buying at low cost and selling at a much higher price. He employed Baba's friend Otto to help him run the business and this too began to make generous profits. Kofi Ntim was a contented man and began to dream bigger dreams. Although he continued to drive the taxi, he had second thoughts about the share he was giving to Mystique Mysterious.

He continued to woo Esi, but he was now such a busy man that his courtship was unwillingly sporadic. He tried to drink with his friends as often as possible, but his former daily visits to the bar were reduced to three visits a week. Still, he made progress. It began with holding Esi's hand at the beach, then putting his arm around her shoulders from time to time. She did not complain. He advanced to encircling her waist and she did not protest, but when he tried to kiss her on the lips she pushed him gently away.

He waited patiently and planned his next move. Then Esi helped him a little by taking the initiative one night and placing a kiss on his lips.

Meantime, Bukari was drinking and womanising with Mystique Mysterious. Most weekday nights, after having a few drinks at Kill Me Quick, they picked up women and took them to places chosen by Mystique Mysterious (who seemed to have access to many houses, though whether he owned all of them or none of them, Bukari did not know). Their adventures were always the same: orgies of alcohol and human flesh. Bukari's finances suffered greatly. He was always broke at the end of the month.

Fati was conscious that her husband had less and less energy and attention for her, but gradually she resigned herself to what was happening. If Mystique Mysterious was her compentiton, she would not complain. She too was beginning to develop a sort of dependency on the big man. After the visit when he had persuaded her to drink her first drop of liquor, he returned with more, and each time she drank a little more freely. This continued until she actively looked forward to his visits. At least when her husband and Mystique Mysterious stayed at home to drink with her she was not alone.

Bukari's son, Baba, was working as a vendor of newspapers. It gave him joy to wake up in the mornings, pick up the day's supply and roam the town seeking buyers. By moving back and forth on the busiest streets, he managed to sell many papers. He always gave Mystique Mysterious a portion of his earnings, still in the mistaken belief that the money was going to the man responsible for the job, for whom Mystique Mysterious was only doing a favour. Baba's life could be divided into three main compartments: when he sold newspapers; when he whiled away the time with his friends; and when he was with Adukwei. His leisure time he spent with Adukwei: after the newspapers were sold, they walked and talked, whether under the glaring sun at noon or the enchanting cavalcade of stars at night. Sometimes he met up with his friends, to loiter in back alleys, occasionally to see a film at the Dunia Theatre. But Adukwei was the most meaningful thing in his life. When Baba thought about the future, it was almost invariably and inextricably linked to Adukwei.

Privately thinking that Baba and Adukwei were too young for lasting love, Bukari gave them three months, but three months came and went and they only grew closer.

Baba was more comfortable with the condition he was in. When Adukwei asked him for an assurance of his love, he replied, 'Adukwei, I believe in the preacher now.'

'Why?'

'He said there is a heaven and now I know there really is a heaven. The heaven is you.'

She laughed, but she was touched and she adored him even more than ever. The young lovers were so happy that Baba's friends became jealous that they too could not find women to love so deeply. For love is attractive: those who witness it desire it for themselves.

Mystique Mysterious continued to experience the powerful push of libido whenever he saw Fati. He looked into her eyes and was transfixed by a potent carnal force. In her body he saw the allure of ultimate sensual possibilities.

Her voice sang pleasurably into his ears. He went to the Bukari homestead again and again and his desire for Fati grew more baffling and exciting, more intense and troubling on each visit.

At the same time he had not forgotten the 441 crowd. Every day, when the crowd gathered, he passed by stealthily and observed them. Some days, he revealed his presence and talked with them a little. Sometimes they became restive until he supplied them with marijuana or cocaine; then they became calm and thankful. Little by little he watched them become dependent on him and on the drugs. On the days when he chose not to show himself, they were disappointed. On these days, knowing that what he did not provide free of charge they were now desperate enough to buy for themselves, he made a point of sending a courier carrying enough marijuana or cocaine to sell to the crowd.

Kojo Ansah had grown uneasy about Mystique Mysterious's constant presence in Nima. He began to follow Mystique Mysterious around, hoping to find out what he wanted. He saw Mystique Mysterious supply the 441 crowd with marijuana and noted the smirk on his face, the expressions of contempt. One day, Kojo Ansah set out as he had done many times before, to watch the operations of Mystique Mysterious in Nima. But a short while after positioning himself where he could observe the 441 crowd without, as he thought, himself being seen, he was shocked by a familiar voice at his ear.

'Kojo Ansah, how are you?'

He turned sharply. Standing behind him was Mystique Mysterious. He blinked as if he could not trust his vision.

Mystique Mysterious beamed. 'It is a beautiful night, no?' he asked.

Kojo Ansah said nothing at first, stunned into silence by the stealth with which Mystique Mysterious had sneaked up behind him. The observer had been observed. 'It is a beautiful night, indeed,' he said at last. 'A night to walk abroad.'

'And to observe things,' Mystique Mysterious added. 'You are an observer of things and of men, are you not?'

'Let's say I keep an open eye and an open ear.'

'That is an interesting way to put it,' said Mystique Mysterious. 'You look and listen, but you don't talk much. Why do you choose to be so quiet?'

'Talk is boring.'

Mystique Mysterious laughed until tears came to his eyes. 'That is the funniest thing I have heard.'

'Talk is such a waste of time and energy,' Kojo Ansah insisted. 'If people would spend thinking half the time they spend talking, the world would be a better place. If people filtered their thoughts before they spoke, they would not come out with the rubbish we hear these days. I keep my thoughts to myself unless I have something of import to say.'

Mystique Mysterious replied, 'I understand your point of view, but I don't agree with it. What kind of world would we live in if everyone were so guarded in their speech? What would happen if we did not speak spontaneously, when thoughts came into our minds?'

'We would have more peace in the world.'

'I must beg to differ. On the contrary, I believe the world would be more dangerous. People would bottle up all their inner feelings and frustrations. But they would express themselves through their actions. That could be very dangerous indeed.'

'It depends. Loose talk can cause trouble too. I believe it is prudent to hold your tongue.'

'We have a fundamental difference of opinion, my friend, one that we may not be able to resolve tonight. I suppose we must agree to disagree.'

'That suits me fine.'

Mystique Mysterious nodded. 'Let me buy you a drink. How about that?'

'I don't drink and you know it.'

'Yes, but I was hoping I could convince you to begin.'

'No, you can't. I used to drink once. I will never go back to that habit.'

For a moment, Kojo Ansah remembered the event that had led to his flirtation with alcohol: the death of his wife. She had fallen ill in the fifth year of their marriage and withered away slowly and surely like a weak plant in arid weather. He had begun drinking with such abandon after she died, that for months he walked the streets mumbling to himself like a madman. Until he saw his wife in a dream that seemed so real it shook him out of his stupor for ever. She came slowly towards him, buoyed up on a sea of clouds, a floral crown upon her head. She smiled at him and reached out for his hands, but as he stretched out his arms to touch her she moved further and further away. In his desperation, he called for her to come to him, but she shook her head and said, 'Kojo, my love, you have to stop your drinking. You are making me very unhappy where I am.'

'I can't,' he answered, and took a swig from the bottle he

had been steadily draining. As he did so, she moved further away. 'Don't go away,' he pleaded. 'Please don't leave me alone.'

She smiled. 'If you throw the bottle away, I will come closer.' He looked at the bottle, the anaesthetic for his pain, then he looked at her. He had such a longing to touch her that he threw the bottle away. Then she came, and he touched her face and she touched his. 'I have to go now, but you must promise me never to drink again. Never again.'

This time he did not hesitate. 'I will never drink for as long as I live,' he said.

'I am glad you've made that decision, my love. Goodbye for now.'

He was disappointed. 'Will I ever see you again?'

'I am with you. I will always be with you. If you keep your promise, I will never leave you.'

The voice of Mystique Mysterious now broke in on Kojo Ansah's recollections.

'What prompted you to stop drinking?' he asked.

'That is my secret.'

'I can respect that,' Mystique Mysterious said. Then he left. For a long time, he thought of the conversation with Kojo Ansah, and he reached the conclusion that the quiet man was much more dangerous that the others. He understood Kofi Ntim; he controlled Bukari. He began to consider ways of dealing with the quiet man called Kojo Ansah.

In addition to his suspicions concerning Mystique Mysterious, Kojo Ansah had to contend with a new problem. Ever since their encounter at Kill Me Quick, Madman had become convinced that Kojo Ansah despised him and desired to do him harm. So Madman went around Nima castigating Kojo Ansah to whoever would listen. Nobody took him seriously, for they all believed that Madman was a ranting idiot. But Madman went further: he physically attacked Kojo Ansah whenever the two of them met. Not wishing to retaliate, Kojo Ansah resorted to avoiding Madman. When he heard that Madman was in a certain part of town, he steered clear of that area. When he saw Madman on one side of the street, he hurried to the other side. When Madman walked into a room, Kojo Ansah left it.

As life carried them in different directions, the friends met less often at Kill Me Quick. But Kofi Ntim and Kojo Ansah did combine forces to try to bring Bukari to an understanding of the error of his recent ways. Although they knew that they risked losing his friendship by doing so, they confronted him.

Bukari was jovial at first. 'When the ugly man and the man who has lost his tongue begin to advise me, then I must say the end of the world has come.'

Kofi Ntim and Kojo Ansah ignored his quips. 'You have a serious problem, Bukari,' said Kofi Ntim.

'It's true, Bukari,' Kojo Ansah added. 'Your drinking with Mystique Mysterious is leading you into trouble and debt. This business of going out with him and living the good life has become an addiction.'

Bukari became defensive. 'It's not an addiction. We just go around in the city and have a few drinks. You, Kofi Ntim, you drink also. Is that a problem?'

Kofi Ntim did not respond. It was Kojo Ansah who said, 'Bukari, we know you are an adult and you may say we have no business intruding into your affairs. You may be correct and you have every right to show us the door. But we do this because you are our friend and we would be neglecting our duty as your friends if we did not speak up. Or am I not right, Kofi?'

Kofi Ntim nodded and said, 'You are very right. And remember that blaming others may blind a man's eyes to his own faults.'

Kojo Ansah continued, 'So we come to you today, Bukari, as friends. For as you very well know, a man is sometimes blind to the thorns on the path he walks. His friends must provide the light to illuminate the path. Or am I not speaking the truth, Kofi?'

'You speak nothing but the truth,' Kofi Ntim replied.

Kojo Ansah went on. 'So we are begging you, Bukari, to reconsider your relations with Mystique Mysterious. We can't tell you what to do, we can only advise you. Or can we not, Kofi?'

Kofi Ntim nodded. 'Instructions we cannot give. But we can offer advice.'

They went on until they were satisfied that their message had registered strongly. Then all three went out and talked, laughed and mocked one another like old times. Kojo Ansah and Kofi Ntim hoped that Bukari would change his ways as he had promised them he would. But he did not change. Everything continued as before.

Fati now found comfort in the friendship of Jojo's Mother. At night, the two women would sit outside, talk and feel the friendly wind on their skin.

Jojo's Father had fallen into the habit, every now and then, of going to Kill Me Quick to drink with Bukari and the others. But Jojo's Father was careful not to drink too much; he did it only to socialise. It was on one such occasion at Kill Me Quick that he met Mystique Mysterious. Bukari introduced them and Jojo's Father said, 'It is a great honour to meet you, sir. I have seen you come to visit Bukari sometimes and I have hoped that I too would have the pleasure of meeting you.' On his face was a grin so wide that it resembled an aperture carved by an inept artist into a wooden figure.

Mystique Mysterious had perfected a smile for such occasions—a smile that really appeared to be genuine. 'It is a pleasure to meet you too. You and I are going to be very good friends, are we not?'

'We are, sir,' Jojo's Father said with eagerness.

Mystique Mysterious placed a hand on Jojo's Father's shoulder and smiled again. 'This is a day that the Lord truly has made, for this day I have met you, the neighbour of my friend, Bukari. The friends of my friends are my friends, so the friend of my friend Bukari is my friend.' Jojo's Father was too delighted to speak. But Mystique Mysterious added, 'Our friends, we cherish. Our friends, we love and protect. But what do we do with our enemies?'

It took a while for Jojo's Father to realise that the question was directed at him and was meant to be answered. 'Our enemies? We... we... uh...' he muttered.

Mystique Mysterious said, 'Our enemies are like eggs in our backyards. You see, they become powerful if we let them. You can allow an egg to hatch into a chick and watch it grow into an adult hen, strong and ready to peck your corn and defecate over your yard. Or you can prevent all that by dropping the egg on the floor. When you drop it on the floor, what happens to it?'

This time, Jojo's Father responded quickly. 'It breaks.'

'Exactly! It breaks. And when it breaks it can't hatch into a chick, it can't grow into a hen, it can't peck your corn, it can't defecate on your backyard. Can it?'

'No,' said Jojo's Father.

'That is right. It can't. Some people say to me, you can still get it when it is a full-grown hen. Certainly, you can, but that complicates matters. When it is grown, it can escape you. But can an egg do the same?'

'No,' replied Jojo's Father.

'No. And can an egg think?'

'No.'

'No. So why delay? When your enemy is but an egg, then is the time to move. Then is the time to drop the egg on the floor.'

Mystique Mysterious had spoken with a disturbing seriousness that frightened Jojo's Father. But the big man's words were not really addressed to him. Mystique Mysterious turned to look directly into the eyes of Kojo Ansah. Their gaze locked and for twenty seconds neither man blinked. The air was tense. Then Mystique Mysterious smiled sardonically and the seriousness disappeared from his face.

Bukari arrived home a little earlier than usual that night because Mystique Mysterious had decided that it was a day of rest. Fati was seated in the middle of the compound with Jojo's Mother. Bukari fetched a stool and joined them and Issaka emerged from his room with his raffia mat and sat down with them. A sense of neighbourliness spread through them and all their conversations were pleasant.

A little later, Jojo's Mother and Issaka left and Bukari and Fati sat together alone. For the first time in a long while, they talked as they used to before Bukari's new habits interfered. They discussed their son and Adukwei, trade at the Mallatta Market, the taxi business. Bukari was shamed a bit. 'I know I have not been paying you much attention lately, Fati,' he said.

'Lately? You have not been paying any attention to me for a long time.'

'I am sorry.' Bukari said. 'But you know Mystique Mysterious is an important man and when he makes demands on my time, I can't refuse him. Be a little patient. I will find a way to gain more freedom and I will make up for all the lost time.' He was surprised at the ease with which he lied.

'You don't have to explain anything to me. I understand,' Fati replied.

What a woman she is, Bukari thought. He had cheated on her and he could not undo what he had already done. But he could do something now to make amends. He reached for her hand and helped her up. He led her to their room and they undressed and made love with energy and affection. For that short spell, it was as if they were reclaiming the year that had been stolen from them—as if twelve months of changes had not passed. But afterwards they both knew that the passage of time could not be denied. Many things had happened. Some were good, some were not so good. And life went on regardless, as the purposeful earth spun around the conniving sun.

Chapter Thirteen

He came to the decision slowly. Why should one man labour while another did nothing and received the benefits? He would stop paying Mystique Mysterious. So at the end of the month when Mystique Mysterious demanded a share of his salary, Kofi Ntim pulled on his goatee and said, 'I don't have it.'

Mystique Mysterious was irritated. 'You have to explain this to me, my friend. You have been paid, but you don't have the money?'

Kofi Ntim took his time in answering. 'I thank you for finding me the job and, believe me, I will be for ever grateful. I think I have paid you back amply. From now on don't expect any money from me.'

Mystique Mysterious smiled. There was amusement, perhaps even pity, where Kofi Ntim had expected anger. 'I see you have come to a firm conclusion, but I think you are making a needless mistake. We made a deal. Honour requires that you keep your word. I have kept my side of the bargain and you should keep your side of it.'

'It isn't a fair bargain and unfair bargains don't deserve to be honoured. The bargain we made constitutes servitude.'

'I have helped you out of your pitiful financial situation

and this is the reward I get? Do not insult me with ingratitude, Kofi Ntim.'

'It's not ingratitude. I am simply extricating myself from your clutches.' He knew his words were harsh, but he had put fear of the consequences out of his mind.

'I'll give you a week to reconsider. I know you are speaking from your heart, not your mind. The heart is often genuine, but often foolish. If you let your mind speak freely for you, I am sure you will reach a better decision. I will give you a full week to think things over.'

As he turned to go, Mystique Mysterious looked into Kofi Ntim's eyes and added, 'Make the right decision.' Then he walked away.

Kofi Ntim watched him go, reminding himself that there was no need to fear Mystique Mysterious. He would fume with rage about Kofi Ntim's rebellion, but then he would resign himself to the situation. Kofi Ntim waited for a week. Mystique Mysterious did not reappear, to repeat his demands. It seemed as if he had suddenly vanished. Not even Bukari knew of his whereabouts. Kofi Ntim began to think that perhaps he had been shamed away.

But after another week Mystique Mysterious made his presence felt in a most forceful manner. It happened on a Saturday night. Kofi Ntim had spent most of the night at Kill Me Quick, conversing with Esi. His heart was at ease as he headed home. He had almost reached home when they carried out their instructions. There were three of them. He had noticed them walking behind him for some time, but had thought they were just three friends strolling around. When he realised they were following him, it was already too late. They grabbed him from behind and pushed him to the ground. He bit dirt as he hit the floor and he knew his lips were split. They let him get to his feet and start running, but only for the pleasure of grabbing him again and dragging him home. Then they forced the keys out of his pocket, opened the door and thrust him inside. He plunged to the floor and stayed there. One of them turned on the light and Kofi Ntim saw their faces.

They were all massive, their arms immense combinations of muscles. All three wore sunglasses even at that time of the night. One had a bald head, the other wore a thick brush of a moustache and the third had a deep and long scar on the right side of his face. Bald Head reached for Kofi Ntim and forced him to his feet. Kofi Ntim took a nervous step back in fear. Searching his throat for his voice, he found it in a whisper. 'What do you want?'

'Shut up!' bellowed Moustached Face.

They came for him again and he had nowhere to run. Scarred Face held him by the left arm while Moustached Face held the right. Bald Head hit him in the belly and he screamed in pain. They were in no hurry. They waited for the pain to subside, then struck him another blow in the same region. He screamed again. Then Bald Head took hold of his left arm and Scarred Face did the beating. Again they waited for Kofi Ntim to recover. Then Scarred Face took his right arm and it was Moustached Face's turn. He motioned to the other two and they turned Kofi Ntim around and pulled down his trousers so that his buttocks were exposed. Moustached Face removed his belt and began to lash Kofi Ntim. Kofi Ntim tried very hard not to cry, but he could not help it: the pain seemed to prick open the tear ducts in his eyes and expel the tears.

Then they left him for a while and chatted as he lay on the floor in agony. Bald Head lit a cigarette and pulled on it until it glowed. Scarred Face and Moustached Face pinned Kofi Ntim's legs and arms to the floor while Bald Head unbuttoned his shirt. Then Bald Head pulled on the cigarette one more time, brushed the ashes off the glowing end and brought it close to Kofi Ntim's chest. Kofi Ntim begged frantically, but Bald Head only laughed and burned the red-hot cigarette into Kofi Ntim's chest. Kofi Ntim screamed thunderously. That seemed to satisfy the three men and they left soon afterwards. Kofi Ntim crawled to the bedroom, his body racked with pain, and wept bitterly. The physical pain was enough, but it was the humiliation that hurt the most.

The next night, Mystique Mysterious came to see him. When Kofi Ntim let Mystique Mysterious into his room, the two men stared at each other for a long period in silence. Then Mystique Mysterious rubbed his palms together and said, 'I am certain you have had a change of heart since we last talked?'

Anger rose inside Kofi Ntim. 'What you had those men do to me yesterday was evil. It's the most despicable thing one man can do to another. You didn't even have the courage to do it yourself.'

Mystique Mysterious affected innocence. 'What is upsetting you so, my friend?'

'Don't insult me by denying you put those men up to it.'

'I have not denied anything.'

'It would be more dignified for you to accept responsibility.'

'But I have nothing to accept resonsibility for.'

They talked like that a while, until Mystique Mysterious said again, 'I am sure you have had a change of heart.'

'I have not had a change of heart.'

Mystique Mysterious shook his head in disbelief. 'I can't believe that you would be this incorrigible. Let me give you a piece of advice. If you value your life at all, you will pay me now.'

'Are you making a threat on my life?'

'You can interpret it as you wish.'

Kofi Ntim said, 'I want to renegotiate our bargain.'

'I do not think you are in a position to ask for that.'

'But I think I am. What do you gain otherwise? If I die, you gain nothing. But if we renegotiate and I pay you a little less, you gain something. Something is better than nothing.'

'If you die, another will fill your shoes and probably be less stubborn than you.'

'Will you renegotiate or not?'

Mystique Mysterious thought for a while and said, 'You know, Kofi Ntim, you and I are more alike than we are not alike. We are like brothers.'

'We are not alike in any way.'

'Oh yes we are. We both use our heads. That is why it surprised me when you made the emotional decision not to honour our bargain. That was very much unlike you. And the second thing that makes us alike is that we both use people.'

'I do not use people,' Kofi Ntim protested.

'You do, my friend, even if you are not aware of it. Like

right now. You are using me just as much as I am using you. You have a goal and I am the bridge you are using to reach that goal. You see, I know about your farm and the clothing business.' Kofi Ntim was dumbfounded, for he had tried to keep his business affairs secret from Mystique Mysterious. 'Do not be so surprised, Kofi Ntim. I know a lot of things about you that you do not think I know. A man in my position keeps his ears and eyes open. I must admit I learned of the farm much later than I would have wished. You were quite adept at keeping it a secret from me. When I found out, my first reaction was to destroy it, but I did not because I need you to be prosperous, even independently of me, so that others will see that there are benefits to be gained from associating with me. So I will allow you your room to grow. And you, as I have said, will use me as one of the means towards your end.'

'By your logic, everyone uses others,' Kofi Ntim said.

'To a certain extent: if I borrow my brother's car to travel in, you could say that I am using my brother in a way. But there is a difference between that and what I am talking about. Take Bukari, for instance. When I offered him a job, what did he think of? He was happy he had a job and that was the end. He was not using me for anything. But you are different. You know what you wanted from the beginning, although you pretended otherwise. And you drove a hard bargain even then. You are exploiting me in that sense to reach your goal, just as much as I am exploiting you.'

Kofi Ntim said, 'I do not use people. I do not go about seeking people to exploit.'

'There is no difference, Kofi Ntim. Whether you seek out

people or not, so long as you end up using them, you use them. Take Esi, for instance. You are using her to…'

'Don't bring Esi into this!' Kofi Ntim bellowed in fury.

'Do not let your emotions enter into this. I am showing you your true face,' Mystique Mysterious said. 'You are using Esi to fill a void within you.'

'That is not true! I love her. I love her deeply.'

'But that is beside the point. Perhaps you love her, but there is more to it than that. She makes you feel worthy, which relieves your sense of inadequacy. Other people taunt you; Esi's attention makes you feel wanted.'

'That is not true!' Kofi Ntim's voice was choked with emotion.

'I will not push the point. But you are only hurt by what I say because like most people you wish to live in a world of pretence. You like to play hypocrite with yourself. I am a mirror showing you your true self, your soul. You have seen its reflection and you do not like what you see.'

'I am not a hypocrite,' Kofi Ntim said weakly.

'Oh, everyone is a hypocrite to some extent in this world of mass make-believe. People like me are called evil because we know what we want and we make no bones about using others to get where we are going. We are openly exploitative; the rest of you are secretly so.'

'I am not like that.'

'You can say what you want, but you know in your heart that I am right.'

'Why are you giving me this lecture anyway? Are you going to renegotiate with me or are you not?'

'I told you, the amount you pay to me is not negotiable.'

'Nothing should be non-negotiable. You have degraded me in the crudest way possible. I was hit in the belly, I was whipped, I was burned in the chest with a lighted cigarette. I think that should suffice to discharge me of any obligations I have to you. But at this point I am not asking for that. I only request a reduction.'

'I hope you are not taking what happened yesterday personally, because it was not intended personally,' Mystique Mysterious said. 'You brought it upon yourself, Kofi Ntim. You brought it upon yourself. We had such a nice relationship until you got all those ideas.'

'If we are alike, if we are brothers as you said, then you should be generous with me.'

Mystique Mysterious began to pace the room. 'You are a shrewd and tough businessman. You see what I say about you? Bukari has not even dared suggest a reduction in his contribution. Very well, I will accept four per cent from now on.'

'One per cent.'

'You are unbelievable, Kofi Ntim,' Mystique Mysterious exclaimed. But he wore a smile on his face and Kofi Ntim breathed easier. 'I will take two and a half per cent.'

'Fair enough.'

'No hard feelings?'

'None,' replied Kofi Ntim. They shook hands and Kofi Ntim paid Mystique Mysterious, who then left. Kofi Ntim wondered whether to be pleased. He had not succeeded in getting what he wanted, but he had made progress. And at least Mystique Mysterious would not be sending his thugs back to finish what they had started. The most important thing, after all, was to go on living. To go on living in a world in which Esi lived and laughed and smiled too. The spirit must rise so that the heart will not die. Kofi Ntim's spirit must rise to the challenge of keeping his heart alive, for Esi.

The next night, Kofi Ntim hurried to Kill Me Quick after work. Kojo Ansah was already there, sipping his usual glass of water. 'Kojo Ansah, my friend, I thought you were going to learn some sense today and drink some liquor like a real man.' Kojo Ansah smiled, but did not reply. Both Kojo Ansah and Esi noticed the bruises on Kofi Ntim's face, but they did not ask him about them, not wishing to embarrass him.

Esi said unexpectedly, 'I have been hearing stories about Bukari. They say he has been going around sleeping with all sorts of women.'

Kojo Ansah asked, 'Who said that?'

'I heard from a friend,' Esi replied.

Kojo Ansah said, 'Rumours must have wings. Once a rumour starts, never mind how absurd it sounds, it has the ability to cover much ground in no time at all so long as it appeals to the imagination. And often you cannot tell who originates it. Everyone heard it from another person, who heard from another. Maybe, since rumours are often so ridiculous, it is not surprising that no one is willing to claim authorship.'

'Are you suggesting that what I just said is ridiculous?' Esi queried.

Kojo Ansah had launched into this short speech on rumours with the hope of diverting Esi's thoughts. He too had heard rumours about Bukari's philandering and in fact he believed them; but in the presence of Esi, he tried to defend his friend. 'We have no reason to believe that Bukari would do that.'

'Well, from what I hear he has.'

'I doubt it.'

'You really do?'

Kofi Ntim interjected, 'We cannot rely on rumours.' But his mind went back to the day at Labadi Pleasure Beach, when he had seen Bukari kiss another woman. He forced the memory out of his mind and said, 'Bukari loves his wife dearly.'

Esi said, 'That has nothing to do with what he is doing. It is possible for a spouse to be in love and cheat at the same time.'

Kofi Ntim said, 'Now, I am sure these rumours you have been hearing have no truth in them. But you know it will break Fati's heart if she hears what you have told us tonight. Esi, please don't ever tell her. I am begging you.'

'I won't be the one to tell her.'

Kojo Ansah said farewell and left.

Left alone with Esi, Kofi Ntim queried, 'Do you think I am using you in any way?'

'I don't think so.'

'Are you sure?'

'I am. Why?'

'What if I were?'

'I can't answer that because I don't believe you are.'

'That is very reassuring.'

'You are a sweet man, Kofi. You have a tendency to be

obnoxious from time to time, but at bottom you are sweet. I know that your feelings for me are genuine.'

'No one has ever said such nice things to me. Oh, Esi, where have you been all this time?'

'Lost and wandering. Wanting, but not knowing what I wanted.'

'I too have been lost. Now I am coming home and you are the reason for my return.'

Esi's face showed that she was close to surrender. 'If you continue to talk like that, you will weaken me,' she said.

'Then I shall continue to talk like that.'

'No, not tonight, my dear. My eyes are tired and my body is already weak from work. You must go home now, Kofi. It is late.'

He did not argue. Her face, her eyes, had said the three words her lips had not said. It had taken a long time, but finally, the race was reaching the finish. 'Very well, Esi, I will leave you now. My dear, the one that the sun shines for, I will leave you now, although I do not want to.'

Kofi Ntim kissed Esi on the lips and left. He felt at ease. The blows to his belly, the lashes on his buttocks, the burn of the cigarette on his chest, were all crushed into insignificant memories. From the grass he heard the insects chirring, and he talked to them with a sense of kinship. 'Sing on, my little friends. Sing on for me. You are rejoicing with me. I thank you for your happiness for me. I thank you for your friendship.' Kofi Ntim walked home contentedly and photographed the sky, the moon and the stars with his mind and stored them in the album of his memory.

Chapter Fourteen

T he night Fati laughed with abandon, without the usual reserve she displayed in his presence, was the night Mystique Mysterious decided to pursue her. He was drawn not merely to the physical beauty of Fati, but also to her sincerity. When Fati spoke or smiled or laughed, she did so from her heart. Nowadays such people are so rare that on encountering them one desires to possess a little bit of them. So that night Mystique Mysterious was engulfed by the desire to share of Fati. He knew he would not acquire her inner power, he was incapable. But he wanted to mesh with it, if only briefly, so that for one moment he could climb over the hills and delve into the seas of realms that were closed to him; to glimpse her world through a soul that shone with multifarious lights.

Mystique Mysterious thought hard. How was he to acquire the object of his desire? Should he simply broach it with Bukari? Had Bukari not become a pawn in his hands, controllable and controlled? But he knew that Bukari still had some shred of dignity left and would not sacrifice his wife to another man without a fight. For a while, Mystique Mysterious tried to think of other women. He could get any he wanted; all he had to do was request. Who needed a low-placed woman like Fati when he could press the flesh of sophisticated women who by their very smiles, the well orchestrated movements of eyes and lips, aroused men's loins? Yet Fati had something those perfumed and and made-up women did not. She possessed natural charm. Her body, her smile, her laugh, her voice, the way she stretched her hand—all were natural, without effort, without guile. There was nothing artificial about her, nothing strained. He needed her and he would have her without Bukari's knowledge. He would approach her and inform her of his desire. He would seduce her with his charm, his wealth. Did not every woman in her station dream of men like him? She would not, could not, resist him. But perhaps! Perhaps she could. She was not like the other women he knew. She had in her eyes a dignity and resolve that seemed to defy the world. But was it strong enough to enable her to reject the advances of a man such as he? Mystique Mysterious went back and forth between confidence and insecurity, between certainty and uncertainty, and his problem remained unresolved.

The next day, he went to Nima, found Jojo's Father at home and led him away. When they were out of Nima, they stepped into Mystique Mysterious's Range Rover and drove in silence for a few minutes, Mystique Mysterious in deep thought. Somewhere in the area of Labone, Mystique Mysterious brought the car to a stop and asked, 'You are my friend, are you not?'

Jojo's Father remembered Mystique Mysterious's speech about enemies being dropped like eggs and he said quickly, 'Without a doubt, sir, I am your friend.'

'Well, are you a friend like these people who just say so, or are you a true friend that I can count on?'

Jojo's Father's heart pounded. Why this question? What choice did he have anyway? Mystique Mysterious was a man to be pleased. 'But, sir, I am not like those that you can't count on. I am a friend you can always rely on.'

Mystique Mysterious cleared his throat and said, 'I knew you would not disappoint me. You see, I pick my friends carefully and when I picked you, I knew you were reliable.'

Jojo's Father grinned widely with appreciation. Mystique Mysterious pulled a wad of money out of his pocket and handed it over. Jojo's Father hesitated, but Mystique Mysterious pushed the money into his hands so that he had little choice but to accept it. Jojo's Father tried to say something, but he could not find the words; he opened his mouth and closed it repeatedly like a dying fish, scanning Mystique Mysterious's face for some sign.

'Take it, my friend and use it as you please.'

Jojo's Father wanted to ask to what he owed such generosity, but he was afraid to do so.

Mystique Mysterious added, 'I know you could use a little bit of money and I am not a man to deprive another of means to fufil his needs.'

At last, Jojo's Father found his tongue. 'Thank you, sir. Thank you very much. I will be ever grateful for this.'

In his head, Mystique Mysterious said: 'You should be thanking your friends, who make me rich.' Aloud, he said, 'That is nothing. There are better times coming. I always reward my friends.' He allowed his words to sink into Jojo's Father's head, before adding, 'There is only a small favour I would like you to perform.'

At that point, Jojo's Father was so grateful he said glee-fully, 'Anything, sir.'

'I knew I could count on you. I knew it. You are familiar with the patterns of Bukari's family, are you not? You know when they come and go.'

'I do indeed, sir.'

'Very good. That is where I need your help.' Mystique Mysterious looked at Jojo's Father to ensure he was attentive before continuing, 'I am looking for a time when everybody except Fati will be out of the house. A night when Bukari will not be with me but will nevertheless stay out late, and when Baba will also be out late.'

'Well, sir, Baba is hardly home. He leaves in the morning, sometimes comes home for supper, leaves again and stays out late.'

'That's good. I want to be alone with Fati for a long time.' Mystique Mysterious's voice assumed a conspiratorial tone and he questioned, 'You understand what I mean, don't you?'

'Yes sir,' replied Jojo's Father. He understood. He was disturbed by the turn of events, for he knew what Mystique Mysterious wanted. Fati was a desirable woman; he too had desired her a while ago, until familiarity and friendship killed that desire. But it was one thing to desire another man's wife and another thing to intend to actually have her. Yet this was no ordinary man. If Mystique Mysterious wanted Fati, who was he to stop him? He was not the one doing the deed, even if he would help to make it possi-ble. He was merely the technician oiling the vehicle; why should he care what the driver did with it?

'Good man,' said Mystique Mysterious. 'What I want you to do is help me devise means of getting *everybody* out of the household for a while, including you and your family and Issaka and his family.'

'Jojo's Father stroked his forehead in thought. After a while he said, 'I don't think you have to worry about Issaka, sir. He stays indoors with his wives and children at night. He hardly ever bothers anyone else at that time. If you sneak into Bukari's house, you will be all right so long as you stay inside.'

'That is what I want; to be inside with Fati.'

'Then you don't have to worry about Issaka.'

'But would it not be safer to get him out of the way altogether?'

'You see, sir, that would be the safest thing to do, but Issaka is not one who likes to go out. He does not drink, he does not chase women. He is so devoted in his religious ways that he lives a hermit's life.'

'Very well. Maybe we will leave him alone. But how about your family? Your wife? I know Fati and your wife have become very close. I know they spend many nights outside in the compound. But if I am going to have Fati to myself, I need your wife to be busy doing something else.'

'That is easy, sir,' replied Jojo's Father. 'I know how to keep her busy.'

Mystique Mysterious smiled and said, 'I think I know what you mean, but I think you should try and get her away from home. Take her somewhere. Anywhere. Where do you normally go together? Where do you take her?'

Jojo's Father racked his mind for an answer. There was

none, for he hardly went anywhere with his wife. Then he remembered. Without jest he said, 'I take her to funerals.'

Mystique Mysterious erupted into a guffaw of mirth. 'I can't wait for you to find a funeral to take her to. You must think of something else.'

Again, Jojo's Father tried, but his efforts were unavailing. Tired of waiting, Mystique Mysterious suggested, 'Why not take her and the children to see a film on Sunday night?'

'All right, sir. I will do that.'

'And maybe you can invite Issaka and his family to go with you.'

'I will do my best, sir.'

'And don't mind how many go because I will take care of all expenses.'

They shook hands and Mystique Mysterious drove Jojo's Father back to Nima.

Mystique Mysterious went in search of Baba and Adukwei next. He found them seated together in front of a decrepit structure that was apparently Adukwei's and her mother's home. Even in the darkness, Baba recognised Mystique Mysterious and immediately approached him.

When the younger man was close enough, Mystique Mysterious placed his hands on his shoulders. 'How are you, my son Baba?'

'I am very well, sir, and thank you.'

'It pleases my heart very much to hear that. And how is Adukwei?'

Baba grinned with both pride and embarrassment and said, 'She is also very well, sir.'

'I know she gets more beautiful by the day. You are a very lucky boy, my son.'

'Thank you, sir. She thanks your mouth for saying such nice things.'

Mystique Mysterious looked into the air in a show of reflection. Then he rubbed Baba's shoulders in a concerned way and said, 'I worry about you, son.' Tell me why, Baba begged in his mind. His silent plea was answered as Mystique Mysterious went on, 'I worry about you because I don't think you are making enough money to satisfy the love of your life.'

'I don't understand, sir,' Baba confessed.

'Let me explain. You remember what I told you a while ago about how many men would want to come after Adukwei?' Baba nodded. 'You see, I personally know of men who have started making plans to get her. She is very beautiful, Baba, and men want her. I am talking about rich and powerful men. You know, Adukwei is a very good girl and I have no doubt that she likes you. But what do you think will happen when a handsome man driving a Mercedes Benz flashes a lot of cash in front of her? Maybe she could resist for a while, but she is a human being and eventually she might surrender.'

Baba glanced over at the profile of Adukwei in the distance, the outline of an immaculate sculpture, he thought. Could she fall prey to the allure of wealth? Baba sought counsel. 'I beg you to tell me what I can do. I need your advice, for you know about these things.'

'I am glad you asked for my advice, son. What you need is more money. I know you make a little bit of money selling newspapers, but that is not enough. You need to make much more so you can buy her more things. You can't afford a Mercedes Benz now, that will come in the future. But you have an advantage over others: Adukwei loves you. So you do not need a Mercedes Benz, but you must make enough to keep her happy. You must be able to buy her expensive clothing, earrings and other things she desires. Do you think she does not deserve those things? I think she does and I know you agree. Do you think she would not like to have them? She would. She does not ask because she knows you can't afford them. But what if you could? You could make her so happy that nothing could come between you two.'

'But how, sir? I want to please her. I want to buy her very expensive things. But how?'

'My son, if you need something, all you have to do is ask. I cannot promise you wealth overnight, but I can start you on the path. You can supplement your earnings by doing other things. I have been looking around for you and I have found something for you if you are interested.'

'I am interested,' Baba said eagerly.

'I knew you would be. See, this is only the beginning. In time, I will find other things less strenuous and more lucrative, but you must start somewhere. Do you know how to trim grass with a machete?'

'I have done it in the past and I believe I can do it again.'

'Good. You can make extra money by trimming the grass in a friend's yard on Friday. In fact it is the same man your father works for. Does that sound all right to you?'

'Yes sir. I am very excited about it.' Baba did not ask how

much he would earn. His trust in Mystique Mysterious was complete.

'You make me very proud, Baba, my son. You are not afraid to work hard. Boys like you grow up into successful men. You, my son, are destined for great things.'

Baba grinned with undisguised pleasure.

Mystique Mysterious left Baba and headed for Kill Me Quick. He entered the kiosk with bonhomie and slapped Bukari and Kofi Ntim on the back. Then he shook Kojo Ansah's hand, saying, 'It is a great pleasure to meet you all here today, especially my friend Kojo Ansah.' Kojo Ansah did not say anything, preferring rather to let the sarcasm stand unchallenged. Mystique Mysterious added, 'I feel so good tonight, I must buy my friend Bukari a drink.' Then he turned to Esi and ordered a bottle of beer.

'What about me?' enquired Kofi Ntim.

Mystique Mysterious laughed and said, 'I am afraid today I can only buy for Bukari.'

'Why?'

'Because he is my friend.'

'And I am not?'

'You talk too much, Kofi Ntim.'

'When I talk I talk sense. I am not so sure I can say the same thing about you.'

Mystique Mysterious smiled at the remark and dismissed it with a wave of the hand. He could tolerate such impertinence, providing his overall control was undiminished. He had these men where he wanted them: under his thumb. All except one, and that one was probably a lost cause.

He turned to Kojo Ansah. 'How have things been, Kojo?'

'All right,' Kojo Ansah replied tersely.

The reply seemed to satisfy Mystique Mysterious. He turned his attention to Esi. 'Madam,' he said, 'How is business these days?'

Esi was flattered by the interest and replied, 'Business is very good. Thank you for asking.'

'I am glad. If you have any problems, if you are not getting enough supplies, for instance, or whatever the problem might be, come to me. I will make sure everything is put right.'

'No!' Kofi Ntim protested—perhaps too energetically.

Mystique Mysterious queried, 'Are you her keeper, Kofi Ntim? She can make her own decisions without your help.' He took a cigar from his pocket and offered it to Kofi Ntim. 'This will make you feel like a king.'

Kofi Ntim took the cigar and studied it. He put it between his lips and Mystique Mysterious lit it for him. This gesture, what did it mean?

'You see,' Mystique Mysterious said, 'I am your friend, not just Bukari's, but I offer things at different times.' And that answered Kofi Ntim's question. Then Mystique Mysterious suggested, 'Bukari, do you want to roam around a little with me?' As always, Bukari replied affirmatively.

Kojo Ansah left shortly after and Kofi Ntim and Esi chatted on. Customers came, bought drinks, drank, and left. Later, Jojo and his mother walked into the kiosk, Jojo carrying a bottle in his hand. They crossed to the bar and Jojo's Mother said, 'Good evening,' and immediately became engaged in conversation with Esi. Kofi Ntim decided to leave to give the women room to speak freely.

Presently, Jojo's Mother said, 'Auntie Esi, would you give me some *akpeteshie*?'

'How much do you need?'

Jojo's Mother took the bottle from her son and gave it to Esi. 'Please fill it.'

'I didn't know you drank this stuff,' Esi said.

'I don't. It is for my husband. I don't know what transpired between him and Mystique Mysterious today, but Mystique Mysterious came and took him away for a while and he returned all cheerful. You know, that man has never taken me anywhere, but today he says we should go and see a film on Sunday night. And he wants some *akpeteshie* in the house, so he asked me to get him some. I don't know what has come over him.'

Esi wore an expression of concern. 'Did you say your husband went out with Mystique Mysterious?'

'Yes, that is what I said.'

'Esi, my sister, you had better be careful Mystique Mysterious does not turn your husband into another Bukari.'

'What do you mean, another Bukari?'

Esi realised then that she had made a mistake. She had promised the others that she would keep the rumour to herself, but now she had opened the door a crack and was faced with the curiosity of this woman before her. She knew there was no point stalling for Jojo's Mother would keep bothering her. So she would tell her, but she would do so in a dignified manner. 'You mean you have not heard?'

'Heard what, Aunti Esi?'

'I thought you had heard. Well, before I tell you, I must warn you not to tell anybody. Will you promise me?'

'I promise I will not tell anyone.'

'All right.' Esi looked at Jojo, who was preoccupied with examining the stools in the kiosk. She said in a whisper to Jojo's Mother, 'When Mystique Mysterious and Bukari go out, they do not just go and roam the streets of Accra. They go drinking.'

'Is that all?' asked Jojo's Mother.

'If that were all, my sister, do you think I would be whispering to you? My sister, they pick up women and sleep with them.'

Jojo's Mother replied, 'But as for you, Auntie Esi, you talk as if your eyes were closed. How many men stay faithful to their wives?'

'But I am not talking about isolated incidents. I am talking about a habitual practice. Every night they go out, they have different women.'

For a while Jojo's Mother was silent, then it seemed to dawn on her who was under discussion. It was Bukari, the husband of her very good friend Fati. She said, 'Esi, Bukari. What does he think he is doing? What has come over him? What is he trying to do to Fati?'

'It is a sad case, my sister.'

'I know. You said they do this all the time?'

'Can you imagine? Bukari has become a male prostitute. At this rate he must have slept with half of the city already.'

'To sleep around like that is not good. As for me, it is Fati I am worried about.'

'But you will not tell her! She must never know!'

'She thinks her husband is an angel among men. And

already she is suffering from neglect. She would die of grief if she knew. I will not tell her.'

Esi was satisfied. She handed the filled bottle to Jojo's Mother, who paid and left. On her way home, Jojo's Mother deliberated. Was it possible, even probable, that her husband too had started on that path of debauchery? It was too soon for her to tell. She would wait and observe him with a cat's keen eyes. She thought of Fati, to whom she had lately grown very close. They shared their thoughts, their frustrations, their anxieties. Under the skies they sat and laughed and dreamed and talked. Could she keep such news from her? A friend such as Fati? A sister? Would it break her heart if she was told? No! Fati was a strong woman. She would be pained because she loved and trusted her husband, but she would bear it all with grace. The alternative was worse. What if Fati found out from another? An enemy, intent on causing pain? The manner of telling could make the difference. If Fati learned from a friend, if it were said with tact, she would bear it better than if she found out otherwise. Jojo's Mother herself would tell her, as a friend should. To fail to do so would be a betrayal of her trust and friendship. Also, if Fati knew now rather than later, perhaps she could yet save her marriage from utter destruction.

After she had given her husband the bottle of liquor, Jojo's Mother picked up a stool and went and knocked on Fati's door. Fati came out, saw her and understood that it was time to sit outside and chat. She fetched a stool and followed Jojo's Mother to the middle of the compound. They sat in silence for a while as Jojo's Mother contemplated her choice of words. When she was satisfied, she said, 'Fati, has Bukari been acting strangely these days?'

'I am not sure I understand you.'

'Does he show the same affection towards you as he used to?'

'As I told you before, he has been busy meeting with Mystique Mysterious and his friends. That takes all the time and energy he has, so he is a bit inattentive and aloof. But apart from that, he is as he used to be.'

'I see.'

Fati knew there was more, so she pried. 'But you know that already. Why do you ask?'

Jojo's Mother allowed a few seconds to elapse and said, 'I have heard things, Fati. I have heard bad things.'

Fati felt the muscles in her body grow tense; her face drew into a deep frown. 'What bad things?' Her heart beat faster and she was afraid.

'I hate to be the one to tell you this, Fati, but as your friend, I can't keep it from you.'

'What is it?' Fati pleaded with her eyes.

'I have heard that... I have heard that when Mystique Mysterious takes your husband out, they do not simply roam the streets of the city. They drink all over the place.'

The tension in Fati's face and body eased. 'Is that the bad news?'

'That is not all, Fati.'

Again, the tension and the strain. 'Do not torture me so,' Fati implored.

Jojo's Mother played the part of the reluctant purveyor of ill news. 'If you insist,' she said. 'I have heard that when your husband and Mystique Mysterious go out, they drink and then pick up women and sleep with them. And this is not something that happens once in a while. It happens all the time. They say Mystique Mysterious and your husband have slept with half of the women in the city.'

For a long time, Fati was silent. Jojo's Mother waited uncomfortably for her to say something. She did not know how to deal with this silence. Finally Fati said, 'Are you sure of this?'

'I am only telling you what I heard, Fati.'

'Where did you hear it?'

'It is all over the town. It is on everyone's lips. I am very sorry, Fati. I should not have told you. Forgive me.'

'You have done the right thing. I know you mean well.' Fati's voice shook with suppressed emotion. 'I thank you for telling me.'

The women sat in silence, one weighing the sad news, the other contemplating its effect on a friend.

'I think I have to be alone now. Thank you, my sister.' Fati said as she picked up her stool and slowly walked away.

Jojo's Mother asked, 'Will you be all right?'

'I will be all right,' Fati replied.

Inside, Fati sat in the living room and fought her tears, contemplating her husband's infidelity. She did not have proof, but she believed the worst. Had Jojo's Mother not said it was on everyone's lips? A rumour so widespread must have some basis in truth. But how did it happen? Had she not done all a wife could do to satisfy a husband? She had loved him, cared for him, been at his side when he was ill, nursed him, soothed him in his depressions and rejoiced with him in his elation. How could he do this? Or had she failed him somehow? Was it her inability to bear more children? A tear defied her stoic attempts to remain dry-eyed and crept down the side of her face. She wiped it away with the back of her hand and blew her nose. Then she waited for Bukari.

He came home after midnight, drunk and tired. He walked into the living room, mumbled a greeting, smiled weakly and went into the bedroom. Fati followed him. 'Gabriel Bukari,' she began. Bukari was stunned, for Fati never addressed him by his full name. He turned and looked at her as carefully as his tired eyes could. She went on, 'Where have you been all this time?'

'With Mystique Mysterious, you know that.'

'I didn't ask you who you have been with, I asked you where you have been.'

'Why are you asking me this question?'

'Answer my question.'

'I don't have to answer any question.'

'Yes you do!'

Bukari shivered with surprise. Fati had never shouted at him so. 'What is the problem?'

'Answer my question. What did you do tonight?'

'All right. I will answer. We went to see some friends of Mystique Mysterious. They want to set up a business and they say they may have a part in it for me.'

'Is that why you reek of alcohol and look so exhausted?'

'They gave us a few drinks, Fati.'

Fati shook her head. 'You are lying to me, Gabriel Bukari.

You are lying. Have the decency to tell me the truth. I deserve that much.'

'Ah, Fati, what has come over you?'

'You think I have not heard what you two have been doing? You think I do not know?'

'Fati, my dear, who has been telling you things?'

'Gabriel Bukari, are you denying that you have been sleeping around?'

'Ah, Fati, why do you insult me so? Do you think I would leave you at home and go around doing such things? What kind of man do you think I am?'

'You are lying to me. I know you are lying.'

Bukari tried to move closer to Fati, but he stumbled and nearly fell. Then he steadied himself and reached out to her.

'Do not touch me!' she yelled.

'Be quiet. Do you want the whole world to hear this?'

'Let them hear.'

'What kind of disgrace are you trying to bring?'

'Disgrace? You talk about disgrace? What can be more disgraceful than what you have been doing?'

'I don't have to stand such abuse. I am going to sleep.'

'You go to bed and sleep well. You think you are the only one who can cheat? I too can do it. You hear? I too can do it.'

The threat rang in Bukari's ears as he dropped heavily on to the mattress and instantly fell asleep.

Chapter Fifteen

B aba met Mystique Mysterious at the Kanda Parks and Gardens as planned. They shook hands and Mystique Mysterious placed his palm on the younger man's shoulder and said, 'I'm glad you came, Baba. This job will be a bit of a slog, but you will earn considerable money.'

'I am not afraid of hard work, sir,' Baba replied.

They walked to the Denyi residence and, as they entered, Mystique Mysterious pointed to the compound, where the once well-manicured grass was slightly overgrown. 'This is what you have to cut, Baba. It is not too much, is it?'

'Not at all, sir.'

'Good.' Mystique Mysterious said with a grin.

They walked to the veranda and knocked. Mystique Mysterious was reminded of the day he stood in that very spot with Baba's father, Bukari. Presently, a young woman opened the door leading from the living room to the veranda. 'Hello,' she said.

'Hello,' replied Mystique Mysterious. 'This is the young man who will be working on the compound. His name is Baba and he is ready.'

'All right,' she said. 'Please come in and have a seat.'

'No, no.' Mystique Mysterious answered for both. 'I am

not sitting. Baba will go to work immediately if you get him a machete.'

The young woman disappeared and soon returned with the machete, which she offered to Baba. He took it without speaking. 'You know what to do?' she asked him, and Baba answered that he did.

'I think everything is in order.' Mystique Mysterious said. Then he turned to Baba and added, 'All right son, take care of the grass. They will pay you when you finish. I will see you later and if any problems arise, let me know.'

'Yes sir.'

Mystique Mysterious left, the young woman went indoors and Baba walked, machete in hand, out on to the grass. He removed his shirt so that it would not get wet with sweat. The sun at once burned down on his skin; sweat began to surface on his face even before he started work. He began at one end and worked his way down towards the street.

Two hours later, after two short breaks, he was three-quarters finished. Then a Volvo pulled into the compound and a woman stepped out, but her back was turned to Baba and he could not get a good view of her before she went into the bungalow. He pressed on with his task and finished within an hour. He picked up his shirt, wiped the sweat off his body, approached the bungalow and knocked on the front door.

The woman who had stepped out of the Volvo opened the door and peered outside. At first, Baba could not see her clearly. He was about to speak when she opened the door wider and took a step forward. Baba looked at her face and trembled, struck by the beauty he saw. She had a beautiful complexion, completely without blemish; narrow eyes that suggested intrigue; and voluptuous red-painted lips. Her hair was artfully cut and shaped, and, in Baba's mind, her figure was the epitome of desirable womanhood: full breasts, thin waist, slimly curving hips. Baba instantly yearned to hold her, touch her; any contact would suffice. His tongue was numb and his heart pounded in his chest.

She waited for him to speak, but he did not, so she asked, 'Can I do anything for you?'

Baba found his tongue, but his voice quavered. 'I finished cutting the grass. They told me to collect the pay after I finished.'

The woman remembered. 'Oh, you are the one clearing the compound? Good. Have you raked it yet?'

'I was supposed to rake too? I did not know.'

'That is all right. You can do it now, or tomorrow if you prefer.'

Baba debated the options. If he finished it all today, this could be the last time he saw this goddess. If he waited until the next day, he could have the opportunity to see her again. 'It is a little late. I prefer to come back tomorrow to finish.'

'No problem. When you are done tomorrow, knock on the door and either I or whoever is home will pay you.'

Baba said, 'I will do so,' fervently hoping that she would be present the next day.

The woman smiled and said, 'I am Janet Denyi. What is your name?'

'My name is Baba.'

'That's a nice name. Well, you come back tomorrow, Baba, and we will take care of everything.'

At the sound of his name on her tongue. Baba was dizzy with pleasure. He started for the road, his head spinning with the sudden conviction that he was in love with Janet Denyi. As he walked away he carried her image with him, so vivid that it was as though she were still present, looking into his eyes, smiling at him, asking him his name. Thoughts of Adukwei were swept away in this tide of erotic attraction to the more sophisticated woman. Adukwei was a beautiful girl; Janet was beyond beauty— she was a goddess.

But was she not out of his class? He, a poor driver's son residing in the slums of Nima; she, a rich man's relation, daughter perhaps, living in the plush Kanda Estates. Would she even glance in his direction if it were not for the need to be polite to one who had done work for her? Women like her were only made for his kind to gaze at, to desire and yearn for in vain. He ought to be content that she had even spoken to him. But had she not smiled at him and looked at him pleasantly? Had she not volunteered her name? Had she not? Maybe she liked him after all. The possibility gave Baba hope. Then he remembered his mother and the story of the love between his parents. Had she not been in a situation similar to Janet's, and his father in a position similar to his? And had their love not conquered the articifical gulf between wealth and poverty? If they could do it, why not Janet and himself? It was not impossible; he must be bold. He began to ponder how best to make his overtures.

But Adukwei. What was he to do about her? He liked her.

If it were not for Janet, he would still want to be with her. But things were going to have to change, for he had Janet to pursue now. He would tell Adukwei the truth; she deserved no less. His heart sank at the thought as he remembered the times they had spent together, but he could not let that divert him from his quest for this new love.

Baba went to Mallata Market and found his mother to seek her counsel. 'I am glad you came, Baba,' she said. 'Your grandmother just left and I mentioned to her that you want to meet her. She was very pleased and suggested that I arrange for you two to meet next week.'

The thought of meeting his grandmother pleased Baba, but he had more pressing concerns on his mind. 'I am happy to hear that, Mother, but I came to talk to you about something that is bothering me.'

Fati was slightly disappointed: she had expected her son to leap with excitement at the news. But she masked her disappointment and asked, 'What is it, son?'

'Promise you will not be angry?'

Fati smelled trouble, but she had to allow her son to speak. 'I promise.'

'Mother, I have met another girl that I like more than Adukwei. I want to be with this new girl, not Adukwei.'

Fati was stunned and pained by what she heard. 'But Baba,' she said. 'How can you do that? You can't fall in love with every woman you see. You and Adukwei have been together for so long and you are so perfect together. You can't go out and begin to like another girl just like that.'

'But, Mother, I have.'

'I can't believe this.'

'Mother, I did not expect that this would happen.'

Fati asked. 'When did you meet this girl?'

'This afternoon, Mother.'

Without meaning to sound so harsh, Fati said, 'You are foolish indeed. You just met this girl this afternoon and you think you like her so much. Don't tell me such nonsense.' Baba merely shrugged his shoulders and Fati added, 'I hope she feels the same way about you.'

'I just met her, Mother. We have not talked much.'

'I see. Who is this girl anyway?'

'Her name is Janet Denyi. She lives in Kanda. In fact, I think she is the daughter of the man father works for.'

Fati yowled and clasped her hands over her mouth. Then she said, 'Oh, my son, what are you doing? You think you are in love with the daughter of Henry Denyi? You think such a high-class woman will give you any thought at all?'

Baba said, 'I don't *think* I am in love with her. I *love* her.'

'My son, now I know you are being very foolish. You can't love a person like that. Look at us, Baba. We are poor. We have to toil night and day just to find enough to eat and clothes to cover our bodies. People like Henry Denyi and his daughter swim in wealth. They don't care about people like us. What do you think Janet will say when you tell her you love her? She will laugh in your face, that is what she will do. Laugh in your face and think that you are mad.'

'Did you laugh in father's face?' demanded Baba.

'What?'

'Was it not the same with you and father? Did you not tell me yourself how you two fell in love despite your wealth and father's poverty?'

'Baba, I am only saying what I think is best for you.'

'Then give me your blessing. Tell me it is all right.'

'I can't do that. I can't encourage you to go on the path I know will bring you pain.'

'You could follow your heart, but I can't?'

'I did not say that.'

'You do not have to, Mother.' Baba seemed to retreat from her in that moment. 'Mother, I thought I could count on you to help me, but it is clear to me now that I cannot. Neither you nor father have ever been much help. I wonder why I even came to you. Mystique Mysterious is the only one who offers me help.'

It was painful enough to hear her son speak of being disappointed in her, but to have to listen to him express confidence in the one who had intruded into their household and led the father astray! 'Don't talk to your mother like that!' Fati commanded, her words carrying the force of her pain.

Baba did not reply immediately. He stared at Fati with a defiant look. 'I want Janet and you are not going to stop me. Not you, not anyone.'

Fati lost control. 'Fool!' she yelled. Baba simply turned and walked away. He walked back to Nima and went and sat under the neem tree where he and Adukwei had sat the day they first met.

He needed help. But from whom? His mother had failed him; he could not count on his father. He did not know where to find his mentor, Mystique Mysterious. He must turn to his friends. Ntiamoah, Otto and Ofori. He headed to the alley where they usually gathered. As he had expected, they were all there. They greeted him with their usual exuberance, but he could not find the heart to match their boisterous show of friendship, and that surprised them. Something must be amiss. They set about finding out what.

'I want to leave Adukwei,' Baba told them.

A hush fell. The news was most unexpected. Then Otto found the voice to cry with incredulity, 'What? You are leaving Adukwei?'

Baba explained to his friends that he had fallen in love with a new woman. They were astounded to discover who it was. Ofori and Ntiamoah encouraged him to pursue his new love, even to the extent of coaching him in exactly what to say to her. But Otto warned him off, echoing Fati. The debate went back and forth, but it had no effect on Baba, whose mind was made up.

'I have to find Adukwei,' he announced.

'What are you going to tell her?' asked Otto.

'That is between the two of us.'

'Do not make the mistake of telling her what you have just told us, Baba.'

Baba did not reply. He pushed away from them and went and found Adukwei, his heart throbbing, his mind in turmoil.

Adukwei looked elated. She said, 'Baba, you will not believe this. Mother is travelling in about two weeks and I will be left alone in the house. You know *Homowo* is in two weeks and I can make you some *kpekple* and we can sit at home and eat, just you and I.'

Adukwei was referring to the major festival of the Ga

people of Accra. She had heard in bits and pieces the story of how the festival came to be. The Gas has migrated westwards from Nigeria in canoes. They arrived in Accra to face severe famine, so when they had their first good harvest, they started the celebration of *Homowo* to drive away hunger: *homo* meaning hunger in the Ga language and *wo* meaning sleep. The *Wulomo* or chief priest mediates between the people and the gods during the celebration, and noise such as drumming is not to be made at this time, for the gods require peace and quiet. The festival is celebrated on different dates between August and September by the different people of the Ga—people like the *Asere, Abola, Otublohun*, each with many clans. Adukwei belonged to the *Lantey Gyan* clan, the first to celebrate the festival. One feature of the festivities always captivated her most: *Akwele-Suma*, the twin-celebration—a time for hooting at hunger and thanking the gods for giving families twins, who are believed to be good omens. Adukwei would make *kpekple*, the ceremonial food of the gods, and this year she would enjoy the *Homowo* more than ever, for this year she had Baba to celebrate with, to cook for, to eat with.

Baba listened to her and did not know how to begin, to tell her what must be told. Adukwei saw the frown on his face. 'Is anything the matter, Baba? Did I say something wrong? I thought the idea would delight you.' Silence. 'What is it, Baba? Why are you so quiet?'

Baba wanted to speak in the most consoling manner, for he had no desire to hurt Adukwei's feelings. But when he spoke, the phrases carefully planned in his head mutated into blunt words. 'I have found another girl, Adukwei. I think we should not be seeing each other any more.'

Adukwei listened and did not know what to say. She tried to control herself, but she failed. She dropped her face into her hands and sobbed noisily.

Baba watched her and wanted to say something to comfort her. But what? He put his hands on her shoulders, but she pushed them away. He paced back and forth, sat down, paced back and forth again. Finally he said, 'Say something, Adukwei. Say somewthing.'

She did not speak. Baba waited, but still she did not speak. He wanted to hear her voice, cheerful as before, telling him that she would be all right. But Adukwei only went on crying. Eventually, not knowing what else to do, Baba walked away. He had expected to be happy after breaking with her; instead he was desolate.

The next day, Baba picked his clothes carefully. He wanted to dress for Janet, to please her. But he had nothing that could impress such a woman; he had to settle for a pair of jeans and a blue shirt his mother had bought him the previous Christmas. In these he presented himself at the bungalow, praying that Janet would be home. He could not tell, though, since it was the maid who welcomed him and handed him a rake. Just as he finished raking, the Volvo pulled up and Janet stepped out. Baba's heart pounded as hard as before. This was his chance, and although he felt weak and inadequate he could not hang back now. Too much depended on his actions: his friends would want to know, and he could not disappoint them; but more importantly, he had to do it for himself.

Janet approached him and said, 'You have done a very good job, I can see, Baba.' Then she handed him his pay. 'I think I can say that you deserve this.'

She remembered his name! Baba was elated. He took the money and put it away in his pocket. This was the moment! But it was painful indeed. His heart beat even harder now and he was afraid she would notice how it heaved in his chest. While he was summoning his courage, Janet smiled and turned, about to walk away. He saw his opportunity slipping away before his eyes and suddenly, as if an alien force had seized him, he found the strength to say, 'Janet.'

She turned to face him. 'Yes?'

He thought back to the night before and tried to remember the words he had rehearsed. As he tried to reorganize them in his mind he heard her ask, 'Did you want to say something to me, Baba?' She smiled then, and it was that smile which gave Baba courage.

'Yes,' he said softly.

'I am waiting, Baba.'

'I have had good thoughts about you since I saw you yesterday.' She said nothing. 'I think you are like the only bird on the tree, the only fish in the sea.' This time she found his choice of words amusing and she showed it by grinning. That encouraged and emboldened him. This was it! She liked him. He said, 'I love you, Janet, and I want you to be my girlfriend.'

She laughed raucously, although she had not intended to. Baba stared at her, stupefied; he detected the rejection in the laugh. 'She will laugh in your face.' His mother's warning echoed in his mind.

When she had finished laughing, Janet said, 'That is a very nice thing to say to me, Baba, but I already have a boyfriend.'

Baba did not know what to say to that. He had not anticipated this response, and neither had his friends. He could only watch dumbly as Janet, having thanked him again for his nice thoughts, went indoors. For two minutes afterwards he stood and stared, hoping that she would return and tell him it was all in jest, would open up a route by means of which he could reach her heart. But she did not return. Slowly, in anguish, he left. Did any avenue of hope remain? Perhaps Ofori and Ntiamoah could help him. Better still, Mystique Mysterious. He would first consult his friends and then seek the advice of Mystique Mysterious.

Baba found his friends a little later and told them what had happened.

'I told you you would get nowhere,' Otto said. 'Such girls don't like people like us.'

Ofori said, 'What do you mean? She is just playing games. Look, she wants to play hard to get. All Baba has to do is persevere, show her that he is serious. She says she has a boyfriend. That is what they all say. If she had no interest she would have said so. But did she say that? No. I tell you, Baba, you will win her if you go back and show her you like her.'

'Don't let him lead you into more pain, Baba,' Otto advised.

But Ofori was insistent. 'Don't listen to his nonsense. Girls don't want to look cheap, so they come up with all sorts of excuses. Don't let that discourage you, Baba.'

Ntiamoah asked, 'But Ofori, what if it is true that she has a boyfriend?'

'So what? It does not matter if she has a boyfriend. If she didn't tell you to leave her alone, then she is interested in you, Baba.'

'I will go after her,' Baba said. 'I will try again.'

'Good,' said Ofori. 'You will thank me for my help.' Then he advised Baba what to say. Baba listened and made a supreme effort to memorise what he was told.

Later, when Baba arrived home, Bukari was asleep, but Fati was seated in the living room doing nothing, as though she were waiting for his return.

'Mother,' Baba said, 'I thought you would be asleep by now.' Fati looked into her son's face for a long time, as if he were a stranger, until he felt embarrassed. 'What is it, Mother?'

'Baba, you didn't come home for your supper.'

'I am sorry, Mother, but this isn't the first time and you have never complained about it before. Have you stayed up to ask me why I didn't come home for supper?'

She did not answer his question. 'What did you say to Adukwei?'

'What? Who told you I have said anything to Adukwei?'

'Her mother came to see me at the market today. You have broken the poor girl's heart. Her mother told me Adukwei will not stop crying and has refused to eat.'

Baba thought. 'You think I have done her wrong, Mother?'

How to answer such a question? Could she advise her son to do what seemed right to her, but probably wrong to him? To apologise to the girl he had jilted and be reconciled with her, even though he no longer felt able to give her his utmost love? How could she, sitting in the fringes, dictate his heart's path? But this new girl he sought, was she not just a glitter in the dark, an illusion that would tantalise him but evade his grasp? Fati knew that wealth scorned poverty; wealth despised poverty. True, she had risen above that prejudice with Bukari, but what they did was rare. She had no answer for her son, so she turned his question back on him. 'Do *you* think you have done her wrong?'

'I don't know, Mother. I like Adukwei even now and I don't want to hurt her feelings. But I fear that I have already hurt her badly.'

'That you have, my son. But if you like her, why are you turning your back on her?'

'I like Janet better, Mother. I like Janet much more.'

'I can't tell you who to like or love and who not to. You must choose and walk your own path on these matters. But you must tread carefully, otherwise you may be badly burned and you may badly burn others.'

Baba said nothing for a long time. He stared into nothingness, hands in pockets, and tried to focus. But the effort yielded no results. Finally, he said, 'Mother, I don't know what to do. I am confused and I need help.'

'Son, you know I care for you and I want the best for you,' Fati said. Baba discerned such earnestness in her face that he wanted to go to her and embrace her. But such a show of affection by a boy of his age would be a sign of weakness, he thought, so he restrained himself. His mother went on to say, 'I wish I could tell you what to do in this case, but I can't Baba. You do what you think best. It is getting late and we should both go to bed. They say the pillow is a source of knowledge. Maybe by tomorrow your mind will be clearer and you will know what to do.'

She started for the door leading to the bedroom. But Baba stopped her. 'Mother, thank you.'

Fati nodded to acknowledge her son's gratitude, then passed through into the bedroom. She undressed and joined Bukari on the mattress. Everything was in such a mess. Jojo's Father had come to her the previous night asking her on Mystique Mysterious's behalf for a meeting. She had agreed, hoping that this would be her chance to get Mystique Mysterious out of her husband's life or at least to reduce his influence over him. So on Sunday, Mystique Mysterious would come to see her. But why had it come to this in the first place? This man asleep beside her whom she thought she knew so well. Time can sometimes be cruel. Tears streamed down the sides of her face and she broke into sobs which she tried to stifle with her covers. Her husband lay deep in sleep beside her, unstirred. But in the living room, Baba could hear her. His heart felt heavy and he hoped he was not the cause of her tears.

Chapter Sixteen

A placid wave rolled in and broke upon the shore, lift-ing and letting fall the brown and white half cup of a partly eaten coconut. The wind blew in over the sea and sand, and rustled among the branches of the coconut trees. Out towards the horizon, the black swell of the ocean reflected the glow of the moon and the flicker of stars in the rapidly darkening sky.

Mystique Mysterious stood on the quiet shore and breathed in the power of the sea, as if its strength might help him in the challenge that lay ahead. In about an hour, he would have the opportunity to hold Fati in his arms, to caress her body, to fondle the face that was moulded in such exquisite clay, to possess her and feel the power of her inner glow. Alternatively, he might blunder and lose the possibil-ity for ever. But he would not fail. He must not.

As the appointed time drew closer, Mystique Mysterious drove to a house in the Airport Residential Area where he fetched a bottle of Black Label whisky and dressed for the occasion. He wore a pair of imported shoes, black-polished and glittering; a three-piece suit drenched in cologne. He had been preparing himself physically for this seduction: his body was as firm and trim as an athlete's, hard and curved in the right places; his features stood out in strong contours on his handsome face. He admired himself in the mirror, and, satisfied, drove the BMW he had chosen for the night to Nima. He parked the car a short distance from the Bukari homestead and made his way stealthily to his destination, careful to look before he ventured on to the compound.

It was empty, as planned. He crept like a burglar to Fati's door and knocked gently. There was no response and he began to fear that Fati had left home, perhaps with the Jojo family. He knocked a little louder; still there was no response. He began to panic a little. Were all his plans coming to naught? He knocked again, louder than before. The knock travelled further than intended. In the adjoining building, Bukari's neighbour, Issaka, heard it and excused himself from his wives, Salamatu and Alia, and his children, Issifu and Ibrahim. He looked out of his window and saw Mystique Mysterious with what appeared to be a bottle of liquor in his hand. Then he saw and heard Mystique Mysterious knock on the door again. After a brief wait, Fati opened the door and looked outside. From the distance, Issaka saw her smile and let Mystique Mysterious into the room.

That was not right, Issaka thought. It offended against his every notion of decorum, every religious principle. It was improper for another man to walk into the room of a married woman in the absence of her husband. Issaka felt the urge to intervene and beg Mystique Mysterious to leave, but wondered if that would be prudent. What if Bukari knew and approved? Was it his, Issaka's, business anyway? Yes. Bukari was his neighbour, his brother, and he had to keep his brother as he would himself. But perhaps Mystique Mysterious had only stopped by briefly on his way elsewhere and would leave soon. It would be premature to take any action yet. For the moment, Issaka returned to his family, content to keep his mind alert, his ears open, his eyes looking.

Meanwhile, Mystique Mysterious stood before Fati and smiled. Fati said, 'I am happy you came, for I have something very important to discuss with you.'

'I am sure you do, dear,' Mystique Mysterious said, 'But won't you offer me a seat?'

In her impatience, Fati had forgotten to be courteous. 'Pardon me, please sit,' she said.

'So, my dear, what is it you wanted to talk to me about?' Mystique Mysterious queried, trying to weaken her offensive by his initiative. Then he added, 'But how unthoughtful of me. Forgive me, madam, I brought this drink for your enjoyment. It is only proper that we discuss your concerns over a glass of whisky.' He affected pride as he examined the bottle.

Fati said, 'No! Thank you, but it would be improper for me to drink.'

'If you will pardon my curiosity, may I ask why? Haven't you drunk with me in the past?'

'Yes, but my husband was always here.'

'Oh, I see. But Bukari and I are like brothers. Is it a sin to drink with the brother of your husband, madam? Isn't it an insult for you to tell me you will drink with me when my brother is here, but not when he is away? You know Bukari himself would approve if you shared a drink with me.'

Fati wanted no distractions from discussions of the issue that was uppermost in her mind. Besides, Mystique Mysterious was probably right: Bukari would not object if she shared a drink with him. She said, 'All right, I'll have a little.'

Mystique Mysterious smiled but did not speak. Fati fetched two cups and gave them to him; he quarter-filled each of them and handed one to Fati. 'Cheers,' he saluted, raising his cup. Fati did the same, their cups clinked and they each took sips.

'Well,' Fati said. 'Now we need to talk.'

'Anything, dear.'

'I have heard…' Fati paused to pick her words. 'I have heard that you and my husband have been very busy during the nights.' She expected to see a glimmer of guilt on his face, but there was no trace. Instead, he raised the cup to his lips and took a gulp. By mechanical impulse, Fati did the same. She continued, 'I suppose you are not married and so you have no wife to go back home to at night, no son to be responsible for. But, you see, Bukari is a married man with responsibilities. His reputation in the community is important to him… and inevitably affects me.' She paused, again with the hope that he would react in some way to what she was saying, but still he did not. He drank more whisky instead; without thinking about it, Fati did the same. 'Do you understand what I am saying?'

Mystique Mysterious nodded.

'Then you will understand why I must ask you not to take him out again.'

Mystique Mysterious was not about to comply with this

request, but he knew he must be clever about refusing. 'Your husband and I have become very close friends. As I have said, we are like brothers, my dear. I love him and I won't intentionally do anything to hurt him or his family. But you understand that he is a grown man and must make his own choices. I never coerce him against his will. On the contrary, I do all I can to dissuade him, but you understand that it is very hard to say no to a friend, a brother. When my brother Bukari asks me to take him out, I desire in my heart to say no, to tell him to stay with his wife and son. I tell him his family needs him more than I do, but he replies that his wife and son understand that a man must do certain things. So you see, my dear, it is not my doing. Your husband himself has made his choice.'

Mystique Mysterious drank, and Fati did the same. He glanced into her cup and noticed that it was empty. He poured a little more whisky into it; she protested, but did not stop him. She said, 'I don't wish to blame you, but I am forced to say that my husband never did such things before he met you.'

'I don't intend to deceive you into thinking I am entirely without blame, but it is also not entirely my fault. Listen, I have on countless occasions told him: "Bukari, you have an extremely beautiful and lovely wife called Fati; you must not do these things that I do, for I am not married and I am free to go after as many women as I want." But he does not listen.'

'I find that very hard to believe.'

'You must, Fati. Have I not done all a brother can do for Bukari? Have I not looked after his interests? Was it not I who found him his job when he had no prospect of employment? Do you think I would ever do him or his family ill on purpose?'

He continued in this vein of self-justification and self-exoneration for some time. Fati listened, all the while drinking, bit by bit, without realising how much liquor she was imbibing. He watched her closely and waited for the opportune time to make his move. She was not yet at the stage where her resistance would yield easily, so he talked slowly and lulled her into a sense of trust. He knew that trust breeds carelessness; alcohol encourages risk-taking; and he needed her to be careless and ready to take risks.

While Mystique Mysterious prepared his ground, Issaka's worries grew. Even as he told his family stories, he continued to look furtively out of his window, hoping in vain that Mystique Mysterious would emerge soon with no harm done. After half an hour of waiting, he made up his mind. He asked his first wife, Salamatu, for his sandals and said he had to run an errand he had neglected during the day. His wives and children asked him no questions, for they were not used to doing so. He hurried to Kill Me Quick, intending to inform Bukari of Mystique Mysterious's presence in his house alone with Fati. Bukari would probably laugh him off, but at least he would have done something.

The Kill Me Quick group welcomed Issaka with surprise, since they had never seen him there before. Bukari spoke first. 'Issaka, what wind blows you into this room? Are you not afraid you will get drunk from smelling the liquor on our breath?'

Issaka smiled nervously, itching with impatience. He

cleared his throat and said, 'As for you, Bukari, your head is full of nonsense.'

'Hello, Issaka, how are you?' Kojo Ansah asked. And then Issaka realised what he must do. He could not tell Bukari, who was too close to the situation. And he could not tell Kofi Ntim, for would Kofi Ntim not inflame a delicate situation into an inferno? But Kojo Ansah: he was the thinking one. Like Issaka, he did not drink. A man who refused to touch alcohol had character; he could be trusted to act with tact.

'Let me buy you a drink, Issaka,' Kofi Ntim teased.

'Don't worry the man,' said Esi.

Issaka took a step forward and Kojo Ansah said, 'Don't tell me you are here to drink, Issaka.'

'No, Kojo, you know I am wise like you and do not drink.'

Kofi Ntim asked. 'What are you doing here if you have not come to drink? Come and drink, we will not tell anyone.'

Issaka laughed, but the laugh was forced. He said to Kojo Ansah, 'I need to tell you something. Could you come outside with me for a minute?'

'Certainly,' Kojo Ansah replied.

'What is so secret that you must pull a man aside to tell him, huh?' asked Kofi Ntim.

Issaka did not reply, but led Kojo Ansah outside and a little distance away from the kiosk until he was confident that they were beyond the reach of eavesdroppers' curosity. Kojo Ansah noticed the troubled look on his face and became a little worried.

'Kojo,' Issaka began. 'I don't know if I should be telling you this or not, but Bukari is my neighbour and when a neighbour's house is on fire you do not just stand aside and watch it burn. Maybe what I am about to say is the trivial concern of a prude, a foolish man. But in my mind, I will not be able to rest till I have told somebody.'

Kojo Ansah wished Issaka would spare him the suspense. 'What is it?'

'A while ago, I was sitting at home when I noticed Mystique Mysterious knocking on Bukari's door with a bottle of what I think was liquor in his hand. Fati let him into the house and they have been there alone ever since—for quite some time now. I know it is not right for a man to go to a married woman's house with alcohol and stay there so long. I was worried and did not know who to tell. I would have gone to Jojo's Father, but he is seeing a film with his family. He had asked me to go with them, but you know I am not a man of the world so I refused.'

'How intriguing,' said Kojo Ansah. 'I don't know what to think. It could be that Mystique Mysterious is only visiting Fati. He probably thought Bukari was home and wanted to share a drink with him, but found that he was out and simply decided to stay. On the other hand, maybe he called in the knowledge that Bukari was away.'

'You don't think anything bad is going on, do you?'

'I hope not,' Kojo Ansah replied. 'But I can't be sure. There is only one way to find out. We must go there right away.'

Fear crept into Issaka's face. 'What? My brother, I don't want trouble for myself. I don't want to provoke the anger of Mystique Mysterious. What will he say if we intrude? What if they are doing what we fear?'

'You don't have to be afraid. If his visit is innocent, we will not be intruding on anything. If they are doing bad things, we have the moral obligation to stop them and our intrusion will be justified.'

'Morally justified, but practically unwise.'

'That is all right, Issaka. You don't have to come with me. I will go alone, knock on the door and see what is happening. You go back home and keep an eye outside. If you see or hear anything disturbing, raise an alarm and get some help. Do you think you can do that for me?'

'Yes! Very well then, let's go.'

They headed back.

Inside her home, Fati was tipsy. Slowly, she had drunk much more than ever before, comforted by Mystique Mysterious's promises to help Bukari end his 'unwholesome noctural activities', as he put it. Presently, Mystique Mysterious reached out and brushed away a piece of thread hanging in Fati's hair. Unsuspecting, slouched in the armchair and looking dazed and sedate, she thanked him. He looked at his watch and realised that he was losing time. Before long, the Jojos would be back and Bukari would be on his way home. Now was the time, the moment of execution.

He lunged forward and pinned Fati's shoulders to the armchair. Before she realised his intent, his lips were over hers, forcing his tongue into her mouth. Caught by surprise, she yielded for a brief moment and he found confidence in her pliancy to reach out with one hand and touch her breasts. But she collected her thoughts and summoned her energy. She put both hands on his chest and managed to shove him away. 'What are you doing?'

'Don't tell me you don't want this,' Mystique Mysterious said. Fati's anger at his insolence choked her into silence. Mystique Mysterious misconstrued her again and his confidence grew. He rose and removed his jacket in a quick deft motion, then darted forward again. But Fati got out of the chair and dodged sideways. She made a dash for the door leading outside, but he stopped her by catching her round the waist with an outstretched arm and pulling her to him. They faced each other. He pushed her against the wall, between the living room and the bedroom and she hit it hard and felt a little faint. He held her against the wall and tore the front of her blouse open, exposing her breasts underneath.

Fati gasped and fought futilely with both hands. 'Don't do this. Please don't do this,' she pleaded. Mystique Mysterious's loins throbbed with the power he held over this creature of beauty, helpless, entirely at his mercy. He reached with his free hand for her right breast and fondled it and then pressed his lips against hers, stifling her cries. She was his to take.

It was then that they heard the bang on the door. At first, Mystique Mysterious ignored it, covering Fati's mouth with his hand to prevent her screaming and hoping that the intruder would tire and leave. But Kojo Ansah knocked and banged and knocked and banged. Mystique Mysterious had to act quickly. He tore off the remnants of Fati's blouse and covered her mouth with it, tying it behind her head, so that she could not scream. Then he held her hands behind her and moved her towards the door. He opened it slightly so that nobody could see into the room and peered outside with anger. 'What are you doing here?' he demanded angrily when he saw Kojo Ansah.

'I am here to see Fati,' Kojo Ansah replied.

'She is not here.'

'I think she is.'

'I said she is not here!'

'Then what are you doing here?'

'That is none of your business! Leave! Leave now!' Mystique Mysterious was about to bang the door shut when Kojo Ansah put a foot forward so that it would not close. Kojo Ansah pushed on the door with all his strength and it moved inwards against the weight of Mystique Mysterious and Fati, sending them both tumbling to the floor. In the process, Mystique Mysterious lost his grip on Fati. Burning with rage, he leaped to his feet and went for Kojo Ansah's throat, but Kojo Ansah moved back a bit and Mystique Mysterious hit him in the chest instead, pushing him outside on to the compound.

Issaka, watching from his room, ran past the fighters on to the street and started yelling for help. Neighbours and passers-by heard his cries and started to congregate on the compound to watch Mystique Mysterious and Kojo Ansah on the ground in a battle of blows.

'Somebody stop them,' Issaka cried.

'Why? Why stop this free show?' a neighbour replied.

Issaka's wives came outside with his children and looked at the fighters with concern and a little amusement. As the others looked on, three men emerged from the crowd to intervene and struggled to pull the fighters, now clutching each other's throats, apart.

Meantime, news of the fight had tavelled fast and soon spread as far as Kill Me Quick. But when it reached the ears of Bukari, the story was that Kojo Ansah had caught Mystique Mysterious sleeping with Fati, and when Kojo Ansah tried to stop them, Mystique Mysterious got angry and attacked. Bukari ran out with Kofi Ntim and Esi. The neighbours had succeeded in separating Kojo Ansah and Mystique Mysterious when they arrived.

Fati sat on the floor in the living room, sobbing, naked above the waist. Bukari looked at Mystique Mysterious and asked bitterly, 'You?' Someone shouted to him, 'Beat him up, he was caught sleeping with your wife.'

'That isn't true,' Kojo Ansah said. 'He wasn't sleeping with her.'

Then suddenly Madman emerged from nowhere yelling meaninglessly and drawing attention to himself. He ran up to Kojo Ansah and hit him in the face. Kojo Ansah fell on his back and Madman jumped on him. Kojo Ansah fought back, and for the second time that night became embroiled in a reluctant fight. Again, other men intervened to separate the combatants. As Kojo Ansah recovered, Mystique Mysterious said to him, 'You will regret this, you fool,' and without another word, walked away.

Madman tried again to attack Kojo Ansah, but he was stopped by a neighbour.

Kojo Ansah was furious by now and he yelled at Madman. 'I will kill you!' Madman looked at him nonchalantly and walked away with a shrug, as if nothing had happened.

Kofi Ntim began to dismiss the gathering and they dispersed until only Esi, Kojo Ansah, Kofi Ntim and Issaka and his family were left.

Bukari walked into his living room and stood over the sobbing Fati. While his neighbours watched, he assailed her. 'You filthy prostitute! I turn my back for a minute and what do you do? You go and bring yourself a man to sleep with.'

'She didn't sleep with him,' said Kojo Ansah, whose anger had waned now. 'Mystique Mysterious tried to force himself on her. I am sure of that.'

Bukari looked around the room and shook his head. He picked up the half-empty bottle of whisky and showed it to those outside. 'Is this something that suggests force to you? They were drinking and having their party behind my back. No, Kojo, Mystique Mysterious was not forcing himself on her. She was a willing participant. Look at these two cups. Yes, my wife has been sleeping with him and I didn't know it.'

Fati got slowly to her feet. Jojo's Mother and Father, returning from the cinema, looked into the room and realised all was not well. They all watched silently as the tears in Fati's eyes rolled downwards, tracing the paths where earlier tears had flown. Then she looked up, and husband and wife gazed into each other's eyes.

'Why did you do it?' Bukari asked.

Emotion smothered Fati; she, the victim, accused by the philandering husband. He had assumed the worst, believing she too would do what he had done. But who was he to accuse her? On what moral authority did he judge her? The urge mounted inside her to hurl insults at him, to unleash her frustrations, the pent-up anger, to lurch forward and beat the arrogance out of his erring, misjudging head. Her anger and the effort to restrain it collided and she shuddered. But, with the neighbours watching, her breasts still bare, she managed to say, 'I did not do anything and nothing happened. He tried to force me and I resisted. Nothing happened.'

'Don't insult me with your lies, woman! He tried to force you, huh? With these cups for two, this drinking spree? You are nothing but a cheap prostitute!'

Fati's fury leaped inside her and she felt as though it would engulf her. 'You filthy prostitute!' she heard him say again. She could fight the urge no longer. With a passion not before witnessed by herself, her husband or the neighbours, she bellowed, 'You stupid fool! You call yourself a man? What kind of man will leave his wife at home every night to sleep with other women?'

Bukari took a step towards Fati and, for the first time ever, slapped her heavily across the face. 'Shut up!' he commanded as she fell to the floor.

Issaka and Kojo Ansah ran forward to restrain him while Jojo's Mother hurried to her room and returned with a piece of cloth. She helped Fati up to her feet and covered her partial nakedness with the cloth. Then she led her out, slowly, with a solemn air.

When they were gone, Kojo Ansah said to Bukari, 'Fati spoke the truth, Bukari. You must believe her. She is not to blame at all.' Bukari said nothing. He walked over to the armchair and slumped into it with a sigh. Kojo Ansah added, 'You take care now and be careful how you react. You have a good woman, do not be hasty.' His words went unheard, and presently he and Issaka walked away. The rest were unsure of what to do or what to say, how to comfort their friend in his grief. One by one they began to disperse until none remained.

Alone, Bukari reached for the half-empty bottle of whisky and stared at it. Was this the aphrodisiac? The catalyst? The source of Fati's betrayal? He looked at the two cups. One was empty, the other almost. He hurled the empty cup against the wall, drained the contents of the other cup, and flung that too at the wall. Then he put the bottle to his mouth and took a swig. His mind began to fill up with thoughts. Fati, the chaste queen of love, honour, understanding; the woman who had followed her heart and turned her back on wealth; she who had borne and raised their son while he whiled away the time with friends, drinking and, lately, philandering. Would she now sink so low and share herself with another man? It was hard to believe. But she had. She had denied it, but that was to be expected. Had he not himself denied his misdeeds to her? Why else would she invite Mystique Mysterious to their home when he was away? Why would they share a bottle of liquor together? As for Kojo Ansah's account... maybe he just intended to protect a friend's feelings, or perhaps he too had been deceived.

Bukari began to reconstruct the events of the evening in his mind. Behind his back, they had planned it. Mystique Mysterious waited until he left and then sneaked in, Fati waiting for him, smiling at him. They shared the bottle of liquor and then had sex. For some reason, Issaka suspected something. He came to Kill Me Quick to inform Kojo Ansah of his suspicions. Kojo Ansah came over, barged in on the lovers *in flagrante delicto*. Shamed, Fati quickly ripped her blouse and concocted the story that Mystique Mysterious was forcing her against her will. That was it. Had Fati not threatened it? Had she not said she too could cheat? She had the motive: the desire to exact her revenge for his infidelity. What a cruel way to pay him back! Right in his own house, with a friend.

He imagined Mystique Mysterious and Fati together, their bodies meshed in carnal union. In his mind's ear, he heard his unfaithful wife's moans. He felt as if part of him had been slain, or cut off and flung into an eternity of abyssal loss, unrecoverable ever. Tears began to crawl down his cheeks. He took another gulp of liquor, and the liquid spilled over his chin and travelled downwards to soak his shirt.

Presently, Baba opened the door and was startled to see his father awake, in a drunken stupor. He closed the door behind him and stared. Bukari looked up at his son as a stranger would. The younger man was uncomfortable and felt compelled to speak. 'Father, I thought you would be asleep, by now.'

Bukari rose slowly. 'Go to sleep,' he said simply, and walked into the bedroom. His sense of emptiness increased at the sight of the mattress; all his married life Fati had been lying on the mattress at that hour. He undressed, lay down, and stared at the ceiling, wishing desperately that Fati were there with him so that he could just feel the warmth of her body, the assurance of her presence. He heard Baba prepare to sleep in the living room. What had he achieved, as a husband, as a father, as a man? Nothing! He was a failure. He who had vowed to be a better parent to his offspring than his own father. Had he been? No, he had treated his son with dispassionate equanimity, as though Baba did not exist as a person but was there like an object to be tolerated. And the wife. What was to be done about her? Could he hold her again when another man had defiled her? But his love! Love? Fati had betrayed his love, and love betrayed may prefer the pain of alienation to the salve of forgiveness. But had Fati not been ready to compromise when she believed rightly that he had betrayed her? She had been willing to forgive. Why could he not do the same for her? But the thought of the neighbours and what they would say of the cuckoldry came to his mind. It would soon be on everybody's lips. They would smile and chuckle and behind him they would laugh and say, 'This is Bukari, the man married to Fati who slept with Mystique Mysterious right in their bedroom.' And how they would embellish, these neighbours. They might add, 'She has been like that all her life. Baba is not Bukari's son; the boy was fathered by another man. Can't you see how unalike they look? No wonder they are so far apart.' Bukari tormented himself with visions of his humiliation.

What of Mystique Mysterious? His benefactor, who had found him a job when he was desperate. The man who had so often placed his arm around his shoulder with such a show of affection, who had drunk with him and found him women. Mystique Mysterious, his friend, his brother, his mentor… and now the seducer of his wife. He could cut off all contact with him. But was that the wisest course? Mystique Mysterious was such a powerful person, a man with a ubiquitous presence and octopoid tentacles.

Thoughts came and went unresolved.

The night teased Bukari with its deep silence. He thought he heard a door open and close. Thinking it was Fati, he got up and rushed into the living room, waking Baba in the process. Baba, startled and wide-eyed, saw his father's profile in the dark doorway, saw him go back sadly into the bedroom. After a short while, he heard his father begin to cry, like his mother the night before. Something was amiss, but Baba did not know what. He assumed his mother was asleep in the bedroom. But why had his father sat up so late alone, drinking? Why had he suddenly entered the living room and gone back to the bedroom to cry? Baba's young mind was deeply disturbed. Something was going on in the house. It bothered him that he did not know what it was.

Chapter Seventeen

Kojo Ansah's mind was in turmoil. The future seemed dangerous and inexorable: a disloged boulder falling closer and closer. He was convinced he had witnessed an attempt by Mystique Mysterious to commit a heinous act: forcefully to acquire carnal knowledge of Fati. Something had to be done about this man! But what? How long could they wait while the leech sucked their blood, the worm burrowed into their veins? Until they were transformed into empty vessels, sleeping and waking to the beck and call of his whispers of destruction? No. Kojo Ansah would act.

But he wanted some assurance that he wasn't overreacting. He went to see Kofi Ntim and told his friend of his concerns.

'There is nothing we can do,' Kofi Ntim advised.

'What do you mean, Kofi? Should we just sit here and wait to die?'

'My brother, perhaps we are already dead. Perhaps we died a long time ago.'

'What do you mean?' Kojo Ansah asked.

'We are the most pathetic of creatures. We are insulted, but we can't insult; taken advantage of, but we can't take advantage of others. It started slowly and then it grew until where we once had the urge to yell, now we can only sit and talk in whispers, whimpering like kicked dogs, moaning, enslaved by a good nature transformed over time into a foolish weakness. We are the fools, my brother, because we are nice to everybody.'

It was an old story, and a sad one: the gentle do not go far. Those who fail to live by the iron principle of an eye for an eye are ever susceptible to the snares of those who do; those who welcome with open hearts are ever prone to the guile and machinations of those who are out to devour.

'Let me illustrate what I'm saying,' Kofi Ntim continued, 'Take a guest who has gone to visit another. The host says to his family, "Let's live together as brothers and sisters. Let's give our guest a home." But the host forgets that a step into the room is insufficient for one looking to possess the mansion. A morsel of food does not suffice for one aiming to acquire the entire harvest. A parcel of the trade does not sate the heart of one seeking to control the whole economy. Now, the guest steps into the room, gazes at its contents, admires its decor and then asks to see the rest of the mansion. The unsuspecting host obliges; meanwhile the guest is scheming. To possess, he must learn. Little by little if need be. So he is patient, studying every gesture, every attitude. At the dining table the guest drinks and laughs heartily. The host is charmed, not knowing that he must beware of the one who laughs the hardest. So now the guest knows all he needs to know and he makes his move. He wants to see the source of the harvest. "I have this," he says, "I will trade you for that."

'And the host and his family are trapped by their desire to enjoy the alluring wares brought by the guest. They fall under the spell of his beautiful goods. They want more and more. Eventually, life without the guest becomes unimaginable. He has captured them; they cannot escape.'

Kojo Ansah listened to this bleak warning and returned home more convinced than ever that he ought to act.

Was there some weakness he could exploit? Kojo Ansah racked his brains. Then it hit him. The 441 crowd, Mystique Mysterious's support in the community. If they could be turned against him, Mystique Mysterious would lose the foundations of his strength. He might even be driven from Nima if there were a threat *en masse*. To attempt to turn the tide of the 441 crowd's opinion was a step on to hazardous ground: like quicksand, it might easily give way beneath his feet and swallow him. But the possibility of success made Kojo Ansah bold.

So Kojo Ansah joined the 441 group for the first time ever. He had previously only observed them from a distance or stopped briefly to give and receive polite greetings. He had never walked in among them, to be encircled by their presence. He wondered if he had made a mistake by keeping his distance while Mystique Mysterious mingled with them and became their trusted colleague. He had a great deal of ground to make up.

'Good evening,' Kojo Ansah said.

Some of them responded with words while others did so by raising their heads. They were surprised to see Kojo Ansah in their midst, for they knew him only from a distance—as a face, a voice. They looked at one another and, though they said nothing, understood one another: what is this familiar stranger doing here among us?

Yaw Cake decided to find out. Although his manners

were often crude, he knew that he must be civil with this dignified man. 'Kojo, how are you? It's a great honour to see you here. Were you on your way somewhere?'

The others strained their ears to hear the response. Kojo Ansah said, 'I am happy to be here with you. We need to talk from time to time as friends?'

Whispers arose among the crowd: 'He is not our friend. What is he talking about?'

Kojo Ansah said, 'I know we are not friends in the ordinary sense, but we have certain interests in common. We live in the same neighbourhood, shop at the same markets, breathe the same air. If a disease sweeps Nima, it will affect us all. When a neighbour's house is on fire, all of us are at risk, for who knows how far the fire will spread? It is in that sense that we as neighbours are also friends.'

There was doubt in Yaw Cake's voice when he asked, 'Is that why you have come here tonight, Kojo Ansah?'

'Yes, but wait. Before you reach any conclusions, hear me. I want to say simply that if one of our brothers in Nima has a problem, we need to help him.'

Yaw Cake agreed. 'We need to help one another. It is the right thing to do, but none of us is in trouble of any sort, so why bother us with this speech? Or has somebody's house caught fire?'

'In a sense, yes. One of us has been wronged.'

'Kojo Ansah, we know you are a quiet man and you don't normally waste your words. But right now you are wasting words. First, you say we are friends, brothers, and that one of us has been wronged. But you won't tell us who it is and what the wrong is.' The speaker now was Danger Diabolic, who had acquired that name from his love of a foreign film by the same title.

'Be patient, my brother. I will tell. You all know Bukari, I am sure?'

They murmured affirmatively, but Yaw Cake tried to regain the initiative by saying, 'Everybody knows Bukari. We all know he is Mystique Mysterious's friend. What a lucky man he is, Bukari, to have such a friend, so rich and kind and good.'

The last remark was a challenge—the first layer of bricks in a wall of hostility—and had to be answered quickly. 'Do you consider Mystique Mysterious Bukari's friend?'

'Certainly,' replied Yaw Cake. And the crowd agreed.

'I see. But tell me, what is a friend supposed to do? A friend should love a friend, like a brother loves a brother. A friend should protect a friend.'

Danger Diabolic said, 'We all know that. That is what Mystique Mysterious does for Bukari. He takes him out at night to drink and meet big men. I hear he even found Bukari his job.'

The wall was growing and the brick was hardening. Kojo Ansah needed to act even more quickly. 'I hear what you are saying, but let us suppose there was more to it than that. Supposing they went out not just to drink, but to find women to sleep with every time. What would you say to that?'

Danger Diabiolic said dismissively, 'Who cares? Isn't that exciting? Would we all not do so if we had the opportunity?'

'But Bukari has a wife.'

'And so what?'

'You mean it is all right, even though he has a wife?'

'Yes.'

Kojo Ansah was getting nowhere. He redirected his line of argument. 'But you all know Bukari's wife, Fati. Does she not deserve better?'

At the mention of Fati, a hush fell on the crowd. Whereas previously their minds had dwelt on the abstract concept of a wife, now they had to contend with a face, a body, flesh and blood. A woman they knew and desired: beautiful, dignified, graceful and polite. It did not matter in abstract terms if a husband was unfaithful to a wife, but it mattered that a particular husband cheated on Fati. On the other hand, Bukari had only done what they all fantasised about doing: could they blame a man who had an opportunity and seized it?

'It does not matter what she deserves,' said Yaw Cake. 'Is she not a woman?'

But another who had listened carefully had had his conscience stirred. They called him Dada, for he was older than the rest. His receding hair was streaked with grey, his forehead was heavily lined and deep furrows ran down the sides of his nose to the edges of his chin. 'I am interested in hearing more.' His voice was powerful and elicited respect. 'You seem to be suggesting that when Bukari goes out with Mystique Mysterious all they do is chase after women?'

'Yes sir,' Kojo Ansah replied.

'How do you know? Have you seen with your own eyes?'

'Sir, I have seen plenty.'

'You must be able to tell us something more concrete than that. We have all heard rumours, but rumours are just rumours.'

'Sir, those rumours, I believe, are true.' Kojo Ansah's

argument was weak, unsubstantiated; he was asking for a leap of faith. Dada saw his shining eyes and believed him, but Dada was not ready to condemn on that basis alone. Time was slipping by and, desperately, Kojo Ansah played his last card. 'What is most terrible is that tonight, sir, I caught Mystique Mysterious trying forcibly to have sexual intercourse with Fati.'

There was a sudden and deep silence as the crowd fed on this news. But Yaw Cake said after an interlude, 'I don't believe you. Why do you want to ruin a good man's name?'

Dada, however, wanted clarification. 'You make a very grave accusation, Kojo. Tell us more.'

Kojo Ansah proceeded to narrate the events of the night. While he spoke, the crowd was quiet, but when he finished, it erupted into a cry almost in unison: Kojo Ansah was lying. Who were his witnesses? Bukari's closest neighbours were the witnesses, he told them. They retorted that only the liar says his witnesses are elsewhere. Kojo Ansah gave them names, but they were not interested.

Dada observed them with disappointment and, his voice a flood of anger, pointed to Kojo Ansah and said, 'Why do you all choose to close your minds to this man? What does he gain by saying these things? We all know him as a quiet man, a man who will not fight back even though Madman attacks him incessantly. Is this a man who will get up one day and start making false accusations? I don't think so and none of you have any good reason to think so either. His sincerity is beyond doubt. What has he told us today? He has come to us as a neighbour to show us that another's house is on fire. We must put out the fire before its spreads.

A man who would try forcibly to take another's wife... I can't find the words to describe what should be done to him. We are individuals, but we have responsibilities to one another and to our women.' Dada paused and seemed to be at a loss for words. For a minute the crowd gazed at him in silence, then he added, 'Kojo Ansah has spoken the truth to us. It is up to us to do what we have to do.'

Yaw Cake said with irreverence, 'That is nonsense.'

'It is not nonsense,' disagreed Danger Diabolic. 'Dada is older and wiser than all of us. Look at his white hairs.'

'Pah! White hairs do not supply the head with wisdom,' countered Yaw Cake.

Yet things were turning in Kojo Ansah's favour. Danger Diabolic said to him, 'I am prepared to believe you. But you have not told us what you want from us.'

'Mystique Mysterious is able to do these things because we let him. We welcome him, we accept his gifts and make him feel comfortable. We must stop all that. Next time he comes into the neighbourhood, we must show him how angry we are that he should attempt to corrupt our little town with his ways. Today, it is Fati; tomorrow, it could be your wife.'

The last warning seemed to work a dangerous chemistry. The men talked among themselves and came to the conclusion that Mystique Mysterious was an evil man. They would drive him out, spit on him, run him away. If he refused to go, they would drag him through the streets... out! Kojo Ansah watched them and smiled. He had them. With their support, he could stand up, unafraid. He began to make a plan of action.

But then a Jeep pulled up, raising a flurry of dust. The

men's attention was diverted as they looked to see who had disturbed them so. When the dust settled, a middle-aged man emerged from the Jeep. He had a congenial demeanour and commanded respect by his sheer presence. The anger the crowd had prepared subsided and there was quiet. The man held a knapsack in one hand; he pulled out several rolls of marijuana and said calmly, 'This is weed for all of you from Mystique Mysterious.'

This was the test.

Kojo Ansah said with deep anxiety, 'Do not be tempted by this. Mystique Mysterious wants to play with your minds.'

'Listen to Kojo Ansah,' said Dada.

For several seconds the crowd waited in silence, confused.

Then the man reached into the knapsack again and took out a bundle of money and held it out. 'Not just weed,' he said. 'Mystique Mysterious is a very generous and caring man and he has asked me to distribute this to you, his friends, his brothers.'

That decided the issue. They were faced with two options. One was to follow Kojo Ansah down an uncertain road of rebellion. With what consequences? They would lose the free marijuana, the cigarettes, the cash. And what would they gain? A vague sense of accomplishment for driving away a corrupting influence? The other option was to take the money and the marijuana, with the certainty of instant gratification and the prospect of more to come. The alternatives contrasted starkly, like midday and midnight, with no twilight of grey in between. Their hesitation was short. They chose, but they needed a leader to take the first step. Yaw

Cake provided that leadership by walking up to the man and saying to the rest, 'You people can choose to be stupid, but not me. I know what I want.' He received a roll of marijuana and a bundle of cash. Danger Diabolic followed and the rest did the same. One by one they approached the man to receive a reward for rejecting Kojo Ansah. Eventually, only Dada was left.

Dada looked at Kojo Ansah and shrugged. 'You offered us freedom, but it is hard to resist temptation. I am sorry, my friend, but you and I alone cannot save Nima.' And Dada walked up to the man and received his share. The man stared at Kojo Ansah for a long time, then walked to the Jeep and drove away, throwing another whirl of dust into the air.

Kojo Ansah stood helpless as the crowd began to smoke. Praises were voiced for Mystique Mysterious. Weakly, Kojo Ansah said, 'I can't believe this.'

'Go away and leave us alone!' Yaw Cake hollered; and the crowd, in murmurs, concurred. As the marijuana began to take effect, a chant rose up, warning Kojo Ansah to go. Kojo Ansah looked to Dada for help, but even he was smoking and chanting with the crowd. Kojo Ansah had to accept his defeat. He had tried, come close to success, and finally lost to a man who had not even entered the field in person. If Mystique Mysterious could sit elsewhere and win a battle against one who lived and walked among these people, was there any hope of vanquishing him? Dejected and disconsolate, Kojo Ansah left.

Fati, recovering from her ordeal at the Jojo house, was still stunned. She could not believe what Mystique Mysterious had tried to do to her. But the response of her husband was more shocking. Why did he not believe her? Why had he slapped her? What had she done to deserve this? The possibility that she was at fault, that somehow she had encouraged Mystique Mysterious and given Bukari cause to doubt her, took hold of her mind. Like many victims, she was left with a sense of guilt and victimised herself even further. Such terrible things could not happen to people unless they deserved them, and people deserved such things only if they had done terrible things themselves. The powerful twisted logic of this ate away at her sense of dignity and self-worth. She had done something terribly wrong in her life—somewhere, somehow. It was as though she was cursed: she who had been ostracised by her own father, spewed from his mouth like a distateful clove of garlic, shunned like the carrier of a fatal infectious disease; she who had failed to bear more than one child. She was bad and had been execrated for her bad deeds. But what were those bad deeds? Her early childhood was indistinct, but her mother had told her that she had been a good child, helpful and kind. And as far as she could remember, she had been good. So what was it? Was it her dalliance with Bukari before marriage, allowing herself to become pregnant? Or was it the marriage to Bukari, in defiance of her father?

She relived the events of the night again and again. What had gone wrong? She had allowed Mystique Mysterious into her home in the absence of her husband, but without ill intent. She had only wanted to discuss her husband's philandering. Was that such a bad thing to do? Maybe she should not have drunk at all. Had she, in her intoxication, flirted, done something suggestive and untoward? Had she smiled too much? Talked too much? Were men not bestial creatures, too easily aroused? And did she not deserve to suffer the consequences if she had by her conduct stirred Mystique Mysterious's loins?

Fati convinced herself that she had invited Mystique Mysterious, even if tacitly, to take her. She wanted to run out of the Jojo household and plead with her husband to forgive her, promise him that she would never err again. This was the first phase of her reaction: guilt and shame at her own violation, and a sense that she had been to blame, pried open for all to abuse. The second phase would not begin until later.

'Take our bedroom,' Jojo's Mother said presently. 'We will sleep here in the living room.'

'No!' Fati replied. She could not dislodge the family like that. 'I will sleep here in the living room.'

'But I must insist,' said Jojo's Father. 'We can't allow our guest to sleep in the living room.'

'I am not a guest,' replied Fati. She sounded upset, and the Jojos did not wish to exacerbate her state. Jojo's Mother went on tiptoe into the bedroom, where the children were already asleep, and brought out a thin mattress, a pillow and two wrappers. She made room on the floor for the mattress, and made up a bed. 'I wish you would take our bed, but since you don't want to, I hope this will do.'

'This is perfect. Thank you very much.'

Jojo's Father was riddled with guilt for the part he had played in the night's episode; he considered it an atone-ment to play host to Fati, the victim of the machinations of

Mystique Mysterious. 'If you need anything, let me know,' he said.

'I will, and thank you again.'

Left alone in her makeshift bed, Fati entered the second phase of her reaction. She relived the events of the night again and again, trying to pinpoint where she went wrong, what she did or said to mislead Mystique Mysterious. Again and again she could not. Then it began to seep through to her that she really had done nothing wrong. Sure, she had invited Mystique Mysterious to her home when her husband was away. But that was not such a bad thing in itself. She had drunk with him, but Bukari had blessed her drinking in his presence, and his absence did not make such a big difference. She knew that what she had done would be considered unusual in the community; but even then, even if she had stripped and walked the streets, was that a licence for another to invade her being? Certainly not. Especially not when she had so openly voiced her lack of consent.

But Mystique Mysterious had tried to take her, like a piece of property. She was the wronged one. And her husband had reacted without listening to her side of events. Besides, even if she had slept with Mystique Mysterious, had Bukari not done worse? Or is what is good for the bull not good for the cow? There was no reason for him to explode with such anger. She would not apologise. She still wanted to save her marriage, but she could not do it alone. If her husband had any interest, he would take the initiative and come to her.

What bothered Fati most was Baba. He was grown in many ways, but he was also still a child: he needed guidance. And she needed him. How would he react if he heard of what had transpired that night? Whose version would he believe? Would he also blame her, like his father? Was there some male solidarity that would defeat the truth? Or would he understand her? Sons had a way of drawing to their mothers; they understood and appreciated their mothers. But what if the marriage broke up? How would Baba bear it? She would have to help him. The thought of Baba, the fruit of her womb, roused her. She had to be strong for him.

At the same time, the pain was there and she was unable to stop the tears. Suddenly claustrophobic, she got up and opened the door and stepped outside. The compound was so well lit by the moon that she could see the closed door leading to her own home. Was Bukari inside, lying in bed in as much pain as she? Was he choking with regret, planning his apology? Or was he out somewhere with one of his numerous women? How about Baba? Was he back home yet? Had he heard? What was he thinking? Fati stood for a while outside and hoped that Bukari would open the door and walk up to her. No words would be necessary; if he so much as smiled and reached out for her, she would understand. She would fall into his arms and everything would be forgiven. Was she weak to long for him so? After all he had done? Perhaps; but if her weakness would bring her happiness, it was worth it.

Fati re-entered the room, closing the door carefully so as not to wake the Jojos. She sat for a while, then paced the room, and finally rested her weary body on the mattress. She prayed for the relief of sleep, but sleep was slow to come.

Chapter Eighteen

T he next morning brought more bad news. Bukari woke up after a mere hour of sleep, tired and with bloodshot eyes. Fati had not come home and his empty feeling worsened and ate at him as he left for work. As usual, he went to the Denyi residence and knocked on the door. The maid opened the door, but instead of handing him the keys to the taxi, she said gloomily, 'Master wants to talk to you.' Bukari held his breath. It was unusual for the boss to talk to him at such a time. Normally, if he had anything to say to Bukari, he waited until evening. Bukari followed the maid into the living room.

After a short wait, Henry Denyi appeared, but he did not look into Bukari's eyes. In an impersonal tone, he said, 'I will not be needing you any more. Thank you.' After more than a year of service, discarded without ceremony or waste of words.

Bukari tried to remain calm, but after the events of the previous night, it was as though his whole world was coming unhinged. He looked at Henry, trying to make eye contact, for the eyes can sometimes reach the soul in a way that words cannot. But Henry kept his gaze averted. Bukari sank to his knees. 'Massah,' he said, 'I beg you to reconsider. I have nowhere to turn.'

'I have spoken!' Henry replied. He reached into his pocket and quickly counted out a stack of bank notes. 'Here is your pay for up to now. Take it and leave.'

'Massah, please.' Bukari began to sob. 'I have a son, massah. How can I take care of him? I beg you with God, please reconsider. Please have mercy.' He did not take the money. Henry Denyi let it slip to the floor and began to walk away. In one last desperate effort, Bukari reached for Henry's ankle and held on to it, but Henry yanked his leg away, pulling Bukari over in the process. Then Henry left the room, and Bukari was left alone with his despondency. He lifted himself to his knees and collected the money from the floor. He rose to his feet and very slowly left the house. It was vain to hope that Henry Denyi would have a change of heart.

Outside, the sun was beginning to rise—a faint yellow. Bukari blinked to clear his eyes. Near by, a turkey gobbled; a sparrow chirped. A wandering spaniel appeared on the street and Bukari felt a sense of kinship with the friendless animal. He would have liked to pet and fondle the creature a little, for the comfort of warmth and contact. But as he advanced towards it, the dog, who had learned to expect cruel treatment from humankind, ran away.

What to do? Bukari had lost his income and probably his wife. Even if he and Fati were reconciled, could they ever return to the love of times past? Fati would never trust him after all he had done, nor would he trust her. They would live the rest of their lives in forced tolerance, as wary of each other as predators, every action analysed, every move countered.

The shame of being cuckolded did not matter much any more. Not when he had so little to be proud of. He could previously point to his job as a source of pride; without it he was worthless. Let the neighbours say whatever they wanted. He did not care.

Why had he followed Mystique Mysterious into immorality—into debauchery? He had betrayed the trust of the woman who had shared with him through good and bad. Was it so surprising that she had stooped to revenge? She was noble, but she was human too. She may have wronged him, but he had wronged her first. He would make amends. If he could not bring himself to go to her personally, he would ask an elder to intercede.

Sorrow weighed heavily in Bukari's heart as he aimlessly walked the streets. At the corner of Flagstaff House he noticed a woman selling palm wine. He felt the money in his pocket and decided to buy a little comfort. He approached the stall. The vendor greeted him and he ordered. The woman fetched him a calabash of palm wine and Bukari sat down on a bench to drink. She noticed the look of sorrow on his face and the tears where they had dried. 'You are my first customer,' she said. 'I hope you bring me good luck. I give you this first drink free.'

Bukari was not in a conversational mood. 'Thank you,' he said tersely. But she smiled with natural charm and Bukari warmed to her. 'At this hour you won't get many customers. You should wait until after noon.'

'You would be surprised. I have nothing to do anyway, so why not come out and sit in the rising sun and see it shine off people's faces?'

They sat silently for several seconds, then the woman said, 'I don't want to be too inquisitive, so tell me to shut up if you wish, but I can't help noticing that you look unhappy.'

Bukari wiped his face with his hand, hoping to clear away the stains of tears. 'Do you think it is all right for men to cry?'

'I take it you are assuming that it is all right for women to cry. And if so, why not men?'

Bukari was tempted to open up to this stranger. Why not? She would probably be more understanding than his friends. He began, 'I have done terrible things to my family. You see, I have ignored my son, and I have been cheating on my wife.'

'That is not such an uncommon thing these days.'

'But my wife and I had a special relationship. We love each other deeply, and until recently, absolutely trusted each other. But then I met this rich man who would take me places and find me women, again and again and again. It became a habit, almost a daily ritual. My wife heard and confronted me, but I refused to discuss it. Last night, she slept with that rich man right in our bedroom when I was out drinking with my friends.'

'I see. That is enough to make many men cry.'

'And to make things worse, I lost my job this morning.'

'I'm sorry to hear that.' She paused briefly and then said, 'But you forgive your wife?'

'Forgive? I am not sure I can forgive her. I need her and still want her, but forgiveness is another matter.'

'If she forgives you, will you not do the same?'

'I have too much pain to talk about forgiveness.'

'You men are interesting creatures. You cheat, your wife does the same and it hurts you.'

'But women are different.'

'Is that really so? Or is that what you want to believe?'

'I love her. She is a rare kind, believe me.' He told her how they met, how Fati gave up her wealth for him. When he was finished, there were tears in the woman's eyes. He asked for more palm wine. After drinking it, he suddenly felt tired so he stretched out on the bench. Sleep swept over him immediately. It was noon when he awoke. There were now many customers at the stall, drinking and chatting cheerfully. He excused himself and left.

He walked meditatively—his mind clearer, his body not as weary as before—towards Nima. On his way, he met his son going in the opposite direction. 'Hello, Father,' Baba said. Bukari greeted his son with a wave of the hand and Baba added, 'Are you not working today?'

The father was silent as he groped for a response. 'Not today, son,' he replied, not ready to admit that he had been sacked. He spoke so slowly and unsurely that Baba's anxieties of the previous night were revived.

'Is something wrong, Father?' Baba questioned.

'What do you mean?'

Baba decided to be direct. 'I heard you crying last night. I have never heard you cry before. And you walked into the living room in the middle of the night as if you were walking in your sleep.'

Bukari glanced away, afraid to look his son in the eyes. Obviously, Baba had not heard what happened. He had probably woken up and left home without realising that his mother was not there. But he would hear soon and it would be a painful revelation for him. Better that he heard it from his father than from a stranger. If he, Bukari, told the story, he could leave out some of the sordid details and make it less painful for the young man's heart. But he needed time to think and pick his words carefully. He would tell him everything that night. He said, 'We need to sit down and talk. When you come home tonight, I will be waiting for you.'

That satisfied Baba. He agreed and walked on, putting his curiosity aside for the moment and focusing instead on the task at hand: winning the heart of Janet. He had decided to sneak into the house and look for her. If she was not at home, he would wait. She liked him, he asserted. She was only playing hard to get.

The bungalow was silent when Baba arrived. His heart beat rapidly as he walked to the front door and knocked. There was no response and he knocked again and again in vain. He tried the door and it opened. He put his head in the opening and looked inside. With the curtains drawn, it was dark inside and Baba could not see clearly, but he thought there was a woman sitting on the sofa. Was it Janet? He pushed the door open and stepped inside, blinking. His eyes adjusted to the dimness and he realised there was nobody on the sofa after all. He stood in confusion, thinking what to do next. Perhaps he should leave and return later?

Baba turned to go, but he bumped into a gargantuan figure in the doorway. This giant pushed Baba back into the room and turned on the lights. Both men blinked at the sudden gush of light, then the giant asked, 'Who are you?'

Baba thought quickly. 'I am a friend of the family, Janet's friend.'

The giant, whose voice and face were familiar to Baba, now asked, 'Don't I know you from somewhere?'

Baba thought back, digging into his memory for remembrance. Then it came to him: the urine on the wall, the man telling him to collect the urine. This was the man he had insulted and teased, the day he met Adukwei. 'No… I don't know you. You do not… I mean… you.' Baba stammered from sudden fear, hoping the giant would not remember their previous encounter.

He did. 'You are the little imp who made me look like a fool in front of that primary school in Nima. I remember you. You see, I never forget the face of one who insults me.'

'It is not I, sir. I do not know what you are talking about.'

Then the Volvo pulled up outside and Janet entered the living room. Baba felt relief: she would speak for him and save him from this freak. The giant spoke first. 'Madam Janet, I was passing by and I decided to come in and pay my respects. I found this boy in the living room. He claims you are his friend.'

Then the maid walked into the room and Janet addressed her. 'Where have you been, Adjoa?'

'I was sleeping inside,' Adjoa replied.

'And you left the door unlocked?'

She did not reply. Janet turned to the giant. 'I don't know this boy here. I don't know what he wants.'

Baba was aghast. 'But you do. I was the one who cut the lawn.'

'Didn't you get paid?' asked Janet. 'What business do you

have stealing into the house? Did you think nobody was here and you could steal something? All you people are the same: good for nothing, never to be trusted.'

Baba was too startled to speak. The giant said, 'Don't worry, Madam Janet. I will take care of him.'

'Thank you, Joe. He must be dealt with severely! A thief like that.'

Joe said to Baba, 'I am a better man to slap your face, thief.'

'But I have done nothing,' Baba managed to say. 'I have stolen nothing.'

'Shut up!' Joe thundered. He said to Janet. 'He is guilty of unlawful entry, if nothing else. I will take him to the police station. He will not do this again after we are through with him.'

'Thank you again, Joe. I will tell Daddy of your help.'

That pleased Joe and he smiled with gratitude. He turned to Baba and said, 'Let's go, you hoodlum.'

Baba looked for a means of escape. Was this thug a police officer, then? He could not allow himself to be taken to the police station; he had heard stories of how people were beaten in the cells. He lurched towards the door, but not quickly enough. Joe reached out with his long arms and caught him by the collar of his shirt. Then Joe slapped him twice across the face. Stunned, Baba wobbled on his feet. Joe grabbed hold of him and pushed him outside on to the street. He shoved Baba all the way to Nima police station and presented the case to his fellow officers of the law.

'Foolish boy!' one man snarled at Baba. 'Why did you go

to the rich man's house to steal? Did you think you could get away with it? Why did you make an unlawful entry?'

'I did not go there to steal,' Baba protested. 'Unlawful entry is nothing.'

'Do you know what unlawful entry means?'

'No, sir.'

The men laughed. Joe said, 'Let us deal with him.'

One officer queried, 'Who is your father?'

'Bukari.'

'Foolish boy. I do not want his name. What does he do?'

'He is a taxi driver, sir,' Baba said.

That freed them. This was not the son of a big shot and they did not have to fear any repercussions. Three men approached him and he was very afraid. Joe hit him from behind and he tumbled forward, but another stopped him from falling and delivered a slap to his face. Baba winced and covered his face with his hands.

'Take off your shirt,' Joe ordered. Baba hesitated. 'I said take off your shirt!' Baba complied. Then they ordered him to remove his trousers. He protested and they beat him until he did as he was told. Since he wore no underwear, he was completely naked. He was ordered to bend over and place his palms against the wall. Then they took turns lashing him on the bare buttocks. At first Baba tried to bear the pain with dignity, but after a while he began to yell and beg for mercy. He counted twenty lashes, and then he lost count. When the officers were satisfied, they allowed him to put on his clothes. Even the feel of the clothing against the lacerations on his buttocks and back was so painful that for a while he continued to cry. Joe shoved him into a cell.

It was dark and cold. Baba tried to sit down, but that was too painful, so he lay face down instead.

He was hurt, physically and emotionally. He had been betrayed. Janet, the woman he had desired, the reason for his finishing with Adukwei, had not stood up for him when he needed her to. Worse, she had placed him in the hands of a brutal man and actually asked for him to be severely dealt with. The betrayal! Adukwei would never do a thing like that. In his first encounter with Joe, Adukwei had sided with him. But he had met a stranger and jilted her. Because he had fancied himself in love with Janet. Was it really love that he had for Janet? Or was it just a yearning to grasp what seemed beyond reach? He had made a stupid mistake. Adukwei was the woman for him, not Janet. But perhaps it was too late. Would Adukwei want him back? If she could forgive him, he would be for ever true to her, he vowed. He would make a brighter and better tomorrow with Adukwei. He too would be a rich man, he too would own a mansion and drive nice cars, if only Adukwei would take him back and let him prove himself to her. He would not be one of those for whom tomorrow is only another today of shattered dreams. With Adukwei at his side, he would make tomorrow come. So he dreamt, and in the dreams was Adukwei.

Adukwei.

When Baba told her of his new love, she was simply devastated. The impossible had happened, and it was as though her life had come to an end. For a few days she lived in a state of numbness. When that wore off she felt only painful sensations: her head throbbed from lack of sleep, her heart ached with loneliness.

Was this the price of love? Was this her punishment for following her heart? Did the sweetness of love always lead ultimately to such pain? What had warranted Baba's rejection of her? What was wrong with her? She must be inadequate somehow. There must be something she did not have. For a while she hated herself.

Then she tried to hate Baba: the person who had spurned her without regard for her feelings. The boy who had ditched her so that he could chase another girl. She said to herself, 'I hate. I hate.' But she could not hate him. The line dividing love and hate is a thin one, and whenever she came close to hardening her heart enough to cross over into the territory of hatred, her memory presented her with vivid pictures of Baba's smiling face, and she was back in the realm of love and suffering and she could not hate him even for the expediency of lessening her pain.

Then the pain began to subside. It was slow, but it happened. In the early mornings, when the leaves rustled in the breeze and the world became colourful in the light of the sun, she could think of Baba with sorrowful tenderness instead of in bitter agony. As she went about her day's work, she could sing—though sadly—with the birds. She began to wonder how Baba was faring with his enchantress, and gradually the conviction came to her that the new woman would turn Baba into the clown of love.

In time, Baba would come back to her. But when he came, he would find her changed. Adukwei was learning the ways of the world; when Baba returned he too would be taught a lesson.

After meeting Baba, Bukari walked home, fully resolved to take control of matters and steer them back on course. After explaining everything to Baba, he would seek reconciliation with Fati and begin the healing. The sooner the better. He hoped that Fati would come to him and make it easier; but at the same time he hoped she would not, for he did not know if he had the courage to face her at that moment. What would he say to her, anyway? He needed time to think. The feeling of emptiness revisited him as he sat down in the empty house. With his head in his palms, he sat and thought. The day grew and then slowly died. Darkness descended. Fati did not come home and he was grateful that she was with the Jojos. They would take good care of her until he was ready.

That night, Bukari went to Kill Me Quick. It was the only place where he could find comfort. Kofi Ntim, alias Philosopher Nonsense, and Kojo Ansah, the quiet one, were already present. They watched tensely as Bukari entered the kiosk, feeling his pain with him. Kofi Ntim said nothing, but Kojo Ansah felt it incumbent on him to try again to explain the truth of the business between Fati and Mystique Mysterious. 'Bukari,' he began, 'I am glad to see you again. I think you should know the truth about last night.'

'Thank you, Kojo, but I don't want to hear it.'

'Please, Bukari, listen to me.'

'Please, Kojo, let's not talk about it. What I need now is advice on how to get Fati back.'

Kojo Ansah respected Bukari's request. He said, 'You

should go and talk to her, honestly and earnestly. She will come back to you.'

'He is right, Bukari,' Esi added. 'Talk to her. Tell her you want her back home. She will come with you if she knows your request is genuine.'

Kofi Ntim had nothing to add to that. He said, 'Let me buy you a drink, Bukari. You need one.'

Kojo Ansah said, 'What he needs is a clear mind, to think.'

'Yes, a bottle of beer will help him think,' replied Kofi Ntim.

Esi got Bukari a bottle of beer. He drank slowly and reflectively, lost to the conversation around him. When he finished his beer, he said, 'I have decided what I am going to do.' His friends listened attentively. 'I'm going to the Jojos' place right now. I don't need any elders to intercede. This is a matter between me and my wife. I will ask Fati to come home. I will plead with her if I have to.'

'That is a wise and bold decision,' said Esi. 'But be careful and gentle. I beg of you to be tactful.'

'I know Fati,' Bukari replied. 'I know how to talk to her.'

'Do you need us to come with you?' asked Kojo Ansah.

'No, Kojo, I can do this alone,' Bukari stood up. His head felt heavy and he was a little weak. He had not eaten all day, so the impact of the alcohol was great. He steadied himself and walked outside. In the fresh air, his head began to spin and it was only with a tremendous effort that he could put one foot in front of the other. Staggering from side to side, he set out for the Jojos' house.

He did not see the vehicle as it sped towards him from

behind. It was not clear whether the driver tried to veer away, but if he did he failed. Bukari was hit from behind and propelled into the air. The world seemed to churn in front of his eyes, then he tumbled to the ground and lay motionless. The driver did not stop. In a flash, the car was gone.

It was almost three minutes before Bukari was discovered by a passing pedestrian, a young man who lived close by. By that time there was a large and spreading pool of blood under Bukari's head. The young man hurried over, knelt down and gently shook him. Bukari opened his eyes and said faintly, 'Fati. Please get Fati.' The young man was undecided for a second. Should he get help to take Bukari to the hospital or grant his request and get Fati first? Perhaps he could do both. He leaped to his feet and started to shout for help as he ran to get Fati. He pounded vigorously on the door when he reached the Bukari homestead.

Issaka came out and said, 'I don't think there is anybody at home.'

There was panic in the young man's eyes as he narrated what had taken place. The panic spread to Issaka and he ran to the Jojos' to deliver the news.

'Bukari has been hit by a car and he is asking for Fati.'

'Jojo's Mother squealed for Fati, who ran with the young man to where Bukari lay, surrounded by a crowd of people who had been attracted by the young man's cries for help. Fati had to push her way through the crowd to get to her husband. He was unconscious, but still breathing. She sat and gathered his bloodied head in her arms and wailed. Somebody had run home to get a car. The crowd helped carry Bukari into the car and they drove to the 37 Military Hospital where Bukari was pronounced dead on arrival.

When Fati came home she cried and cried and cried. She blamed herself for every feature of the previous night's altercation. Why had she not forced Bukari to listen to the truth? Why had she lost her temper? If Bukari were still alive, she would expect him to accept his share of blame, but now that he was dead, he was beyond blame, absolved entirely. Dead! Her husband dead? She could not believe that he was gone for ever. He would walk into the living room any time now. He would take her into his arms and caress her.

'Can I offer you something to eat?' That was Jojo's Mother, trying to make herself useful. She too had tears in her eyes and remorse in her voice.

'Thank you,' Fati said, 'but I am not hungry.'

'Let me know if there is anything I can do for you.'

Fati nodded. Throughout the evening, friends and neighbours, some of whom Fati had not seen in ages, came and went. It was amazing how death brought people together.

Kofi Ntim and Kojo Ansah wandered around the streets of Nima for a long time, teary-eyed. They overheard one neighbour ask another, 'Is it true that Bukari is dead?'

'Yes, he was struck by a car.'

'Wht kind of car was it?'

'I think it was a Mercedes Benz.'

'Huh, well then his death is not that bad after all; he was killed by a good car. He exited with dignity. Can you imagine if he had been killed by a worthless car?'

Kojo Ansah and Kofi Ntim would have liked to

remonstrate with these callous gossips, but this was not a night for a fracas, so they hurried away. They went and expressed their condolences to Fati, who was touched by the sincerity of their grief. Esi came later and joined the men in expressing sorrow. They would all miss Bukari. They told Fati she could rely on them for anything. Bukari was their brother: she would never be in need.

Even with these kind people around her, Fati was terribly lonely. But when they left and Jojo's Mother said, 'I think I should stay with you tonight,' Fati answered, 'No. It is very thoughtful of you, but I need to be alone tonight. I need time to be by myself to think. Has anyone seen Baba?'

Neither Jojo's Father nor Jojo's Mother had seen him. They said good-night to Fati, and left her to her grieving. But Fati was not only sorrowing, she was waiting for her son, wondering how she would break the news to him, how he would take his father's death. She had to be strong, for his sake. She waited, but Baba did not come home. Where could he be? Had something happened to him too? That was impossible. Life would not be worth living if Baba too had met with misadventure.

Chapter Nineteen

Another death occurred in Nima the night Bukari died, but that fact was not known until the stabbed corpse of Madman was discovered the following morning. The news of Madman's death travelled fast and the question in the mouths of the people of Nima was, 'Who killed Madman?' Who would have a motive for killing a man who lived in absolute penury and carried nothing of value? Why would anyone want him dead? The murderer must have committed the deed out of sheer cruelty; and if you killed someone for the sole purpose of ending a life, then the act was most heinous, the people of Nima said. The perpetrator must be dealt with ruthlessly.

Typically, when a person like Madman dies, the police work lackadaisically, if at all, for such deaths are not important to them in the large scheme of things. Yet this time it was different: the police descended on Nima with speed and energy. Who were Madman's friends? What were his habits, his haunts? Had anyone seen him the night before? Where? With whom? Why would anybody kill him? The people were questioned and they did not have many answers. They could not remember that he had any friends. He roamed the streets alone, and when he appeared among others it was without invitation. They could not remember much about the man, but they remembered one detail: Madman had one enemy, the quiet man called Kojo Ansah. Madman had assaulted Kojo Ansah on several occasions. Some remembered that a couple of days before his death, Madman started a fight with Kojo Ansah, who threatened to kill him.

So Kojo Ansah became a suspect, his motive personal enmity. There was no evidence to link him with the crime until that evening, when the police discovered a blood-stained knife buried under a pile of leaves near where Madman's body was found. The blood on the knife matched Madman's. They took Kojo Ansah's fingerprints; laboratory tests revealed that they were identical to prints on the knife. The warrant was issued for Kojo Ansah's arrest.

The news spread through Nima. The 441 crowd demanded immediate action. This is a terrible thing, they said. This Kojo Ansah is a very bad man. He has been pretending that he is a good man, planning all along to do murder. Never trust the quiet ones; you never know what they are thinking.

'He did it.'

'Yes, I heard how he made the threat to kill.'

'But was he not simply joking?'

'You do not joke with a man's life like that.'

'Maybe he did not do it.'

'He did it. How about the dagger? Didn't they find his prints on it? At night when everybody was asleep, Kojo Ansah killed Madman, thinking that the night would swallow his deed but forgetting that the night does not eat shit.'

Their minds were made up, and with the people against him, there was no hope for Kojo Ansah. As the crowd discussed the issue, Mystique Mysterious appeared among them and smiled and shook hands. Then he said, 'I have heard terrible news today: that Madman has been murdered, and by a man we all know. A man we all thought was good, a friend. Who would have thought that the quiet one could commit such a terrible crime? It is unpardonable. My friends, we must demand action. Kojo Ansah must meet with the same fate as he inflicted on Madman. Kojo Ansah must be punished.'

The crowd cheered at Mystique Mysterious's speech and praised him for being so wise. After he had left, they felt obliged to do something—to take action, as he had demanded. So they walked on to the streets and chanted for Kojo Ansah's blood. They marched to his home and knocked on his door, calling on him to come out and face their justice. When they received no response, they broke his door down, entered his room and finding it empty, ransacked it. Then they left and marched on the streets and continued to chant for his blood.

Kojo Ansah had heard. He managed to escape minutes before the crowd reached his home. Lost and confused, he sought refuge with Kofi Ntim. 'Kofi,' he requested, 'I need help. Could you keep me here for the night? I am a dead man if I am seen in the streets.'

Kofi Ntim understood, for he had heard the crowd. He had felt an urge to confront them and force them to think. Was it not possible that Kojo Ansah was innocent? Was it not better to wait and see? But would they listen to him? They would not. A crowd like that had little ability to reason. It was a mob: angry, irrational, blood-thirsty and dangerous. If he confronted them, they would only turn on him. So he stayed at home and prayed for his friend. Now, with Kojo Ansah before him, seeking a place to hide, he wished he had done more. 'I am sorry, Kojo, I wish I could do something to stop this madness.'

'There is nothing you can do, Kofi. I am even endangering your life by being here. If these people knew, they could kill us both.'

'Don't worry. They will not come here.'

Kofi Ntim was wrong. The crowd left Kojo Ansah's feeling cheated.

'Where could he be hiding?'

'Where would he go?'

'Kill Me Quick.'

They all went to the kiosk and demanded Kojo Ansah. They looked around and some of them took alcohol without paying for it. Esi was afraid to protest. They were high on their own sense of power; knowing that it might not last they used it there and then.

'But where can he be?'

'He must be with that midget, Kofi Ntim.'

So they marched to Kofi Ntim's and banged on his door.

Inside, the two men were terrified. They had to act fast. Kofi Ntim said in a whisper. 'Under the bed, quickly.'

'Is that safe?'

'We have no choice now.'

The banging got louder. The crowd hurled insults and somebody called out, 'Kofi Ntim, bring us Kojo Ansah so we can show him the colour of his insides.'

The confrontation Kofi Ntim had feared was inevitable

now. He opened the door and hollered, 'What is all this fuss?'

'Foolish man. Do you think we don't know that you are hiding Kojo Ansah? Bring him to us or we will take you instead.'

'You fools!' Kofi Ntim scoffed. 'Do you think I would be stupid enough to keep a murderer in my house? A man that deserves to be torn to pieces has no place in my home.' He threw the door wide open and said, 'If you want to waste your time and look for him here, help yourself. But at this minute Kojo Ansah is running around somewhere, laughing at you.' He held his breath and hoped.

'He is your friend. Did he not tell you where he would be?'

'He was my friend yesterday, not today. I want nothing to do with murderers.'

'Then why are you not with us trying to find him?'

'Huh, don't be foolish, I have only just got home from work. I had just finished eating when you came banging on my door. Wait for me while I put on my sandals. Then I will come with you.'

'Hurry! We don't have time to waste!'

Kofi Ntim put on his sandals, locked the door and followed the crowd into the streets and the alleys of Nima demanding the blood of Kojo Ansah, the quiet one. After hours of searching, the crowd finally tired of the hunt and dispersed. Kofi Ntim went back home, a little shamed. He looked under the bed and found Kojo Ansah still there, staring with fright.

Kofi Ntim said. 'You can come out now, my friend. They

have given up the pursuit. Like the tiny gazelle who eludes the stronger and faster cheetah by running zigzaggedly, we have eluded them. At least for now.'

Kojo Ansah came out from under the bed. 'You handled the crowd brilliantly. Thank you, Kofi.'

'No need to thank me. Let me find you something to eat.'

'I am not hungry. I could not eat.'

The men looked at each other for a while. Then Kojo Ansah said, 'You know, I did not do it, Kofi. I did not kill Madman. He was killed only hours after Bukari died. If you remember, we were both at Kill Me Quick when we heard that Bukari had been run over. We rushed to the scene, went back to the kiosk and later went to see Fati.' Kofi Ntim nodded and Kojo Ansah continued, 'Afterwards we walked back and parted company where we normally do.'

So far, Kofi Ntim could verify everything Kojo Ansah had said. But what happened after they parted? Kojo Ansah went on, 'When you left me, I walked home and went to sleep. I did not leave home until the next afternoon. Madman was murdered that night and it was not I who did it. What is strange to me, though, is that I normally do not sleep past six. But the day after the deaths, I slept till noon. I do not know why. And when I woke up, I felt tired and there was an ache in my head. It was as if I had drunk some bad medicine or something.'

'I believe you did not kill Madman, Kojo,' said Kofi Ntim. 'I wonder who did.'

'Mystique Mysterious,' replied Kojo Ansah.

This confirmed Kofi Ntim's suspicions. 'I thought so as

well. But it will be hard to prove that he did it. They have the knife, and—'

'I know. I don't know how it happened. It is possible that while I was at the kiosk someone managed to put a drug into my glass of water, then later came to my home and put my fingerprints on the knife when I was asleep. The knife was deliberately left at the scene of the crime, to frame me. Do you think I would be so stupid as to leave it there, where it would be so easily discovered, if I had done the deed?'

'And is it not strange the way the police have taken such an interest in Madman's death? Bukari died the same night, yet nobody is talking about his death. Whoever hit him is roaming around the streets now, free. And I can bet you he will never be brought to justice. This man, Mystique Mysterious, is clever, extremely clever. See how he has set you up. Everybody believes you killed Madman.'

'Why would he do this?'

'He has been wary of you for a very long time. He believes you are dangerous. But previously he was content to keep a close watch on you. You tipped the balance when you foiled his attempt to sleep with Fati.'

'I have been wondering. Do you think he had anything to do with Bukari's death?'

'That I don't know. I have suspected it, but I cannot say with certainty. He doesn't stand to benefit by Bukari's death.'

'Perhaps he does. He failed with Fati, remember, and he is not used to failure. Perhaps he could not stand the thought of another man having what he had been denied. So he got rid of that man.'

'You may be right. I had not seen it that way.'

Kojo Ansah began to pace the room: up and down, back and forth. Kofi Ntim watched the anxiety on his friend's face. He wanted to help but did not know how.

'I know what to do,' Kojo Ansah said with decision. 'I will try to get some rest tonight. Then tomorrow I will go to the Nima Police Station and turn myself in. I will have to do it at dawn, before the town wakes up.'

'No!' Kofi Ntim cried. 'You can't do that. What do you think will happen if you do?'

'I will get a trial.'

'If the police do not kill you first. My friend, at the very least, you will be severely beaten. And then if you get a trial, do you imagine that it will be a fair one? My friend, the laws are not meant to serve us. You may be tried, but it will only be to show how evil you are. In the end, you will receive the same sentence the people have been demanding today.'

'There is no choice, Kofi. There is no choice.'

'There is. Stay here a few days, until things calm down a little. Then I will sneak you into my taxi and drive you to Apam. My uncle will take you in and look after you until things quieten down here.'

'Thank you, Kofi, from the bottom of my heart, but I can't do that. I don't want to run away from the law, be a fugitive for the rest of my life.'

'I can understand that, but the alternative is not good. I entreat you not to turn yourself in. The people want your blood and they will not rest till they get it. Unless you allow passions to cool down, they will get your blood.'

Deep down, Kojo Ansah knew that his friend spoke the truth. But he did not want to burden Kofi Ntim any more than he already had. Kofi Ntim had risked his life to save him. That was more than enough. He would turn himself in and face the consequences. So the next day at dawn Kojo Ansah walked to the Nima Police Station and gave himself up. The police were surprised: he had handed himself to them on a plate. They sniggered and threw him in the cell.

That night, Kojo Ansah was taken from his cell, his head was shaved, then he was stripped naked and beaten. Same thing the next day and the days after. The following week, he was brought to trial. The trial was quick, lasting only a day, and the outcome was a foregone conclusion. The evidence was unassailable, said the prosecution. The weapon bore Madman's blood; the fingerprints on it belonged to Kojo Ansah. The motive was the personal grudge that had brewed between the two men for over a year. Witnesses came and testified against Kojo Ansah: he disliked Madman; they were always fighting; he had threatened to kill Madman. They even found somebody to testify that he had seen Kojo Ansah stalking Madman on the night of the murder. A large crowd gathered outside the courthouse and called for a guilty verdict. The jury's deliberations were short; after a mere ten mintues they returned to the courtroom to deliver the verdict. Kojo Ansah stood up, his shaven head bowed, and heard the pronouncement: guilty of murder. The judge passed the sentence: death by firing squad. The sentence was scheduled to be executed the following dawn at the Teshie Nungua Shooting Range. The crowd outside the courthouse cheered. Kofi Ntim observed from a distance helplessly and went home and cried for his friend.

The next day, at five in the morning as scheduled, a bare-chested Kojo Ansah was driven to the shooting range. Even that early, there was a crowd at the site of execution, including the men from 441. They were cheering and chanting for his demise. Despite the chill in the air, Kojo Ansah's body was bathed in sweat. The bare muscles on his chest and arms, displaying the welts from the beatings he had received, twitched with fear. For a moment, he lost consciousness of his surroundings; but the crowd, so loud in its desire to witness his death, jolted him back to his situation. Two soldiers led him to the post and tied him to the pole.

He was bewildered by the excitement of the crowd. Among all the faces in the throng, not one was sympathetic (a friend like Kofi Ntim would not wish to be present at his execution). He did not understand why all these people viewed him with hostility verging on hatred.

How could they be so exalted at the prospect of his death? Even if they believed he had committed murder, was it justice to kill him too? An eye for an eye? He could understand that some people believed in capital punishment, as a deterrent or for retribution. But to cheer at the act was beyond his understanding.

Then perhaps (and it comforted him briefly to think of it this way) they were there to express their solidarity, for are not all human beings under ultimate sentence of death. Some later, some sooner, but the same end. And some of them would experience deaths far crueller than his:

withering away with old age, or being eaten away by a painful disease. They were afraid, and they were trying to propitiate their god. He was to be the sacrificial lamb, killed to pacify the god of mortality that hunted all of them. At the same time, if they believed him guilty of murder, he was the ogre created by the projection of their own evil deeds: the evil within them personified and punished, so that they might live in the illusion that they had cleansed themselves, that they were purer than he.

The soldiers finished tying Kojo Ansah to the post and blindfolded him. In the darkness, his meditations fled him and only fear remained. He wished that he had more courage. How could he fear death so? Had others before him felt the same terror? In the distance he heard the countdown. His heart pounded and his body weakened. He set his teeth together and squeezed his eyes under the blindfold. Then somehow his mind began to shut out the world around him and he saw an image taking shape: a cushion of clouds and a crown of flowers. Gradually the image grew clearer, and he saw that the floral crown was on a woman's head and the woman was his wife, appearing to him now just as she had appeared to him years before to urge him to sobriety. Her face glowed with grace and comfort. She smiled at Kojo Ansah and stretched her arms out to him in a gesture of love and welcome. Kojo Ansah's heart ceased its frantic pounding and grew quiet. A voice in his head, which might have been his wife's and might have been his own, said gently, 'It won't be long now, darling.'

And then the crowd roared again and the guns fired. And then there was only silence.

Chapter Twenty

The day Baba was released from police custody, he walked home with hope in his heart. He found his mother in the living room and she leaped up and held him in her arms for a very long time. Then she let him go and said, 'I have been extremely worried about you, Baba. I have sat here and waited for you. Why have you kept me worried so? And look at you. Where have all these bruises come from?'

Baba told her everything, every detail. By the end of his story, Fati was close to tears. But she struggled to remain composed. She needed the strength for him.

'Baba,' she said, 'I have sad news for you.' She did not know how to continue.

'Something bad has happened.' Baba could sense it.

'Yes.'

'What, Mother? Has something happened to Adukwei?'

'It is not Adukwei. Baba, your father passed away two days ago.'

She expected tears, but he did not cry. He stood bowed, hands thrust deep in his pockets, and was silent. His face wore an expression of solemn sadness which made him look older than his years.

'How did it happen, Mother?'

She told him everything. She could sense the struggle in him as he listened, and she was proud of his gallant efforts to control himself.

When he next spoke, he had a sudden tone of maturity in his voice. 'We will both miss him very much. How I wish I had spent more time with him, learned all the things a son should learn from a father. He told me on the day he died that he had something to tell me, but now I won't ever know what it was.' Then he looked intensely at his mother and said, 'You don't look well, Mother. Are you all right?'

'I am all right, Baba. Let me cook you something to eat. You must be hungry.'

'You don't need to cook. You look hungry yourself. I will go out and buy us both something to eat.'

They had taken away the money he had on him when he was arrested, so he went to the corner of the room and looked under a cup where he kept some cash. Then he went out, returning a few minutes later with some food. Mother and son ate in silence. Fati had never before known Baba to project such strength.

A week later, Baba, Fati, Jojo's Mother, Jojo's Father and Issaka sat outside on the compound and chatted. The sense of loss was still in the air and Fati was weighed down by it. Still, she took comfort in the company of her friends, and especially in Baba's newfound inner strength. If he could survive, so could she.

Baba regretted that Adukwei was not there with them. He had not gained her back completely, but he was trying. Adukwei was wiser now. She wanted to renew their relationship, but on better terms. She would not rush things.

She would make him suffer a little; if he too could know the pain of rejection, it would teach him to be careful in the future.

Presently, Kofi Ntim and Esi walked hand in hand into the compound and joined the gathering. They talked about life at the market, about business, about everything and nothing. After a while, Kofi Ntim and Esi bade the others farewell and walked away. Esi asked Kofi Ntim, 'Have you seen Mystique Mysterious lately?'

'No, and I am glad. This is my last month working as a taxi driver. Next month, I will go fully into business on my own. The farm and the clothing store are both doing well.'

'*You* have done very well, my dear,' Esi said. And she kissed Kojo Ntim on the lips.

The night was beautiful. The wind was soft and the empty streets were quiet. Then, out of the silence, Kofi Ntim thought he heard someone call his name. He stopped and looked behind him and saw the shadowy form of a man outlined against the dusky sky. He looked harder and realised it was Mystique Mysterious. And that Mystique Mysterious was smiling. Then Kofi Ntim knew that Mystique Mysterious had not gone away. He would never go away. He would always be present in the background, watching and waiting; but a man like Kofi Ntim could widen the distance between them.

About the Author

B ENJAMIN KWAKYE is a novelist and lawyer, born in 1967 in Accra, Ghana.

While attending Dartmouth College, he served as editor of *Spirit*, the African American Society's literary journal. He later graduated from Harvard Law School.

His debut novel, *The Clothes of Nakedness*, won the regional Commonwealth Writers' Prize for First Best Book in 1999. Kwakye also went on to win the prize again for Best Book with *The Sun by Night* in 2006 while his 2011 novel, *The Other Crucifix*, won a Gold Award in the Independent Publisher Book Awards for Adult Multicultural Fiction.

As well as practising law, Kwakye is a director of The Africa Education Initiative, a non-profit organisation dedicated to promoting science education in Africa. He currently lives in the San Francisco Bay Area in the U.S.

You can find out more by visiting benjaminkwakye.com